What the Marquess Sees

Agents of Change, Book 2

Amy Quinton

Published 2015

ISBN-13: 978-1518737381

ISBN-10: 1518737382

Manufactured in the United States of America

This is a work of fiction. The characters, incidents and dialogues in this book are of the author's imagination and are not to be construed as real. Any resemblance to actual events or persons, living or dead, is completely coincidental.

DEDICATION

To my friend, Angela Lawson Mizell, for the talks off topic, the coffee, the laughs, the talks off topic, the texts, the reviews, the talks off topic…and the many moments discussing plot points. Oh, and the long talks. Off topic.

And to my friends and family for your continued support and encouragement.

CONTENTS

ACKNOWLEDGMENTS

I would like to thank my editor, Ansley Blackstock, for the superior editorial work. I would like to thank my cover artist, Taria Reed for the beautiful cover art. Finally, I would like to thank everyone at Liquid Silver Books for, again, gifting me this opportunity and for their hard work and dedication to producing quality books for our readers.

PROLOGUE

"Lady, you are the cruell'st she alive."

— Shakespeare, Twelfth Night

The Rutherford Ball...
May 1813...

Clifford Ross, 7th Marquess of Dansbury was altered...forever changed. He had known nothing before that precise instant, nothing before he saw her. But then he did, and he was captivated. His world righted itself...he hadn't even known it was askew. And in that moment, his life split into two distinct halves: Before her and *After.*

But wasn't that so like life? A journey made up of a succession of moments, each point altering its direction. And after each change, one could never go back to their previous reality, no matter how much one wanted to. Sometimes the change was slight, and other times? Well, this was one of those times. He knew it. Could feel it in his bones.

Her laugh preceded her, the sound slow and husky and sensual. It slid over his skin and enveloped him like warm, silk sheets. He burned to step out of the shadows, his body straining toward the sound. He tamped down the impulse.

Then, she stepped out onto the terrace and into a small pool of light, offering her gaze to the moon. His heart skipped its next beat before

1

thundering away. But he didn't move or make a sound. Regardless, she lowered her head and looked right at him; her gaze pierced him in the darkness.

He was sure her eyes were blue…Adonis blue…though he couldn't be sure in the low light. Regardless, they all but pinned him in place against the balustrade. His cock hardened to solid oak as lust slammed into him from out of nowhere. He no longer heard the strains of the waltz or the murmur of voices from the crush of people mingling inside. He homed in on her, only her. He ached to smell her…to taste her…to take her.

Then, she smiled. Not a wide, blinding, light-up-the-night kind of smile, just a simple quirk of her mouth. She glanced down at her feet for a moment, then, back up and threw him another twist of her lips as she peeked at him through her lashes. And in that instant, Clifford Ross…wanted. He wanted it all. With her. Not just sex and sweaty sheets…well, that, too…but also life and love and time. He didn't know why he felt this way; she simply reached inside and latched onto his soul with her smile, and he was powerless to stop her. He shoved aside his base urges; his mind now racing, fast cataloguing a succession of questions. *Who can introduce us? How quickly can I court her? When can I marry her?*

Before, he'd been a confirmed bachelor. After, he imagined silly things like making her laugh, chasing her about the garden, giving her a puppy. It was all irrational, but those thoughts flashed through his mind nonetheless. Trivial moments. Life. With her. His imagination brought to life by her laugh and her gaze, which was no insignificant thing for her regard held power.

"Lady Beatryce, sweet," a disembodied voice called. In response, she stood taller, visibly stiffened.

He knew that voice—Lord Middlebury. Oh, yes. He knew that voice very well. He was infuriated by the intimacy that curled around the sounds it made, not to mention his disgust at the man who owned it.

He'd called her "sweet", dammit.

Middlebury joined Lady Beatryce on the terrace and slid his arms around her waist. Possessive. Sensual. Familiar. Then, he rested his chin on her shoulder.

Dansbury clenched his fists in anger. She didn't look away; her eyes remained locked on *him*, watching her from the shadows.

Middlebury leaned in. "Where have you been, love? I've been searching for you."

"I-I've been here the entire time; I needed the air." Her voice was smooth and sultry, if a trifle unsettled. If he noticed, Middlebury didn't acknowledge the hitch.

Middlebury's hand slid up her side until his arm landed around her shoulders. "What are you looking at, love?"

She shuddered and turned toward Middlebury, breaking their tenuous connection. The loss curdled in his gut despite everything he was witnessing.

She looked up at Middlebury and smiled a sexy, inviting smile. "Nothing. Nothing at all." She all but purred the words.

Dansbury noted every detail, and he still wanted to crush the stone behind him with his bare hands. Better yet, he wanted to strangle Middlebury.

Middlebury grinned, but what arrested Dansbury's attention was the other man's hand, the one attached to the arm dangling over her shoulder...hanging. Just. So. The hand that he wanted to rip off and feed to his dogs. The hand that started...Kneading. Her. Breast.

His banked lust surged to life; and it incensed him. Two long fingers pinched her nipple, and his own cock twitched in answer. His instinct was to charge, take possession of what was his. Claim her peaked nipple. Break those damned fingers.

Absurd. All of it.

"Not here, darling," she murmured.

"You? Modest? Since when?" Middlebury chuckled as he tweaked her nipple again.

"H-How'd it go?" She ignored Middlebury's rhetorical questions...and his wandering hand.

"You know how, love. Same as always. Miss Saintsbury's reputation is in tatters, just like you planned."

Dansbury's blood turned to ice. He was fury tempered with disillusionment and a hint of embarrassment over his earlier whimsical thoughts. Lady Beatryce turned and pressed her forehead to Middlebury's chest, but she twisted her head in *his* direction, seeking *him* in the shadows.

Her eyes appeared bleak.

Ha! After what he'd just seen and heard? Not bloody likely.

And he was chagrined; worse, he was a fool, for he'd been taken in by her beauty. She was magnificent and the most stunning thing he'd ever seen. But now, he could see she was also hard. It was written in the way she stood and the nuances in the way she moved in the face of her paramour. Yes, she was a diamond, but she was also fast, unscrupulous, and a liar.

In that moment, he hated her. And he vowed to never be deceived by her again.

He turned his back and ousted her from his mind. There was a reason he was hiding in the dark; a reason he did not approach her before. He had a contact to meet and trouble to find. He would meet his contact, dispatch with said trouble, and find the girl whose reputation lay in ruins by this pair of scoundrels. Who knew? Maybe he could help.

Yes, that was him. And this was his life. A world he'd thought he'd known. A world that would never be the same.

His *After*.

He walked away a tad melancholy; as if he'd lost something he never really had.

CHAPTER 1

"A witty woman is a treasure; a witty Beauty is a power."

— *George Meredith, Diana of the Crossways*

Beckett House, London…
May 1814, One Year Later…

Father was up to no good.

Well, he was always up to no good, but this was different and much more serious. The Earl of Swindon was angry and mean and as vile as a…as a…as a peppered scoundrel. When he wasn't pretending to be the doting father that is.

But he was always sure of himself—or at least, sure of his own arrogant superiority. La, she hated the smug expression he'd wear when putting her in her place. But she hadn't seen that arrogant mien at all in two weeks or more. Instead, there was an underlying sense of fear about the man.

He was utterly terrified, actually.

And Lady Beatryce Beckett needed to find out why. Knowledge was power and in her case, often offered some measure of protection.

In addition to Father's odd behavior, suspicious men watched the house at all hours of the day. Bea didn't recognize any of the strange men; they didn't belong in this area of Mayfair. And, somehow, they always happened to disappear whenever a runner was nearby. Surprise.

Father was oblivious to their unwanted observers, but once, she'd caught him start with alarm after catching sight of a particularly large brute wearing a dark, hooded cloak. That man had stood right in the middle of the street, shrouded in black, and stared up at the house, his arms crossed and his stance wide. A dancing bear wouldn't have been more obvious.

Even Father had noticed that one.

The hooded man had stood there for several minutes, before turning and walking away, nonchalant-like, as if this were a normal, everyday thing to do. As if he commanded everything and everyone around him. Arrogant, like Father. No one else in Beckett House had noticed the event, or if they had, they hadn't remarked upon it. And none of their neighbors had mentioned the event either, which was rather disturbing to say the least.

Today, Step-mother and Father were away at a garden party held by some faceless society hostess. Her three younger sisters had gone, too, but Bea had pled a headache at the last minute and remained behind. Father rarely left the house, so this was her best, and possibly only, opportunity to search his study for clues—short of in the wee hours of the morning, which Bea was loath to do. Those hours were hers.

Bea stopped in front of her father's study, deliberately stepping over the squeaky floorboard in front of the threshold. She looked left and right, then sucked in a breath and gathered her courage. She opened the door, quiet as a mouse, for she didn't want to alert the servants even if they held no love for the earl.

Hell, they held no love for her for that matter. And she supposed she had earned their animosity, but she would never admit it—nor acknowledge that she cared. She didn't care. They were beneath her notice.

Inside the study, the room was dim as the fire was banked low—Father was ever frugal. Bea left the door cracked and made her way across the room. She opened the curtains covering the large window behind the earl's desk to let in more light.

She skipped the obvious hiding places and headed straight for the bookshelf to her left. A few weeks ago, she'd spied Father scrambling to replace a book on this very shelf.

He never read, so the action was remarkable.

She searched the middle shelf for a disturbance in the dust.

Yes. There.

She grabbed the book; it felt lighter than it should, so she opened it. Aha! It was a false book, and inside was a small key.

Right. Now to find the lock.

Bea replaced the book, minus its treasure, and turned to study the room. She tapped the key against her lips while she considered the most likely place to look.

Squeak…

La, the telltale creak of a squeaky floorboard in the hall sounded like a cannon going off inside the quiet house. But wasn't that always the case when one was up to no good?

Everything sounded louder to a sneak's ear.

Bea wasted little time; she dashed behind a nearby screen…just in time.

Through the cracks between the panels, she watched as the door opened as if by magic. Of course, the door wasn't enchanted, but it wasn't someone in the family or a servant opening it, either. Everyone in Beckett House knew about that squeaky floorboard for they risked the wrath of the earl whenever they tread upon it, accident or not.

The accompanying "Shite," muttered in a low, deep, and recognizable voice was another giveaway.

Bea's heart picked up its pace, and a low hum sounded in her ears. She took a few slow, deep breaths to calm her heart and subdue her anxiety. Allowing herself to become flustered would not help the situation.

The disembodied voice, though hushed, was decidedly familiar…

No. It couldn't be? Could it?

The intruder peeked around the door and surveyed the room on a quick glance.

Shite—to use his phrase—*yes. It most definitely was.*

Dansbury. The Marquess of Dansbury, Clifford Ross, entered the room and carefully shut the door. Bea fell back against the wall and beseeched the ceiling.

Of all the people it could possibly be, why, oh, why did it have to be him?

She shook off the pointless thought, straightened, and peeked through the gaps again. Bea's heart now thundered in her chest. God, he was big. He was blond. He was absolutely beautiful. She felt a pang at the sight of him standing there, hands on his hips, studying the room. He would never be hers, and oh, didn't she know it.

Yea, she knew it well. He was everything good, and she was…well, she was who she was…

She watched him for a while as he searched the room with efficient and thorough care. Lord, this could be awhile. She imagined herself sitting back in a chair—behind the screen of course—with a book and a brandy while she waited for him to finish. Maybe she'd even smoke a cigar. She almost snorted out loud at the fanciful image. Almost.

But what would she do once he reached the screen? There was no way he wouldn't look behind it and miss her standing there, hiding in the corner.

She could just imagine the scene: He'd be rude. As usual. She'd be rude in return. As expected. It was the way of things; the very fabric of their lives.

She anticipated her discovery, and her heart burned at the thought. She involuntarily rubbed her chest. She debated relieving her anxiety now by simply making her presence known. Why wait for the inevitable?

"Can you believe the earl ate seven eggs an' an entire loaf of bread on his own this morn'?" came a muffled voice from the hall outside the door.

"Cor," came an equally muffled reply.

"Heard it from the head footman, meself."

Great. A pair of maids conversed as they passed by in the hall. They were loud, which was why Bea could hear them despite the closed door. *Ha.* They must not realize she'd remained behind and were taking advantage of the family's absence by forgetting their place. Typical.

Dansbury heard the commotion as well and dashed to the wall behind the door. He trained his eyes on the knob, likely waiting for it to turn. Bea took that opportunity to leave her hiding spot and slip behind the curtains. He'd already checked the drapes; likely he wouldn't look again. He was too focused on the door and did not expect someone else in the room; thus, she made it to her new spot without attracting his notice.

Was that a slight twinge of disappointment she felt?

La, he was gloriously handsome…What woman wouldn't relish an encounter? Even if he would be regarding her with pure disdain and anger dripping from his lips. And why should it matter? She'd be marrying his best friend, the Duke of Stonebridge, in a matter of days. Never mind that the duke was a stodgy man for someone of only thirty-odd years who didn't want to marry her either. But she didn't have a choice in the matter.

Neither did the duke.

"And did you see Lady Beatryce…"

Bea took a chance and peered around the drapes. The maid's voice trailed off as they moved out of hearing distance. Dansbury had already moved on; he was studying the rug.

Aha! The rug. She'd never thought to look under there. Perhaps, there was a secret compartment beneath the floor?

Dansbury turned to move, and Bea ducked back behind the curtains. A cloud of dust was released with her movement. She started to sneeze, but caught it at the last minute. She held her nose and her eyes watered. La, she wanted nothing more than to force it out. Holding it in was always worse...made one's nose itch and feel...unfulfilled.

She shook off her wandering thoughts and listened to Dansbury search the room; her mind picturing the sight. His form-fitting coat would be stretched to the limits across those broad shoulders. His muscles would flex in his thighs as he bent over. His arse...

Zounds. Bea fanned her heated face. Oh, she wished she could chance it and watch, but then, as soon as he turned to search the screen, he'd see her peeking out amid the drapes. She couldn't risk it.

He was moving progressively closer, though she had to strain to hear that much. He was silent; as if he'd done this sort of thing many times before. She had long suspected he worked for the Crown in some secret capacity. His actions today only reinforced that idea.

And damn, but he was being thorough. She would give anything to sit on the floor and have a cup of tea, or better yet, that brandy, while she settled in for what was sure to be an interminable wait. She imagined asking him to hand her a book to read while she waited—and nearly laughed out loud again.

She heard his foot step off the rug. He was headed for the screen now; which was near the window. Bea held her breath.

Surely, he could hear her heart booming in her chest? It was so loud, she could no longer hear him move. It sounded like soldiers marching in her ears. She wanted to look, yet she couldn't afford the risk. She was committed to staying hidden now, and the thought of success tasted sweet on her tongue. La, how she would love to gloat over the fact; tell him to his face that he, a man noted for his powers of observation, had completely missed her presence in the room.

After what felt like ten years of her life, he finally left. She only just heard the click of the study door as it closed. He'd barely made a sound, and she'd been too afraid to press her luck with another peek. She was lucky she hadn't fallen asleep and completely given herself away with a loud snore.

Wouldn't that have been a sight?

"Oh, Dansbury. Fancy meeting you here," she said in her haughtiest voice. She was good at pretentious.

"Why yes, Lady Bea, what are the chances?" she said in her best imitation Dansbury voice.

She snickered and shook off her wandering thoughts, again.

She bolted from her hiding spot, confident he'd gone. She walked around the desk and looked down at the Aubusson rug. Time to finish her own search.

Hmmm...

She noticed a freestanding globe on one corner of the rug. It had been moved recently, as there were depressions in the carpet where it normally stood. She didn't think Dansbury had moved it, he would have been precise when repositioning it. She only just noticed the clue herself. One could only see the signs when viewed from a certain angle, and she happened to be standing in just the right spot.

She set the key on the desk and approached the globe. It didn't look too substantial. She pulled and eventually dragged the globe off the rug. It required both hands. Then, she set to work on the carpet. She needed to look underneath, and the rug was sure to be heavy. Actually, she could use Dansbury's help about now. She chuckled at the thought of calling him back and asking him to lend a hand.

"Oh, Cliff, would you mind giving me a hand here? I need to look under this rug and see if Father is up to something nefarious?" she said in her pretend innocence voice.

"Why sure, Lady Beatryce, why don't we make love on the floor while we're at it," she added in her finest virile Dansbury voice. She found it difficult not to laugh while she said it though.

She managed the task on her own, after all, using her body to keep the rug from falling back into place as she slowly rolled one end.

Aha. There, in the floor, was a loose board; it was...off kilter. *Hmmm.* She studied it with growing excitement. This was a puzzle, and she was good at puzzles. She laid on her stomach and attempted to pry up the board. It didn't budge. La, there must be some sort of release. She squirmed on the floor as she felt around for some other obvious disparity.

In her struggles, her foot kicked something behind her, and she heard a satisfying click. She looked up, rather than at her feet, and smiled at the peculiar board now lifted slightly higher than the others.

It was pure, dumb luck, but she'd take it. Well, part skill, part luck if she did say so herself.

Bea pulled up the board and several around it. What a clever hiding place! And surprising. Father? Not bloody likely. Someone else must have installed it.

After a wide enough hole was revealed in the floor, Bea reached in and felt around.

A box! *Ha!*

She pulled the box out and inspected the lid. There, in the midst of intricate carvings, was a key hole. Bea jumped up and retrieved the key from the table. She opened the box with baited breath. What would be inside? Her hands shook with her exhilaration.

She opened the lid to find all sorts of papers tucked inside. She pulled out the one on top and read.

Well, well, well. Look what Father's been up to…

She pulled out and scanned the next one.

Oh, Father, you are a bad, bad man… She scanned another.

La, this is serious. Shite. If anyone found out she knew…

Panic set in and Beatryce hastened to return everything and put the room back to rights.

She had to think.

She had to plan.

How could she use this information?

How could she protect herself?

Who could she tell?

* * * *

Dansbury escorted Miss Grace Radclyffe from Beckett House and into his waiting carriage. The carriage creaked and groaned as he climbed inside, grating on his nerves. He was more than a little frustrated; his search of Beckett House had turned up nothing. Absolutely naught. It was deuced frustrating. Earl Swindon was not a clever man, but somehow, he'd managed to be brilliant when it came to hiding the evidence of his numerous misdeeds.

After settling inside his conveyance and rapping on the roof to alert his driver that they were ready to depart, he turned to his companion with a pensive air. "Miss Grace Radclyffe, your uncle is a very strange man." An understatement. "I'm glad you are no longer living beneath his roof."

"As am I. I cannot thank you enough for that."

"Love, no thanks are necessary. It is I who should be thanking you for keeping the servants occupied while I searched the house. It was brave of you. And very helpful."

"Did you find anything?"

"Aren't I supposed to be asking you that question?" He answered with a grin.

"I suppose, but I'm impatient and decidedly curious."

"Of course you are. Alas, I'm afraid I didn't find a thing."

"Well, then. I suppose that makes one of us."

He laughed, but his mirth was cut short. "Wait a minute...You did?" Curious. He couldn't help but be surprised at her confession. He never really expected something to be hiding in the main drawing room of the home where anyone...such as the Duke of Stonebridge, perhaps...might see it. Swindon was a fool.

Grace grinned and nodded her head yes with a rapid bounce of her head. She was like a kid with a plate of sweet pies; her eyes were lit with joyful glee and her grin stretched from ear to ear. She reached into her reticule and pulled out a small, wooden box.

She handed it over to him. "I found this."

He took it and held it up to the light coming in from the carriage window. He turned it back and forth, noting the intricate carvings on every side. It looked to be made of oak and stained with a dark, almost ebony, stain. But on the lid, the center medallion was of a much lighter, reddish stain. And in the middle of that, the lid had been burned with a symbol—one he had seen too many times in the past...Two letters, a swirly P and an E, were entwined together making up the branches of an oak tree. It was the symbol for the Society of the Purification of England. Sure, the box was circumstantial evidence at best, but it was a damning piece against the earl.

The Secret Society of the Purification of England's membership was made up of conservative aristocrats who wanted to purge England of all immigrants or people of mixed blood, particularly Irishmen...thereby purifying the blood of all its citizens. These men were dangerous, powerful, and willing to do anything to see their aims realized. Murder. Treason. Hell, they were even willing to work with the enemy so long as their goals coincided.

"Does it mean anything?"

Dansbury smiled and reached over to give Grace a hug. She was sweet and warm. Kind. She felt like home. "Yes, sweet. It means everything. Thank you. You've been more useful than I this day, I daresay."

Now, he just hoped Ambrose Langtry, the Duke of Stonebridge, wouldn't kill him for putting his woman in danger. Or Grace would be his woman if Ambrose would finally get his head out of his arse and realize that fact. Incredibly, the man was still planning to marry Lady Beatryce Beckett over some misplaced sense of honor.

Still, he suspected Ambrose wouldn't be happy to learn of Grace's involvement today. He and Ambrose never did see eye to eye on the acceptable risks in pursuit of justice. Ambrose drew the line at putting friends in danger, even if it meant their suspect would escape capture.

Cliff, on the other hand, was relentless when it came to seeking the truth. He'd been ingrained with it since birth…a gift from his mother who'd always been passionate about ensuring justice at all costs. True, at times, those costs weighed heavy on a man. But the end result…truth and justice and safety for the masses, along with the proper atonement…made those sacrifices bearable.

Usually.

CHAPTER 2

"Defer no time, delays have dangerous ends."

— Shakespeare, Henry VI

Dansbury House, London…
One Week Later…

"Rise and shine…you lazy toff."

Dansbury opened one eye. *Oomph.* Mistake, that. Bright light bored into his brain bringing forth an involuntary wince. Hammers started pounding steel inside his head. He squinted and eyed the room. Purple spots obscured his vision, but he managed to locate his best friend, Ambrose Langtry, the Duke of Stonebridge, across the room. The man was bustling about, opening curtains, and acting suspiciously…jovial?

Huh. How odd.

Maybe he was dreaming. Yes, that must be it; just a bizarre dream. Nothing to be concerned about then. His eye drifted closed.

"Why are you still abed?"

Both his eyes jerked open. *Ugh.* The sun took it as an invitation to move in and set up housekeeping. "What do you want? Tell me, then go away."

"Don't you recall what day it is? It's my wedding day. Why aren't you up and dressed for it?" Ambrose pulled open the last set of velvet curtains covering three massive windows overlooking the back garden. Dust leapt

14

into the air, dancing in the sunbeams.

Cliff groaned and closed his eyes again. "I don't like you right now, and I certainly don't like your fiancée, so of course, I'm not planning to attend your ill-fated nuptials. Remember? I told you an age ago..."

He dozed off. Or tried to. He'd almost made it back to dreamland when Ambrose started slapping him about the face, startling him awake, *again*.

"Enough!" he bellowed as he slapped at his friend's hands and then rolled away from the source of his misery.

Ugh. I shouldn't have done that.

The hammers started pounding steel inside his brain again. He vowed never to touch liquor again in his life. Probably.

Ambrose leaned in, undeterred by the outburst, and sniffed. "Damn, but you smell like a distillery, Cliff. Long night?"

"You could say that," Cliff murmured.

Ambrose plopped on the edge of the bed and leaned back against the footboard, causing Cliff to roll back the other way. "Hmmm...sounds like an interesting story. I look forward to hearing about it...another time..."

"Please. Hold your breath while you wait, but do it at your house. Your death would have me answering all sorts of inconvenient questions. Besides, disturbingly cheerful morning people make me ill. And since when did *you* become a disturbingly cheerful morning person, anyway?" Cliff couldn't stop his grin as he burrowed further under the bedclothes, seeking the darkness to be found beneath the sheets.

"Ha! I see you haven't lost your sense of humor with your head. Excellent. But seriously, I need you to get up." Ambrose nudged his leg. "Now. I have a task for you."

Ambrose's tone turned serious; which got his attention better than any of his friend's previous attempts combined. He poked his head out from under the covers and studied his friend. Ambrose was dressed casually for travel.

Interesting. Why wasn't the man clad in his wedding finery?

"Am I going to like this?" He didn't know whether or not he wanted to hear the answer, but he asked it anyway.

"Oh, you're going to love it."

Cliff raised one brow in question, unconvinced.

"Don't look at me like that. You will. You care too much about Grace to see her remain unhappy for the rest of her days, living and working without the man she loves.

You'll relish this task. I promise."

Ah, Miss Grace Radclyffe, a wonderful woman—sweet, friendly, beautiful—and utterly in love with her Ambrose.

"I'm almost afraid to ask, but, exactly, what are you planning?" *And do I want to know the answer?*

Ambrose crossed his arms in a defensive pose. "I'm going to ask Grace to marry me."

Cliff lurched upright, the covers falling to his waist. Had he been drinking, liquid would have sprayed out his nose and mouth and drowned the both of them. "What? Are you crazy? Have you forgotten you're about to get married in…oh…" he squinted over at the clock on the mantle, "about half an hour to someone else?" He refused to say his fiancée's name.

"Of course, I haven't forgotten—could you?" His friend raked his hand across his face. "Never mind. Don't answer that. I already know the answer. No, I'm simply not going to marry Lady Beatryce, and that's all there is to it."

Dansbury tried not to cringe at the mention of Lady Beatryce, unsure if he was successful. He eyed his friend, but still couldn't tell.

"Good God. It's about bloody time." Truth. "But what about contractual obligations, your word, and all that other shite you've been spouting for the last month?" His friend had been trying to convince himself as much as everyone else that he had to go through with this marriage. Dansbury had been trying to talk Ambrose out of it ever since the man had first announced his misbegotten plan to marry her.

"Funnily enough, I never actually asked Lady Beatryce to marry me. We just announced our betrothal as if I had. And I never actually signed the betrothal contract either."

That surprised him. Lady Beatryce and her family had pulled all sorts of underhanded tricks to ensure this wedding would happen. He found it difficult to believe that a detail such as signing the betrothal contract would be overlooked by the Beckett Family. But he trusted his friend, implicitly. Hell, he trusted everyone—for better or for worse—except for Lady B and her family.

"Damn me, you're actually going to do this, aren't you?" Cliff's heart picked up its pace. Damned fickle organ.

"You may depend upon it, and I need you to go to the church and inform Beatryce of the change of plans."

"Ha! Of course." Cliff fell back and threw his arm over his head. He was not hiding.

He strove for indifference. "But why don't *you* do it?"

"I don't have time. I don't want to waste another minute without my Grace. I need her like I need air, and I'm on my way to Oxford to tell her that, or something like it. I'm sure much begging and groveling will be involved."

Cliff laughed. "What about our investigation? Did you get my note?"

He still hid under his arm. The sun chose today, of all days, to be brutal with its intensity. That was his only reason for hiding his eyes. He wasn't trying to hide his excite…er, surprise over his friend's decision. Not at all.

Earlier in the week, Cliff had sent a note to Ambrose about his search of the Beckett Estate in West Sussex. Unfortunately, like in the case of the man's London residence, he had found no evidence to help their investigation.

As part of their enquiry into the goings on of the Secret Society for the Purification of England, they were investigating the assassination of Ambrose's father, the 9th Duke of Stonebridge, which occurred seventeen years ago. They believed that the duke was murdered by edict of the Society.

Ambrose was in charge of their investigation, and their primary suspect behind the assassination itself was none other than Lady Beatryce Beckett's father, the Earl of Swindon.

Yea. It was a complicated mess.

Oh, Earl Swindon hadn't actually performed the deed, the very idea was absurd, but he was the one who saw it carried out. They were confident of that.

He felt Ambrose stand. "I did. Don't worry about the place being cleared. I have a plan, but that's for later. Right now, you need to get up. You do want to make it to the church before all hell breaks loose, don't you?"

Cliff's grin, visible from below his armed sun block, was answer enough. He delighted in setting the ton on its collective ear, and Ambrose knew it. Even if Ambrose were planning to inform Beatryce himself, Cliff would have begged for a chance to do the deed. He relished the opportunity to put that witch in her place. Lady Beatryce deserved to be stood up and more. She was cruel and underhanded and didn't merit his friend.

"And by the by," Ambrose added before stepping out the door, "I'll be paying you back for asking my woman to marry you…later."

Despite the threatening words, he heard his friend laughing as he walked away.

Good for you, Ambrose, you lucky bastard.

Cliff jumped out of bed, whistling a jaunty tune, as he rang for his valet. The pain from his overindulgence was forgotten, his day had turned suddenly jolly. He hadn't been this enthusiastic in quite some time, and he all but rubbed his hands together in anticipation of carrying out this task.

It was the reason his heart now raced. The only reason.

CHAPTER 3

*"Anger's my meat; I sup upon myself, and so shall
starve with feeding."*

— *Shakespeare, Coriolanus*

Beckett House, the Earl of Swindon's Study...
At the Same Time...

Bea closed her eyes and tried in vain to find some measure of serenity.

Then, she knocked on the door to the earl's study with a firm rap. She
waited with more than a little trepidation for him to grant her permission to
enter. He'd summoned her to his study, which was rarely a good thing. She
fought harder to find peace, to steady her nerves.

Bea tapped her fingers against her thighs as impatience won the battle
over tranquility. She only just stopped herself from drumming her foot in
nervous anticipation.

"Come in, daughter."

It took a full minute for him to say the words. He liked to use the delay
to intimidate visitors. Even if they were family. Even if he'd been the one to
summon them.

She entered the room walking on eggshells.

Just a little bit longer; you can do this, woman.

At the moment, she needed her little internal motivational talks like a fish needed water.

"You wanted to see me, Father." Her voice tangled with the word 'father'. She hoped he didn't noticed the hitch.

"Good. You are prompt. Have a seat."

He didn't bother to rise; the poor chair groaned a complaint as he leaned back to watch her. The earl was an enormous man in poor physical condition and turned to fat; the solid oak desk probably weighed a few stone less.

As she crossed the room, she had to compel her eyes not to glance at the rug where she'd found his little secret compartment. She forced herself to be nonchalant as she walked directly over it and approached his desk. She pasted on a serene smile and looked him square in the eye with a firm, yet obedient look.

He gestured to one of the chairs in front of his desk; his chair screamed again in protest. At least he didn't force her to stand for this dressing down. And it would be a dressing down. It was always a dressing down.

He mopped at his ever-perspiring brow with a dinner napkin as he waited for her to sit. He was sweating profusely from having to walk from the dining room all the way to his office. He had to traverse the width of an entire hallway to do so.

He threw the napkin onto his desk, which was littered with loose papers and dirty dishes, mostly unclean dishes, all of them empty. Among a collection of half-finished cups of tea, she could just make out the silver hand bell he used to signal the servants; the nearby bell pull was too far away to reach from his chair.

"I wanted to have this discussion so that I might advise you as to how today will proceed. I cannot seem to counsel you enough on the subject." He held up both hands in a placating manner as if she were about to argue the point. Or cry. She wasn't sure which. "Now, don't be upset. It isn't a surprise. Women, as a general rule, are rarely reasonable."

Bea clenched her teeth behind her composed smile.

Keep calm. Must. Keep. Calm…

"When we arrive at the church, you will proceed directly to the antechamber. Do *not* stop to talk to anyone. Don't even make eye contact. And definitely do not seek out the duke. If he attempts to see you, I will step in and handle the situation."

The image was laughable. No one could deter the duke, least of all the earl.

The earl handed her a frosty stare making her feel somewhat less than warm. As if she were wearing a blanket of snow. Downright chilled.

"I will *not* have you ruining this in the last hour. There is always a chance that you could do so—and destroy all that I've worked for in the process." His glare turned glacial. Even ice would have sought the sun. "Need I remind you what the consequences will be should you attempt to back out now?"

"No, sir."

Normally, she'd be terrified at this point. Today, she was confident he would stay his hand. He wouldn't do anything to risk this wedding. And after the wedding, she'd be free of him.

Her demure smile threatened to widen to epic proportions. She tried her best to curtail it. Freedom wasn't hers. Yet.

The earl continued as if she hadn't just agreed. As if she'd shown some sign of hesitation or rebellion. "You will do whatever it takes to make sure this marriage proceeds as planned. It is what we Becketts do. Even the women. We do what it takes to achieve our aims."

You'd better believe it.

Bea nodded her agreement. She didn't trust herself to speak. The newly formed lump in her throat made her neck ache, but she forced her small smile and held her head high. She tried to swallow without it being obvious.

"Excellent. Then, come and give your father a kiss. And smile, girl. Today, you become a duchess. It is what any woman with sense would desire."

Bea dutifully rose, walked around his desk, and placed a kiss on his moist, ruddy cheek. His stench made her want to gag; she suppressed the instinct.

And as she walked away, he added, "Oh, and fetch your maid. She has done a poor job of dressing your hair. Tell her she will be let go without a character reference if she does not do her best to make you reasonably presentable. We would not want the duke to run away in horror before the vows are spoken, would we?" She made it out the door.

"And hurry or we'll be late!" His voice chased her up the stairs.

God, not much longer...

* * * *

Dansbury House
20 Minutes Later...

Dansbury was ready to bolt from his room.

He couldn't get to St. George's fast enough. He'd already dismissed his valet and was just leaving his dressing room when he noticed a man sitting in one of the chairs in front of his hearth. Fellow agent for the Crown, and a friend, Ciarán Kelly, waited for him, a glass of whisky in hand.

Cliff didn't miss a step; he dipped his head as he passed. "Kelly."

Kelly was another agent for the Crown and one of the men assisting with their current investigation.

"You appear to be in a hurry, Dansbury. On your way to a searing rendezvous?" Kelly waggled his brows. He was a known lothario. Of course, his mind would go there first.

Dansbury paused and looked down at his seated friend. "Actually, I have a wedding to catch."

"Oh. Right. It's today, is it?"

"Supposed to be." He was deliberately cryptic, and Kelly didn't ask what he'd meant by that ambiguous statement. The man seemed too preoccupied anyway.

Kelly and another agent, a Scot named MacLeod, were meant to be in the field, guarding their man in custody and questioning potential witnesses to the murder of the pervious Duke of Stonebridge, so Dansbury was surprised to find Kelly here, relaxing by the fire.

At the moment, they had two witnesses to corroborate their theories about the earl's involvement in the murder—an Irish servant and the Irish assassin who'd been hired to murder the duke—but who hadn't actually done the deed. Ironic, to be sure, seeing as how the Society wanted to rid England of Irishmen altogether.

But the assassin was a suspected supporter of the United Irishmen, a rebellious group who wanted to end the English monarchy's rule in Ireland. So in reality, their purposes were aligned; shared goals make strange bedfellows and all that.

And the commoner was just in the wrong place at the right time and bore witness to the assassin's attempted murder of then-Prime Minister William Pitt the Younger—while he was a guest at the Duke of Stonebridge's house.

Since it didn't appear that Kelly was going to be forthcoming about his unexpected presence in London, Cliff decided they needed to continue this discussion en route.

"Kelly, let us talk in my carriage, shall we? I'm in a hurry."

"Aye, of course." Kelly rose, after knocking back the remainder of his drink, and followed him out of the door.

After they settled in his carriage for the ride to the church, Dansbury decided to come right out and ask what was on his mind. "So what brings you to town?"

"Stonebridge has me following up on a new lead."

Odd. Ambrose would usually handle that himself, especially since Kelly was supposed to be over one hundred miles away. Dansbury crossed his arms.

"I know that look. I agree; it's odd. All I know is that MacLeod passed on the request from Stonebridge last week. So, here I am; though I haven't actually seen the duke."

Hmmm. Stranger still. Why did Ambrose send his request through MacLeod? Out loud, he asked, "You just missed Stonebridge not thirty minutes ago."

"Really?"

Kelly didn't expound on his rhetorical question or whatever thoughts prompted it. He just shrugged his shoulders, a Gallic habit he picked up while sleuthing in France a few years ago. Kelly turned to look out the window, pensive. "So what brings you to my door?"

Kelly continued to stare out the window. "Nothing, really. I guess I was curious to see if you knew anything more?"

"Stonebridge didn't mention anything to me. But then his mind was one hundred percent on Grace this morning. He's decided not to marry Lady Beatryce…"

Kelly jerked around in his seat. He gaped at Dansbury, surprise written clearly across his face.

Dansbury laughed. "I know. I was shocked, too, but he's in love…"

Both men shuddered at the thought. They sat silent for a moment, each lost to their own contemplations.

A few minutes later, Kelly asked, "What would you do, Dansbury, to get your man?

To get *this* man?"

Cliff assumed Kelly was referring to the earl. He didn't hesitate. "Anything."

"Truly? Anything?"

"Yes. Anything. Justice must prevail. Otherwise? We're not much better than animals. Civilization would eventually descend into chaos."

"Glad to hear it."

At that moment, Dansbury's carriage pulled up in front of St. George's Church and he all but forgot his friend's odd behavior. His mind centered in on his current, delightful mission. He could not contain his grin. And, for now, he did not care that Kelly, MacLeod, and Stonebridge were behaving out of character. He'd puzzle it out later. Now, he had a witch to see.

Preoccupied with his task, he didn't even say goodbye to his friend as he all but leapt out of his carriage.

CHAPTER 4

*"Do not be afraid; our fate cannot be taken from us; it
is a gift."*

— *Dante Alighieri, Inferno*

St. George's Church...
Hanover Square, London...
45 Minutes Later...

"Where the hell is he?"

Lady Beatryce Beckett paced the antechamber of St. George's Church, alone. The chamber was made up of marble and stone and her footsteps echoed around the room. Surprisingly, the groom, Stonebridge, had yet to arrive, which made her nervous wandering quite understandable. All the guests were seated and waiting patiently in the pews. She could hear their muffled voices and the sounds of their shifting feet through the door.

"Good morning, Lady Beatryce."

She whirled at the noise, startled, though she knew that voice. Sure enough Dansbury leaned against the doorframe, arms and legs crossed, a curious smile spread across his face. That smile did not bode well. He despised her and the entire idea of her marrying his best friend. As usual when looking at her, his smile did not reach his eyes, and a trace of sarcasm colored the edges of his eyes.

"What are you doing here?" She asked the question though she dreaded the answer.

"Let's just say I'm here to spread good tidings and cheer, and all that rot…though perhaps not for you."

Yes. She had a really bad feeling about this. "So are you going to spread your good cheer or stand there staring at me all morning?"

He frowned at her a moment as if unable to understand her hostility. He was gorgeous in a devastating way, big and broad and blond with chocolate brown eyes, but she didn't care. She wanted him out of here and the wedding over and done with. She had schemed too hard for too long to bring the duke up to scratch. She would not allow anything to stop this wedding from happening. Not now. Not at the midnight hour as it were.

His smile returned in force. Goodness. He could melt the coldest ice with that smile. She braced herself against its impact.

Yes, she had a very bad feeling about this. *Ha.* An understatement; she was downright scared. He was never nice to her. The man could flash a smile, quip, and stroll away with the crown jewels with no more effort than he put into his next breath. And the king and his guards would simply allow him to go on his way with a pat on the back and their blessings for his good fortune. But for her? He hated her, and she knew it well; not that she hadn't earned his animosity. She supposed she had earned it. No, she had definitely earned it.

But right now was not the time to rekindle their hatred. She was supposed to be getting married fifteen minutes ago.

La, his smile bode ill, indeed.

"Yes. Well. I am here to inform you that there has been a slight change of plans. Stonebridge, you see, has finally, shall we say, come to his senses? You see, he won't be joining us here today. He's headed to Oxford, to marry Grace, his love."

"Oh, God." Beatryce was terrified. Her heart, which had started pounding at the words "slight change of plans" now thundered in her chest.

Dansbury watched her warily as her mind raced through the implications.

They will kill me. Father will kill me, beat me 'til I'm blue. I know too much. Stonebridge was my last hope. What will I do? What will I do?

She ran to Dansbury, momentarily setting aside their mutual loathing. She grabbed him by the lapels of his jacket with both hands. "Please,

Dansbury, please, you must take me with you. Please."

She could see the doubt in his eyes. Her mind raced for something else to say.

Shite, what can I say to change his mind?

"I'm sorry, Lady Beatryce, but you're confusing me with someone who gives a damn." And he turned his back on her.

He was leaving. God no, he couldn't leave her here.

"Wait."

He stopped just before he walked through the door. She didn't know what he had heard in her voice to make him do it, but he did, so it didn't matter. She had the result she wanted. He turned to face her; his hands on his hips, brow raised in question.

Beatryce wet her lips, her mouth turned dry and pasty. "I can help you, if you help me. I can…I can lead you to what you need to know…to solve your investigation." She paused to draw in a deep breath and brace herself for his reactions.

I have to tell him. I have no choice.

"I know where my father keeps his secret papers."

That got his attention. He looked stunned, but only for a moment, before he burst into action. He ran toward her, anger blazing in his eyes, his arms outstretched, though whether to throttle her or shake her she couldn't tell. "Tell me what you know. Tell me now!" he all but bellowed.

She held her hand up to stop him and to shut him up. "Shhh. Are you crazy? Lower your voice. First, get me out of here, safely, and without being seen, and then, I'll tell you what I know. Not before. And be quick about it."

He growled at her, literally growled at her, but she stood her ground. She crossed her arms and waited him out, seemingly at ease and in command of the situation, but fear kept her gaze flicking to the door while he weighed his options.

He stared at her as if seeking the truth in her soul before he frowned in resignation.

"Fine. Let's go."

He held out his hand. She both feared and desired to accept it.

She took it without betraying her hesitation.

*

"Where are we going?" Beatryce hadn't even allowed him to relax in his seat before she laid the question at his feet. Their carriage took off with a soft jerk, but her eyes never left him. She had not cared to know their destination when she was in the church, exposed and vulnerable. She'd only needed to get out of there. Now, she was decidedly curious as to where he thought to take her.

"I'm taking you to Stonebridge House. It seems the most obvious choice as it is the last place anyone would think to look for you." He spoke without looking at her as he arranged himself on the rear-facing bench. When he was settled, he crossed his arms and glared at her, anger practically rolling off him in waves. She was sure he hated being forced to do anything, particularly for her.

He stretched out his legs and crossed his booted feet. Her eyes followed his actions. La, he was big; of a sudden, she felt dwarfed by his presence within the confines of his too-small carriage. The feeling was most unnerving.

Her own family's carriage was rather small when Father was present as well, but this was a different feeling altogether. More tumultuous to her composure. She wasn't sure she liked it, this disconcerting feeling inside her.

She shoved such concern aside, something she'd grown to excel at over the years.

"That sounds wise." Nothing more need be said and by unspoken agreement, they each tended to their own internal thoughts. Hers returned to the man seated before her.

They'd never been alone together, nor had she ever sat this close to him before. He looked out the window, seemingly studying the view outside; though anger furrowed his brow. With his obvious distraction, she took the opportunity to study him; she'd never had the occasion before now.

His face was tanned, as if he spent a lot of time out of doors. He had a squared jaw and despite it being early in the day, it already showed signs of an afternoon shadow. A muscle ticked in his jaw. Was he aware of her regard?

He shifted forward at the same time as she looked up and into his eyes. He drew near, close enough for her to smell his cologne.

"Do you see something you like, Lady Beatryce?" He stared at her eyes as he said it. She managed to not lick her lips by sheer force of will.

When his words finally registered, she nearly snorted aloud. "Hardly." She was an excellent liar if anything.

"You've been staring at me for the past twenty minutes. Hardly is not the word I would choose to describe your behavior at the moment."

Beatryce smiled and batted her lashes; hers was a look of false innocence. "I was merely remembering just how many times I've wanted to…" She reached up and touched his cheek. "…punch you in the face…" Her hand slid down to his jaw. "…right about…"

She tapped his jaw once. "…here."

He simply smiled while her hand remained frozen in place; her touch coupled with her words did not appear to unsettle him in the least.

"Hmmm. That's not what your eyes tell me, Lady Beatryce. But if what you say is true, I'd like to see you try as much. I've never hit a woman before, but I'm sure I would make an exception for you."

He was close enough now, she could feel his breath. And despite their words, a strange…something…seemed to arch between them.

"Hmm…tempting, but…" She patted his cheek in time with her next words. "…perhaps some other time."

She took pride in her steady voice, a convincing mask for the uneasiness stirring inside her.

CHAPTER 5

"What lies behind you and what lies in front of you,
pales in comparison to what lies inside of you."
— *Ralph Waldo Emerson*

Stonebridge House...
London...

Day One of Torture...

He could have left her at the church to face the music. Alone. But he'd made the choice to help her. It was for the good of his investigation. Honest. He refused to examine the unspoken reasons behind his actions.

Before they left St. George's, he'd *strongly encouraged* Lady B to write a letter to her father stating that she and Stonebridge had determined that they didn't suit, and thus, they had agreed to call the wedding off. She really hadn't wanted to write anything; she'd just wanted to get out of there. In the end, she'd finally agreed. And he'd dispatched a footman to deliver the letter to the earl at the church as soon as they had arrived safely at Stonebridge House.

So, a few minutes ago, when another footman arrived at Stonebridge House bearing a letter from the earl, it was not a complete surprise. And of course, the duke was still away, so he couldn't respond. And so, Dansbury just had to read the letter on his behalf. Obviously.

Duke,

> *Your Grace, it has come to my attention that, this morning, my daughter intimated that she did not think you would suit each other in that holiest of states: matrimony. The result being that you have mutually agreed not to marry after all. I am embarrassed and appalled by her erroneous thinking in this matter, and I hope that it does not reflect poorly on me in your illustrious eyes. Further, I appreciate your desire to handle this situation discreetly.*

Dansbury laughed. Discreetly? A thousand guests were witness to the fact that the wedding hadn't occurred. He continued reading, shaking his head in the process.

> *I apologize profusely for her misguided behavior, and I pray that you suffer no insult as a result of her foolish actions. Or bear any ill will toward me, specifically. She is thoroughly aware that she made a wrong and hasty decision and that she behaved dishonestly. Should you seek my counsel, I am able to suggest several suitable punishments that work most effectively as a reprimand for her disgraceful behavior.*
>
> *Please know that she fervently desires this union between our families; thus, I strongly believe this unexpected behavior is a singular case of nervous anxiety and not an indication of any weakness in her character. But you know women; they have perversely weak constitutions compared to us men.*
>
> *Therefore, I beg you to reconsider the matter. Unfortunately, Lady Beatryce is currently indisposed as she recovers from her irrationally frightful experience. But I remain confident she will be ready to reassess the situation in a few days. I will be in contact with you when she is thinking sensibly again and ready to speak with you further on this subject of great import. I am sure, then, she will be of a much more amenable disposition.*

Swindon

Dansbury doubled over laughing. He held his sides as he tried to stop. She was no longer in danger, so he could suppress his inexplicable and unsuitable level of concern to the obvious threats leveled at her.

But to suggest that she suffered from a nervous anxiety, even a singular one? *Ha!* Frightened? *Double Ha.* Reassess the situation? And, then, to grovel so completely? It was so despicable as to be laughable. And he did laugh. And laughed. It might have been inappropriate. Lady B was definitely not amused.

The lies about her being at home but indisposed were a bit alarming. It was interesting that he did not admit that his daughter was missing. And he did not understand how the earl could possibly think he was going to find Lady B in the interim. He was awfully sure of himself.

It didn't matter. She was safe with him…er, at Stonebridge House. The earl would never look for her here; it was too impossible to think she would actually be hiding in the duke's residence of all places after calling off the wedding.

* * * *

Stonebridge House…
Ten Hours Later…

It was time for dinner. They'd been here. In the same house. Under the same roof together. For ten. Hours. Ten long hours.

The dining room was a grand affair. The walls were red silk damask. The table, large enough to seat sixty, was walnut and stained a dark, rich hue making the silver sparkle in the flickering candlelight with the contrast.

And it all looked beautiful as a backdrop to the stunning Lady Beatryce Beckett. Her blonde hair and blue, almost violet eyes looked alive amidst the splendor and opulence of the room. It was as if the room had been decorated with her visage in mind.

Too bad her inner soul did not match her physical beauty, else he would be mesmerized by her presence. It only took her opening her mouth to remind him that a pretty package does not necessarily contain a worthy gift inside.

"La, Dansbury, you have encouraged the cook to outdo himself this evening. Thank you."

"Thank you, but I had nothing to do with it. Stonebridge's staff is the best. They deserve all the credit."

She pursed her lips as if she'd just swallowed something bitter. "Well. In my experience, most of the serving class does not possess the intelligence to complete the smallest task without guidance. Stonebridge's servants must be exceptional."

Her attitudes never ceased to amaze him, and not in a good way. "The servants are people, too, Lady Beatryce. Just like you and me. And like you and I, most are quite keen. You do them, and yourself, a disservice if you cannot acknowledge that fact."

She waved her hand in the air. "Goodness, Dansbury. I didn't realize you were so…liberal."

"Lady Beatryce, there are a great many things you do not know about me. And I intend to keep it that way."

That shut her up. For the moment. They began to eat in blessed peaceful silence for at least two minutes before the witch opened her mouth. Again.

"It must be hard to know a commoner, one planning a future in trade no less, would choose your best friend over you. Does it keep you up at night, wallowing in remorse, that Grace chose Stonebridge over you?"

He smiled. "Likely not as much as Stonebridge choosing Grace keeps you pacing the floors at night."

He couldn't resist saying it. Her smile fell, and he was almost ashamed. Almost.

In truth, he wasn't bothered in the least. He threw her a false smile.

She quickly composed herself and pursed her lips as if she would argue the point further, likely with something disagreeable, so he added, "Lady Beatryce, your sour tongue turns my stomach. Please refrain from speaking if you cannot be pleasant."

She knew how to get under his skin better than anyone. Hell, she was the only person who ever managed to do so. Lady Beatryce. Lady. *Ha! Some lady.* The term lady brought to mind manners and graciousness, innocence. Not so this harpy who called herself a lady.

Admittedly, her spoken prejudices were common amongst many in the ton. He still hated to hear them expressed, regardless.

Lady Beatryce was the only person in the world he actively disdained, and if he were honest, he'd admit that that fact disturbed him on some deep level. Even though she deserved his contempt.

He enjoyed people. He enjoyed charming them and putting them at ease, it was an asset in his line of work…but he could never be that way with her. He didn't look too profoundly at the reasons for it.

"Hmm. Touchy…"

He just looked at her, daring her to continue her line of thought. She wisely chose to remain silent, though he could see her mind was churning. Clearly, she needed to speak. He decided he would be the one to choose the topic.

"Since you are so keen to hear the sound of your own voice, tell me, Lady Beatryce, what information do you have to impart? What do you know of our investigation?" Silence.

And now she refuses to speak.

He waited patiently a few minutes. Then, "Lady Beatryce? You were quite determined to speak earlier. Pray do not stop now. I asked you a question. What do you know of our investigation?"

She set her fork down and dabbed at her lips. So ladylike. She was wasting time. His time.

"Lady B…"

"I won't speak until Stonebridge is here. He is the man in charge, is he not?"

"He is. But I want to understand why I brought you here. Why I am lying to your father on your behalf…"

"La, I certainly cannot speak to the reasons behind your actions. Surely, you, of all people, would know the answer to that…"

He wanted to strangle her. She was being deliberately obtuse. She threw him a smile that confirmed this fact.

"Lady Beatryce. You try my patience. I suspect you would try the patience of the most benevolent saint."

"La, Dansbury. You should find a way to deal with your ill humor. A foul disposition is not good for your heart, you know."

He really wanted to strangle her. "Why? Why are you deliberately provoking me?"

"Why, Dansbury, whatever do you mean?"

At that, he stood up and left. Without another word lest he actually strangle the witch.

CHAPTER 6

"We all have faults, and mine is being wicked."

— James Thurber

Stonebridge House...
London...
The Library...

Day Two of Torture...

Lady Beatryce paced the perimeter of the library, glancing over the selection of books without actually taking any real note of the titles before her. She was bored. Utterly bored. And a bored Beatryce was a dangerous thing; she always managed to find her way into trouble when her hands were idle. This time, the tedium had driven her to the point where she made up things with which to goad Dansbury...At dinner. After dinner. During breakfast. In passing...La, she would even consider waking him during the night if she thought she could get away with it.

When she thought about it, provoking him was really quite fun. Though he did not seem to agree with her assessment at the moment. In fact, he reacted strongly to the silliest of things now, which made it all the more amusing. For her.

After a day and a half of this, she no longer had to put forth any effort to needle him. La, he took offense to everything she said, regardless of her intent. Why only yesterday, she made him angry by telling him that his cravat wasn't tied properly. It was true, so she didn't see why it should make him so angry, but it did.

She was the one unable to leave the house, even to walk in the back garden, and it was about to make her crazy. Even if it was for her safety. And all her doing.

But still, Stonebridge House was quickly beginning to feel like gaol. She was sure of it. Yet he was the one walking around like he had a burr in his boot, while she was taking it all in stride. At least, as much as could be expected given the circumstances.

Besides, she had the upper hand. Knowledge was power. And she had the knowledge he wanted.

It was noon of their second day at Stonebridge House and Dansbury was due to press her for information any minute now. Every two hours, he sought her out and tried to get her to speak of her father's machinations. The city of London could set their schedules to his predictable timing. She looked up at the large, ornate Ormolu clock on the fireplace mantle. La, it was time. She braced herself. "Ah, Lady Beatryce…"

Speak of the devil.

"Ah, Lord Dansbury. Right on schedule…"

He gave her a confused look, as if to ask her meaning. She declined to explain, though she suspected he knew what she meant anyway.

He stood beside a chair, all polite manners. Like a gentleman ought.

"I don't intend to sit, but please feel free if it suits you, to rest," she told him with a quirk of her head.

He attempted to suppress a scowl. She supposed her comment had sounded an awful lot like a negative remark upon his age.

But then his smile abruptly returned. "I will stand, thank you."

He clasped his hands behind his back and bounced on his heels. It made his jacket, his waistcoat…everything pull tight across his broad shoulders. She appreciated the view. He wasn't really advanced in age; he was in his youthful prime. A fine man. And she was a woman who cherished fine things.

"I'll save you the trouble, Dansbury, the answer is still no. I'll not be revealing anything until Stonebridge returns. You are wasting your breath if you are here to press me further."

His response surprised her. "Why, Lady Beatryce, perhaps I simply want to enjoy the company of a delightful lady?"

La! Was Dansbury attempting to approach her with his infamous charm? This was novel. And a bit alarming. Already his words involuntarily melted a small amount of her resistance.

It was unacceptable.

"I am flattered." She gave him a sultry smile and approached him slowly and deliberately. She could see him swallow and swore he almost pulled on his cravat. "…but you still won't convince me to divulge my secrets."

His smile remained fixed. "Ah, Lady Beatryce, were I to put forth a considerable effort to charm you into submission, I have no doubt of my success. I can be…very…" he took a step, "very…" he took another, "convincing." His lowered his voice as he spoke, a bass that rumbled like distant thunder. The sound was like a caress; her skin tightened in response.

She swallowed and shored up her defenses. She lifted her chin and countered with, "…and I can be relentlessly stubborn."

He nodded his head in agreement. "A character trait I have come to understand over the past twenty-four hours."

"Good."

"Excellent."

Oooh. He just had to have the last word.

He stepped closer. They were almost touching now, definitely within each other's personal space. She tried desperately to steady her breath. This man was more dangerous than she had realized. For a moment, they simply stared at each other. Each trying to read the other's thoughts, each coming back with naught.

He broke the silence first. "I simply saw you in here and thought to offer conversation."

She laughed. "I cannot deny that your proposal is intriguing, but, Dansbury, I am no naïve girl. You pretend to gain my favor in order to convince me to divulge my secrets. I will not fall for your charms, even as appealing as they are."

"You find me appealing? I can work with appealing…" He stepped forward again.

Oh God, he was good. Too good.

Were he serious, she'd be in trouble right about now. "But I find dogs appealing, more so," she countered.

For a moment, he quit smiling. The room seemed too dim, like clouds momentarily blocked the blazing sun.

But then his grin returned, and his confidence and charm shone like a beacon. "I see you do not believe me. Perhaps, a test. We'll enjoy this afternoon, mayhap play a game of chess, and not speak of anything remotely involving your secrets or your father for the duration."

"Thank you, Dansbury, but no. I would sooner play chess with a snake. But I will continue to make use of your services. And your hospitality. For now. I will see you anon."

And she left before she poured forth her deepest, darkest desires on the altar of his charisma. The fury she saw flash across his face as she passed helped steady her resolve.

CHAPTER 7

"Anger is a brief madness."

— *Horace*

"If a man be under the influence of anger his conduct will not be correct."

—*Confucius*

Stonebridge House...
London...

Day Three of Torture...

Cliff paced the floor outside Lady B's bedroom at Stonebridge House. He was agitated. No, it was more than that. He was furious. And he was trying to rein in his anger before he walked in and faced her. One. Last. Time.

Two days. Two fucking days. For two, interminable, long, fucking days, he'd questioned Lady Beatryce, kept her safe, brought her food, fetched her things to read...Hell, he'd all but waited on her hand and foot like a maid. And for what purpose? All she'd done was argue and complain and argue some more and stubbornly refuse to cooperate. She'd yelled, then played coy. She'd manipulated and toyed with him, then acted the innocent babe. She'd told him she would pass on vital information to help him with his investigation. Then, she'd stubbornly refused to speak further saying that she wanted to wait until Ambrose returned from Oxford.

Well, he had had it. They were going to finish this. Now. This was a criminal enquiry. They could be making progress based on her information; thus, she was, in effect, hindering the investigation with her silence. A crime according to the law. By all rights, she should be hanged. He opened the door without bothering to knock and stepped inside.

Oh, hell.

The earl had lied in his letter when he had said she was indisposed.

But she was definitely indisposed now.

His hands flew to his neck in an attempt to loosen his cravat. Of a sudden, it choked him as if he'd stuck his head in a drawn noose.

She wore nothing but a corset and a dressing gown. The robe was high-quality and silk. And white. A bright white that seemed to shimmer when she moved. Like light from a full moon iridescent over rippling water. And she was a perfectly tall woman, so the bottom of the robe brushed her legs just above her knees. It also did not close; he caught a glimpse of a pink corset underneath. No chemise. Damn the no chemise. It was almost his undoing.

He never once thought to question where she'd found such garments. She'd arrived with nothing but the clothes on her back. He certainly hadn't given them to her.

His eyes stalked her from head to toe. They all but acted of their own accord. Her legs were lean and splendidly muscled. Like she exercised or she spent her days at hard labor rather than being corseted into ball gowns. Odd for a lady. His heart skipped a beat at the sight and his throat turned dry even though he preferred softer, more rounded, women. But he was far too angry to care or acknowledge his primitive reactions. He brushed them aside like crumbs on a sleeve.

He'd catalogued her lack of attire and his base reactions in under five seconds. He started to pace, unfreezing as if on cue. "Lady B…"

"Do. You. Mind?" She talked over him in pretend outrage, hands on her hips, all but emphasizing the curve of her hips.

It did nothing to cool his ire, only inflamed him further. "Shut! Up!" He slashed his hand at her with his words.

She abruptly sat, stunned for the moment. Hell, he was stunned. He never thought he'd say that to a woman, much less yell it. It was a sign of his distress. He raked his hands through his hair, stopped his pacing, and continued, a tad more calmly though still skirting the edge. "I'm through with dancing to your tune, Lady Beatryce. I've played along for two days. We're going to do this my way now. You promised me information. I want it. Now." His temper rose as he spoke. He'd never been prone to violence. Damn, but she seemed to bring out the worst in him.

She sat in a chair facing him, her legs and arms crossed. She'd regained her composure as he lost his further. She raised one condescending brow, the look daring him to make her talk. "And if I don't?"

"You really don't want to know, but I almost wish you would try it and find out." He all but bit out the words.

She looked at him, thoughtfully. God, she was utterly self-possessed and it irritated the hell out of him. "First, let me ask you something. What would you do to get what you want? I don't mean like a new pair of boots or a well-bred horse. I mean something you want…desperately."

This play was familiar. They'd acted it out over the last two days, repeatedly. He'd threatened. She'd refuse to answer or answer with her own question. Usually a provoking one. And the subject was familiar. Hadn't he just had this conversation with Kelly a few days ago?

"All right, Lady Beatryce. I'll play it your way. For now. If you are talking about justice, the end always justifies the means. In any other case, there is always a limit to what is acceptable to get what you want."

She pursed her lips as if his answer disappointed her, but she tried to hide it. "You've obviously not wanted anything bad enough."

He marched over to her chair and leaned over her. She didn't cower. He shouldn't have, but he liked it. "Lady Beatryce, there are plenty of things I want badly enough." He looked her up and down. Thoroughly. But kept a tight rein on any unwanted, base reactions. He would be appalled at his behavior later. Much later. "But I've never seen anything I've wanted badly enough to make me compromise my morals to obtain it." He flicked his eyes to her legs, he couldn't help himself, then back to her eyes. "No matter how enticing the package."

She smiled, and it made him uncomfortable, that smile. It was too astute. Too precise. Too deadly. "My, my, you are a foolish one. Aren't you? So pampered in your lofty world. Almost naïve. Surprising, considering your occupation."

"You test my patience, Lady Beatryce." He all but growled at her.

Yes, he was angry. No. Beyond angry. He was furious.

And he was behaving badly; he knew it as well. Unprofessional.

Immature. Violent.

He no longer cared. She'd worn him down over the past two days 'til his patience was stretched thin. And it wouldn't take much to push him all the way over the edge. Hell, he was barely hanging on as it was. She could do it, too. They both knew it. "Good. You could use a good challenge for once in your spoilt life. You…"

Yea. That did it.

Before she could bat another eye, he unwound his cravat and muzzled her mouth. He stood behind her now, her wrists bound with one hand while he reached behind himself to rip a wide swath of fabric from the nearby window with the other. He tied her arms with the fabric and wound the remaining length around her chest, strapping her to the chair. It'd hold. For now.

He rang the bell pull to summon a footman for some sturdier rope as she tried futilely to free herself. Cursing him to all sorts of hell in the process, he was sure. The rope would do until Ambrose arrived.

He was finished with her. She wanted to wait for Stonebridge? Well, she was going to get her wish. He was amused to see and hear that she was no longer unruffled; she tried to scream through her makeshift gag.

"What was that, Lady B? I didn't quite catch that," he taunted as he sauntered out of the room.

CHAPTER 8

"Resist much, obey little."
— Walt Whitman, Leaves of Grass

An Hour and Much Frustration Later...

At their approach, Cliff looked up and acknowledged Ambrose and Grace with a nod before he crossed his arms and leaned back against the door to Lady Beatryce's room. As if he hadn't just been pacing the floor and mumbling to himself a few minutes ago. He tried to look calm and collected. He thought he succeeded. Mostly.

Ambrose, who clearly hadn't stopped grinning since he decided to marry Grace, spoke up. "I understand we have an unexpected guest."

"We do. She promised me concrete evidence. She all but guaranteed she could solve our investigation, but that was two days ago. If she tells us anything before I throttle her, it will be a bloody miracle."

Ambrose and Grace shared a curious glance. Cliff scowled at the both of them for it. Hell, with the way he felt, he might punch his friend if he so much as looked like he was going to make some sort of pithy comment.

"May I?" Ambrose inquired, reaching for the door.

"By all means..." Cliff stepped aside.

The door swung open to reveal Lady Beatryce tied to a chair and gagged. Her eyes blazed with fury and promised retribution. She thrashed in anger and screamed through the cloth covering her mouth. Cliff could just imagine

43

what she was saying. He'd heard it all, repeatedly, over the last couple of days. It certainly wasn't polite conversation for mixed company.

Ambrose looked like he was ready to tumble to the floor laughing. His lips twitched. "I'm not surprised she hasn't told you anything." To Lady Beatryce, he added, "Can I count on you to be civil if I remove this?" His hands hovered over the cravat being used as an effective muffle to her ire.

She narrowed her eyes at Cliff before she nodded once.

"Excellent," agreed Stonebridge.

Seeing Lady Beatryce with her muzzle firmly in place momentarily lightened his mood, even if the gag was about to come off.

*

Stonebridge removed the cravat from Beatryce's mouth and stood back. She flexed her jaw, relieved to be free of her linen muzzle. Her mouth was sore from clenching her teeth and the corners of her lips were dry and cracked from the cloth.

She glared at Dansbury as she poked her tongue into the corners of her mouth to soothe the soreness there.

His face darkened in return.

She ignored him and spoke to the duke. "I know you're investigating my father, and I know why. I can lead you to the evidence you need to put him away. Or better yet, hang him."

"Yes? And how did you come by all this information?"

"I notice e-v-e-r-y-t-h-i-n-g. I've seen the men watching my house; I've watched Dansbury searching my house," she shot him a mocking brow as she said that, "and I know all about my father's involvement with the Society for the Purification of England. I know where he keeps his papers, including all of their silly, idiotic little Writ's of Execution where they spell out who they intend to murder and why."

"I see. And what do you want in exchange for this information?" She bit her lip for a moment, then firmed her resolve. "Money."

"Hell—of course," Dansbury interjected with a curse.

Beatryce glared at him and shouted, "Don't you *dare* judge me right now. I am putting my life on the line for your treasured Grace and your precious case." She cleared her throat and calmed herself. When her fury was contained, she looked up at Stonebridge. "And I want safe passage out of town—a quiet home to go to in the country, simple, country clothes, and a new identity."

Dansbury, who was back to leaning against the door with his arms crossed, said, "How do we know you aren't just as guilty as your father? I mean, it's clear you knew of his guilt and yet you've never said anything before now? Sounds highly suspicious to me."

She shot daggers at him, again, before returning her attention to Stonebridge. "Does he really need to be here?"

Stonebridge barked out a laugh. "Probably not, but I'm just going to tell him everything anyway, so this saves time. Just answer the question. You must admit, your knowledge does cast you in a questionable light."

"I only discovered all of this recently, when I started to realize that my marriage plans were on shaky ground. I knew my father was behaving strangely…well, stranger than normal…and I had noticed peculiar men watching the house—so I set out to determine why. I broke into his office, found his hidden box, and picked the lock. Imagine my surprise at all I discovered; including that my father was behind the deaths of your father…and hers." She nodded at Grace.

So maybe she hadn't picked the lock, but it sounded more impressive and she needed every advantage.

Grace gasped.

"You didn't tell her, I see," she said.

"Shut up!" yelled Dansbury as the duke raced over to Grace to console and offer comfort. Beatryce suppressed an unexpected flair of jealousy.

Stonebridge held Grace close in comfort. After a while, they agreed that perhaps it was best if Grace leave the room. Of course.

We wouldn't want to offend her delicate sensibilities, would we?

Grace always had been a regular waterworks.

On her way out, Grace stopped in front of Beatryce and said, "Thank you for coming forth and telling us what you know."

Beatryce squirmed in her chair, speechless and discomfited by Grace's kindness. Stonebridge watched Grace leave with a look of pride on his face, but Dansbury just continued to glare at Bea.

Once she was gone, Stonebridge turned to her once more. "All right, now, tell us what we need to know."

She raised her chin. "First, I have one more condition. Once the arrangements are made for my passage out of town, I want him to take me." She nodded at Dansbury.

"Like hell!" the man in question shouted.

Stonebridge gave his friend a speaking look, but he addressed her. "Are you sure that's wise, Lady Beatryce?"

"No. But he's the only one I trust to keep me safe." She flinched over the word trust, but she'd say anything to achieve the desired results. "You must understand. My father is incredibly guilty and has done some horrid things, but I'm telling you, someone else is out there pulling his strings. I don't know who—I've not an inkling, but think about it. My father can barely get out of his bed without assistance. He's out of breath just walking from the drawing room to the library. He's weak. I can't speak of the time when your father was killed, but any move he's made recently, has been done out of fear and a touch of insanity. Someone else is behind all this."

"Done."

"What?" barked Dansbury; looking at his friend as if he'd lost his mind.

Stonebridge looked back at Dansbury. "I said done. You'll take her. You'll protect her. But until the arrangements are made, she'll stay here." He turned back to her. "Now, tell us what we want to know."

"Fine. But will you please untie me from this chair first? I cannot feel my arms anymore."

CHAPTER 9

"Women are made to be loved, not understood."

— Oscar Wilde

3:00 AM…

Technically, Day Four of Torture…

"Stonebridge, you must help me. Take me. I beg you. He'll kill me if you don't. Please. Please. Please. I'll tell you everything. I swear I will…just don't let him kill…"

Those were the last words Earl Swindon, Lady Beatryce's father, ever uttered. He was dead before he hit the floor, killed by a cloaked assassin while he and Ambrose attempted to confront him with his treasonous activities.

Now, it was up to Dansbury to inform Lady Beatryce of her father's demise, a task he was loath to do. Alas, needs must.

Knock. Knock. Knock.

He knocked on her bedroom door. The sound echoed loudly in the early hours of the morning. "Lady Beatryce. It is Dansbury. I have news to impart."

He was surprised Lady Beatryce hadn't waited downstairs for their return, anxious to hear what transpired. He would never understand this woman.

"Come in," came her muffled reply.

He entered the room and was amazed to see her sitting by the fire with an open book in her lap, attending to her fingernails. She appeared relaxed and comfortable. As if she hadn't a care in the world. She didn't even look up at his approach.

He crossed the room and stood before her chair, uncomfortably aware of her disregard. He waited for her to invite him to sit in the unoccupied chair next to hers or to at least acknowledge his presence so he could convey his news. It was the way a gentleman behaved in the presence of a lady, even if they were in her boudoir. Even if said lady wasn't much of a lady at all.

He'd forgotten she often didn't act the part. At times, even a doxy behaved with better refinement and manners.

She ignored him and continued to file her nails, the sound grating across his nerves.

It was late. He was tired. He didn't have time for this.

Finally, without looking up, she said, "Well, are you going to impart your news?"

He ground his teeth and reminded himself he was about to inform her that her father was murdered. But, still, he refused to speak to the top of her head. "Would you do me the courtesy of looking at me while we converse?"

She paused her manicure and looked at him. Her hands remained aloft as if she intended to resume attending to them the minute he began speaking.

He raised one brow and looked pointedly at her hands. "I can stand here all night."

"Suit yourself," she said and resumed the task of smoothing the ends of her nails.

He reached over, grabbed her manicure set, and threw it into the fire.

When he turned back around, she was sitting as primly as a debutante, her shoulders back and hands folded in her lap. As if nothing was amiss. As if he hadn't just thrown her manicure set into the fire.

He was so angry at her antics he no longer cared to blunt his words. "Your father was murdered this evening."

She didn't even flinch. In fact, she showed no emotional response at all. "Oh. Is that all? You tossed my manicure tools in the fire just to tell me that? That set was made of bone and silver, and was the only thing in my reticule besides a couple of stray pins and a knife. The sum total of all I own in this world. Now."

For a moment words failed him. That was not the response he expected.

And a knife? "Is that all you have to say? I just told you your father was murdered."

She just stared at him a moment before waving her hands and saying, "Well, it is not a complete surprise, now, is it? With the men he tangled with, it was bound to happen eventually. Did you happen to catch the culprit?"

"No."

She shook her head. "Tsk. Tsk. Do you at least have a description of the bandit? A way of tracking down who he is?"

If he weren't so confident in himself, she'd have made him feel inadequate with her questions. Perhaps that was her intent? Regardless, he answered honestly, "He was cloaked. We didn't see his face."

For a moment, her eyes widened in fear. It was brief, but he didn't miss it. "My description of the assassin doesn't surprise you. Tell me, Lady Beatryce, do you know this man?"

"No. I don't. I've just seen a cloaked man watching the house many times in the past; his presence always seemed to disturb my father's peace of mind. Especially the last time…"

"I can see why."

"I daresay. The man used to stand in the street, bold as brass, and stare up at the house. No one ever stopped him. No runners ever asked of him…no one ever asked of him. I find it difficult to believe that the neighbors hadn't noticed his presence, yet no one ever mentioned it."

She sounded so practical and matter of fact. And though he knew her father was not a good man, he was still her father. Shouldn't she show some level of remorse? Not talk practically about strange cloaked men and assassins?

"What, Dansbury? Are you expecting me to burst in to tears? To wail and gnash my teeth in sorrow? I'm not that kind of woman."

"No, I didn't expect that, but some show of emotion is certainly expected. He was your father, after all."

She shook her head. "No one knows that better than me. La, I'm sure once the reality of his death really sets in I'll be reacting…"

She's in shock then.

"…by dancing around the room like a banshee…with wild abandon and an overabundance of gaiety."

Or not.

"I see." He clasped his hands behind his back, lest he fidget in frustration. "Don't you want to know about your siblings? Your stepmother?"

"What about them?" She met his eyes then, hers were quite serious. "I'm sure they're fine."

"What about Adelaide? She's only six. She needs someone strong in her life."

"And you think I'm the person to fill that role?" She laughed as if he jest.

"Well, you are many things, Lady Beatryce," he would not enumerate that long list, "but weak is not one of them."

"A compliment, Dansbury? I'm surprised." She shook her head. "Adelaide will be fine."

"But…"

"Dansbury, she is better off without me."

"Better? Lady B…"

"Look. I will not argue the point with you. They will be fine." She raised her chin a notch. "The subject is closed."

"I find myself surprised, Lady Beatryce," he blurted out. She'd not interrupt him again. "I had not realized you were this cold-hearted, so much so as to not even concern yourself with the welfare of your family…" He didn't know what else to add to that.

What more was there to say?

She crossed her arms. "Are you quite finished?"

Should he tell her that her stepmother had been laughing hysterically, like a madwoman, when he left? Lady Beatryce just didn't react the way he expected; he was somewhat at a loss with how to handle her.

"I suppose so." This was the most bizarre conversation he'd ever had. He briefly wondered if there would ever come a time where something she did or said would ever not surprise him.

For tonight, though, he was finished with her. He cleared his throat. "Well, then. I'll leave you to your…dancing," he said and walked away.

"When are we leaving?"

Oh, this woman was cold-hearted, and self-centered. She would finally have a question, but it was about her and her departure from Town.

"We leave in two days."

He did not look back when he answered her. And he left without another word, all but shaking his head in utter exasperation. For sure, he would never understand this woman.

CHAPTER 10

*"Secrets, silent, stony sit in the dark palaces of both
our hearts: secrets weary of their tyranny: tyrants
willing to be dethroned."*

— *James Joyce, Ulysses*

*Later That Morning…
At a Far More Reasonable Hour…*

From her bedroom window, Lady Beatryce Beckett watched fleeting pedestrians as they passed by on the pavement outside. Rain showered down upon the city as thick as the velvet drapery surrounding her window.

The gentry marched by with a determined stride, their black umbrellas open to impede the steady downpour. The servants and laboring classes, who had to attend to their duties regardless of the weather, scurried impatiently behind them, not daring to pass yet resigned to becoming drenched with water; it was probably the first bath they'd had in a week, perhaps longer.

She couldn't imagine living that way herself…filthy as a soiled rag and as smelly as a costermonger's cart full of rotted vegetables. Was it any wonder they were never able to better their lot in life?

She might have felt a pang of remorse for her unkind thoughts, but swept it aside. Beatryce watched it all…life…advance before her with a somewhat detached air, her mind turned inward.

Why wasn't she dancing about her room and laughing with great relief? Her father was dead and could hurt her no more. Perhaps she had yet to really believe it? In a way, the news of his demise still seemed too good to be true...was she finally, after all these years, actually rid of her father? Forever?

She'd always thought she'd instantly feel...transformed and relieved. Perhaps lighter...Alive.

Instead she felt the same, trapped and hardened...and experienced in a way she would never wish on any other, even maids and thieves and whores. In fact, she even felt a tad glum if one could believe it.

She touched her head to the window, the glass cool and damp against her forehead, and fingered the nearest glazing bar separating the broad, yet intricately shaped panes making up her bedroom window. The craftsmanship was of the highest standard; Stonebridge must pay an exorbitant amount in excises for the windows in his home.

She laughed at the errant thought. Such was her way...to find herself dodging persistent yet random thoughts even at the most unlikely of times.

Beatryce dropped her hand and looked to the right, further up the cobbled road. Plenty of carriages tumbled past, pulling unknown occupants to their various destinations amid the gray of dreary rain.

Life carried on as usual. Father's death didn't affect them either.

A break in the river of umbrellas flowing up the pavement across the street revealed a man standing still and shrouded in a cloak and facing the house. Right at the window she presently occupied.

Her heart began pounding in fear. She swallowed the lump that swelled in her throat.

It couldn't be; it just couldn't.

Yet she feared it could...and had. Yet how had the cloaked man known she was here?

A mass of carriages and a wave of fresh umbrellas arrived, blocking her view of the man as if swallowing him whole. No interruption in the flow signaled a lone person standing still against the tide.

Beatryce stood on the tips of her toes. She looked left, then right. She stretched up, then down and tried in vain to see through the sea of black, to no avail. Twice her sawing breath fogged the window. Twice she rubbed it clear with her sleeve.

At another break in the flow, she searched the pavement opposite with renewed fervor, but he wasn't there. As if he'd never even been.

Was she going mad? Now, of all times, when she was finally free?

* * * *

That Night, After Dinner…
The First Floor Drawing Room…

"Ah, Grace, you should have seen Dansbury. There he sat, muddied and bedraggled…his jacket torn and his hair soiled and disheveled. But the cat that was curled in his arms…was altogether tidy and clean." They all laughed, then Stonebridge continued, "…but as he reached with his hand to pet the beast he'd just rescued, it turned round, latched onto his hand, and bit him, leaving scars that are still visible today."

Dansbury shook his head. "Yes, it was my first experience with a cat's claws. I daresay, I never forgot the lesson." He looked at Beatryce as he said this.

Was he implying something with that remark?

They all laughed again, or at least Grace, Stonebridge, and Dansbury did. Beatryce did not. Oh yes, Dansbury was kind. And charming. They were hearing about it all; Stonebridge was regaling them with tales from their youth, particularly of Dansbury. Oh, what a saint.

And she was bosom bows with sarcasm.

"Ambrose, do you remember Head Master Smythe?" asked Dansbury.

"Oh, how could I forget? He was callous and cruel."

"And smelly…"

"He looked like death…"

"Yes. And hated children…" Dansbury looked at Grace. "He was our Head Master at Eton when we were thirteen…our first year there. He'd been there for thirty years before that." Dansbury looked back at Stonebridge. "…Though he looked like he'd stopped aging at about thirty-five…"

"…because he wore his hair so tightly bound, it smoothed his face…" They said it at the same time, and laughed through it all.

"You played so many pranks on that man, Cliff, I cannot believe you managed to pass your year."

"That is because I never got caught. And they were harmless pranks. But funny. And he deserved it."

"True. All true."

"So he was only there for one year with you? Sounds like you were fortunate." Grace asked.

"Ah, yes, well…he died from a heart attack while beating a student, or we might have had to endure him for much longer than a year. We all swore he was already preserved; he was going to outlive us all."

A knock on the door interrupted their remembrances. The butler entered, bearing a missive. The sounds and sighs of laughter died slowly as the butler made his way towards them.

"Your Grace, a message has arrived…"

"Ah, thank you, Ledbetter." The duke stood and approached his butler.

"Ah, but your grace, this message is not for you." The butler turned to Beatryce. "It is addressed to Lady Beatryce Beckett…"

One might have heard a pin drop, the silence was deafening. They all turned as one toward her. "For me?" The blood drained from her face; in fact, alarm graced the visage of every person in the room, the butler included.

How could anyone know she was here? The question was on all of their minds.

Stonebridge walked over and handed her the note, then stood back to give her room. For a minute, she stared at the parchment as if it would suddenly burst into flame and scorch her near-to-trembling fingers. She shook off such fanciful thoughts and opened it to the curious eyes of everyone in the room.

Lady Beatryce,

> *I know you are here.*
> *I know why you are here.*
> *I'm coming for you, sweet.*
> *Tick. Tock.*

-Your Cloaked Friend

PS. Tell Dansbury, I know his secrets.

Beatryce couldn't say a word; her tongue was thick in her mouth. Any words she might have uttered died in her throat. She stood on unsteady legs and handed the note to Stonebridge who read it out loud whilst her thoughts raced in out of control panic.

How does he know I am here? What am I to do? That was him looking at me in the window, after all…La, what am I to do?

She automatically looked to Dansbury.

"Cliff? What is he talking about? What secrets?" asked Stonebridge. The question piqued her curiosity, pulling her to the edge, but not out, of her anxious worry.

"The hell if I know." La, she doubted that. Dansbury mingled with the dregs of society as an agent for the Crown and rubbed elbows with the top echelons of society through his title; between the two, he was bound to have secrets.

"Did you tell anyone? Were you followed?"

"No and no. I'm no green lad."

"I know, friend; I had to ask." Stonebridge turned to her, "Lady Beatryce have you left the house? Gone outside at all? Written to anyone?"

"No." She swallowed. "But this morning, I was looking out the window, and I thought I saw that madman in the street. But then a flood of carriages and pedestrians crowded the road and pavement, momentarily blocking my view, and when they parted again, he was gone. I thought I must have been mistaken." She was pleased her voice didn't waver. She had managed to convince herself that he hadn't really been there, watching her from the street.

"Evidently not."

"No." So she had been wrong.

"Well, this moves up our timetable and makes your departure more urgent." Stonebridge said this to Dansbury.

"Indeed, it does. We leave now." He replied as he stood and exited the room. "Let's go."

Presumably that last part was directed at her. She followed in his wake. She had nothing to pack.

CHAPTER 11

*"A gentleman is one who never hurts anyone's feelings
unintentionally."*

— Oscar Wilde

A Less Travelled Road Out of London…
June 1814…

Dansbury eyed his traveling companion with more than a little distaste. He could just make out her silhouette in the dim light emanating from their carriage lamp. The lamp hung on her side of their conveyance, swaying with every dip and pot hole, casting her profile in light, then dark, then light again.

Lady Beatryce didn't want to die, surely. But the chances increased with every minute of their enforced proximity. They were already at odds with each other from their four day stay at Stonebridge House…but this…this…closeness…was so much worse.

And he'd felt that way since half an hour into their trip. On their first day out. What would it be like after five days?

Lady Beatryce should be worried.

He could have refused to take the assignment. Ambrose would have grumbled and cursed, but he would've accepted his decision…eventually. Ambrose could have easily brought in MacLeod or Kelly.

So why had he said yes? Because someone needed him. He was a fool for it every time.

Even when he despised the very person he was saving, apparently.

Now, he was seriously beginning to regret his capitulation.

He eyed his companion again and wondered aloud, "How can someone as beautiful as you be so ugly inside? Do they teach that sort of the thing at that fancy finishing school you attended or is it a Beckett family trait?"

He didn't know why he'd voiced the question. It was rude and ungentlemanly. Call it a temporary madness, like when someone decides to poke a stick at a wild animal. Well, that might be idiotic, but at least his madness was only temporary. He hoped.

Lady Beatryce ignored him. She sat frozen as if turned to stone, her expressionless gaze fixated on the scenery passing by outside the window of their traveling carriage. Or what she could see of it. It was cold and dark and damp out. If he peered too closely outside his own window, his breath fogged the glass.

Their ratty conveyance squeaked, rattled, twisted, bounced, and jerked every time its wheels found even the smallest hole in the road—which was often—yet she was so still, one wouldn't guess that the carriage was even in motion, much less traveling at great speed over such uneven terrain.

Well, well. Apparently, she was very good at cool aloofness and unflinching immobility, when she wasn't pulsing with unreserved ire that is. He'd seen that side of her often over the last several days. Firsthand. Some might call it passion.

He didn't.

Yet he really didn't understand her current behavior. What happened to the passionate virago of the past week? He'd seen every manner of behavior from her—from angry to antagonizing to sarcastic. She'd provoked him at every turn and ordered him around for four days. Utter silence was a first.

He snorted to himself. He couldn't care less about her current inclination toward aloofness. It was a blessing. For him.

Dansbury sighed, rubbed the bridge of his nose, and turned to study the view outside his window. He pushed thoughts of Lady Beatryce from his mind. Easily and with pleasure. He was glad she was inclined toward silence. Now. He might even finish this unwanted assignment without murdering her. He glanced over at the witch again. Maybe.

He clenched his jaw and his teeth rattled with the windowpanes as they rode over a particularly rutted patch of road. Their unmarked and decrepit carriage squeaked and groaned, but held together. Just. His walking stick vibrated against his leg; the jarring making it slide ever closer toward his knee.

He caught it just before it landed on the floor.

Still, Lady Beatryce didn't move.

Damn, she is good.

He forced himself to let go morbid thoughts of strangling her and concentrate, instead, on their investigation. And of the secrets their assassin threatened him with...

"Ahem..."

Dansbury blinked and was surprised to see Lady Beatryce come into focus before his eyes. Brilliant blue orbs stared back at him in question, and his gut clenched in response. Clearly, he had been staring in her direction, though it was with unseeing eyes as his thoughts had been inwardly turned. For a moment, he forgot his hatred for this woman. His breath caught in his throat as her beauty hit him like a punch in the gut. Just like that day on the terrace...

He shook his head and reason returned. He lifted his brow in question, exuding supreme confidence and patience. But he also had the inexplicable urge to clear his throat. He forced himself to appear unconcerned as he waited for the witch to respond to his unspoken query.

Lady Beatryce clenched her hands until her knuckles were white with tension. She lifted her chin. "I asked if we are nearly there."

He reached for his pocket watch without lowering his eyes. He flicked open the lid, and then, after a few seconds more, glanced down to check the time. With exaggerated slowness, he nodded at the time and replaced the watch before returning his attention to his unwanted companion. He tossed his walking stick back and forth between his hands, stalling for time.

Two spots of pink appeared high on her cheekbones. Aha. She noticed he was taking his time and was angry. Good. He smiled at how easy it was to spark her anger. If possible, her fists tightened further. She'd tormented him all week. But she'd played with a master.

"I suspect we shall arrive within the half hour."

Lady Beatryce relaxed; she unclenched her hands and smoothed out her skirts while he absorbed her every move.

"Do you make it a habit of staring at people in such a fashion?" She said it without once looking in his direction. He would have noticed.

He admired her forward attack. "Only at those I wish to throttle."

She smiled, and he dropped his walking stick; it rattled about with the carriage before settling half on his foot, half on the floor. He stepped on it and kicked it against the base of his seat. As if he'd meant to do that.

She didn't remark upon it. "Let us hope it does not come to that before we reach our destination, shall we? Do you have a plan for our arrival? A story to tell? A change of clothes?" Beatryce nodded to the small valise on the seat beside him.

He grinned with pleasure as he prepared to enjoy her reaction to what he was about to say. She was going to hate this. "I'm glad you asked. I do, indeed, have a change of clothes in this bag." He patted the bag. "For both of us."

She was once again wearing her wedding finery. It was all she had, save for a small reticule. He hadn't had time to secure much being that they fled in such a rush. They were fortunate he'd been able to acquire what he had.

She waited, eyes focused and hands clasped, for him to continue—she appeared the serene lady in perfect composure, demure. It was a good act. He wanted to savor this moment for as long as possible.

But he was uncharacteristically impatient. "Unfortunately, we fled in quite a rush, as I'm sure you'll remember; so you'll have to understand when I say that we'll have to manage changing into them…in the carriage."

He leaned back in his seat and crossed his arms behind his head. Satisfied. Like a cat basking in the sun. He was thrilled to provoke her, and he waited with great anticipation to see what she would say or do next. He was rewarded when the pink tinge returned to her cheeks. It shouldn't have been comely, but he had to admit that it was.

His victory was short lived, though. All too soon, the witch composed herself like a queen.

She said nothing as she reached across the seat and jerked open the valise. If her movements were fitful, one couldn't blame her. And despite his own wishes, he couldn't help but admire her fortitude. He was deliberately goading her and she knew it, yet she carried on with apparent confidence.

As she pulled out the dress he had acquired, he couldn't help but watch for her reaction with inordinate pleasure and heightened expectancy. He had been forced to accept the shabbiest, homeliest dress imaginable on such short notice. He was sure she would hate it. He was not disappointed.

After holding up the dress in front of her to inspect it, she slammed it into her lap and glared at him, her blue eyes sparking with fire. He suppressed a smile. Instead, he acted surprised by her reaction to the god-awful dress. "What seems to be the problem, Lady Beatryce? You don't appear to be happy with my selection."

"Are you insane?"

"Lady Beatryce, I realize you are used to more refined clothing, but you must remember we are going into hiding. You cannot expect to wear the latest fashions and remain unobtrusive." He was pleased he sounded so put off. It took supreme effort to withhold his grin.

She hurled the dress at him. It landed perfectly over his head and swallowed him whole. It smelled like mothballs and sweat and other things he'd rather not think about. He gagged as he sought freedom and fresh air and nose blindness.

"That is not the problem," came her muffled screech as he fought to free himself from the hideous dress.

Ah, sweet success. She'd lost some of her infamous composure. He could hear it in her voice. Now, if only he could see it with his eyes.

And breathe again.

"The problem is that you picked out a dress that is at least ten sizes too big!"

By the time he unburied himself from the grasping wool, she was entirely poised again. Bah.

"We will have to pull off somewhere before we arrive. I cannot possibly change in here. With you."

He threw the frock aside and tossed his head to fling his disheveled hair from his eyes. "I'm afraid that is not possible. It is too dangerous to stop on the side of the road. Don't you realize we are in the middle of nowhere and highwaymen frequent these remote areas? Haven't you heard the stories?"

Somehow, he managed not to show his enjoyment of pricking her anger. For a moment, he was rewarded when he saw her jaw clench in frustration, but then her eyes turned knowing and suddenly he became all too apprehensive.

Scared shitless actually.

He fought the urge to tug at his cravat like a boy being reprimanded by his nurse.

Lady Beatryce rose and moved to his seat, drifted more like. His mouth turned dry; he reached for his cravat and gave it a quick tug as she presented her back. She looked over her shoulder and with a demure smile and a husky voice, said, "Well, then. You'll have to help me. I cannot possibly undo all these buttons by myself."

CHAPTER 12

"…I can resist everything but temptation."

— *Oscar Wilde*

Dansbury wiped clammy hands on his trousers. He wasn't a coward though; he wouldn't back down. She thought she had him by the balls, did she? Ha! He was unafraid and he would prove it.

He attacked the tiny, pearl buttons of her dress, of which there were a regrettably large number, all the while reminding himself of why he despised this woman. He would show the witch. He was in control. Utterly in control.

Buttons one and two came open with little ordeal.

He'd seen her speak with spite toward people who hadn't deserved it. He would remind himself of that fact as he undressed her. In a minute.

Button three opened with a little more difficulty.

A thread was caught. He forced the button from its hole. The sound of the thread snapping told him he was being altogether too rough. The result screamed his discomfort.

He took a deep breath and forced himself to slow down and not reveal his unease.

Button four was released from its mooring with a little more care.

And with it, more of Lady Beatryce's upper back was revealed. Her skin appeared smooth and golden in the flickering light of the carriage lamp, and he could just make out the little fine hairs on her skin sparkling back at him from under the lantern's soft glow. The carriage tilted a bit, changing the light patterns, and with it, the angle of his view. He noticed a small, thin scar near her right shoulder blade. He longed to touch it.

Ah, shite.

His breathing turned ragged and his hands shook. He wanted to rub them all over her bare skin. He wanted to taste her. Feel her. Breathe her in. He stopped himself from following through with his desires. Just.

Oh, not good. Not. Good.

And she wasn't wearing a bloody shift. He focused on that fact. No shift? Clearly, she was fast and loose just as he had always known. He'd seen that firsthand, too. And if she was amenable, mightn't they…

Bollocks. Focus.

He tried to ignore the unwanted attraction he felt stirring in his loins. He shifted in his seat to ease his…

Button five taunted him, laughed outright in his face.

It all but winked at him in the dancing glow of the swinging carriage lamp. He was no coward though, and if he kept reminding himself of his bravery, it would be true. This time, his fingertips grazed her exposed skin as he worked to set the button free.

A jolt of full on lust shot straight to his groin.

Ah, hell.

Button six stared back at him. Mocking him. Daring him to continue.

Self-preservation kicked in, and he paused to rein in his unwelcome desire. He managed to refrain from running his fingers through his own hair and down his face in distress. Barely. He clenched his fists to stop his hands from shaking. When that didn't help, he set to work removing his cravat. He was in trouble if he couldn't get a hold of himself.

"Is there a problem?" Lady Beatryce looked over her shoulder while holding the front of her dress in place. She looked confident. Telling.

He glared in return while removing his suddenly too-tight cravat. She seemed completely unaffected by the fact that he was undressing before her eyes while he was nearly choking on his uncontrollable and unwanted desire…at the sight of her back of all things. She'd probably seen many a man without their cravat. His actions probably didn't even faze her.

"Of course not. I'm hot. Turn back around."

For a moment, he thought he saw a smile grace her face before she turned completely away. He ignored the thought and asked a question guaranteed to stir up trouble. "Tell me something you regret."

Button six was released with little fanfare. Yes, this would work. Keeping them both angry would douse the fires of his attraction. Surely.

"That is none of your business."

"It's called conversation. Ever heard of it? We are going to be spending a lot of time together—by your own request, might I remind you. So tell me anyway."

Lady Beatryce squared her shoulders, but didn't look back. Finally, after a long, drawn-out exhale, she said, "I regret nothing."

"Liar. Nothing? That can't be true. We all have regrets." Even heartless sirens.

Button seven was released.

Christ, were the buttons multiplying?

Lady Beatryce lifted her chin a notch. "I once threw something into the fire…something belonging to my cousin, Grace. I suppose most people would regret something like that."

"But not you." It was a statement more than a question.

"No."

Hadn't he called her heartless? "What was it?"

"Her sketch diary. Didn't she mention it at the time?"

"No."

"I cannot believe she didn't tell you…"

"Lady Grace is a much better person than you…give her credit for." He'd paused after saying you. On purpose, of course.

Beatryce lifted her chin higher, if possible. She would drown if she were standing in the rain.

She still didn't face him. The little hairs on her back stood on end. He ignored those wicked fiends.

Button eight was freed.

"Well, this particular diary was filled with her clothing designs, and more importantly, personal notes from her parents—words of encouragement and all that."

He paused, stunned. "Did she know it was you?"

"Yes. She was there. She saw it all."

"And you don't regret your actions even a tiny bit?" He was incredulous. How could anyone be so cruel and show such little remorse?

"No."

"What possible reason could justify…"

She turned at that and with one hand, gripped his jacket. Four knuckles pressed into his chest; four points of heat, sharp like a knife. "Do you even recall who my father was?" she interrupted. "I would have done anything…A-N-Y-T-H-I-N-G…to get away from him."

She let go and turned back around. "For someone so sure of himself, you seem to be a poor judge of character."

"Ha! I dislike you—it would seem I am an excellent judge of character," he retorted.

And that did it. He was through with her. Through with her dress. Through with inappropriate and unwanted lust. He looked down at the remaining buttons. There were ten left.

Bugger them all.

Before he could think through to the consequences of his actions, he reached out and ripped her dress open the rest of the way—to hell with loose threads and malevolent buttons. The remaining pearls flew through the air and bounced about against the wall, the seat, and on the floor.

It was a mistake. The action was base and only rekindled his animalistic desire. Need surged and all he wanted was to take her on the floor. Now. Fuck her until neither of them could walk.

Christ, after everything, I still desire her…

He beat down his lust. God, it wasn't easy.

Beatryce whirled around. "What do you think you are doing?"

The fire was back in her eyes. Good. Bring. It. On. Her chest was ruddy and heaving with anger, but her hand was there, preventing the bodice from falling to her lap.

Thank God.

"My way was much faster."

She continued to glare at him, but didn't say another word. Both to his relief and to her continued safety. He grabbed her 'new' dress and tossed it to her lap. "Here. You had better put this on; we're running out of time."

And without another word, he turned away from her and began removing his fine, London coat…

CHAPTER 13

"Let every eye negotiate for itself and trust no agent;
for beauty is a witch against whose charms faith
melteth in blood."

— *Shakespeare, Much Ado About Nothing*

Beatryce kept her gaze locked on the scenery outside and ignored the man undressing behind her, or tried to. It was dark out, so she really couldn't see very much. Having nothing she could really focus her mind on outside seemed to give her imagination free rein to wander, to visualize Dansbury…undressing.

Hmmm, the sounds he made as he removed his clothes spawned the most vivid images in her mind. And she had quite an imagination.

La, her ears burned red and fair sizzled…and seemed to blaze hotter with every shift of his body. She swore she felt his gaze on her back more than once, which didn't help matters; just the thought made the hairs on her arms stand on end.

Dansbury was large and broad and quite difficult to ignore. He all but overwhelmed their rented traveling carriage with his size and larger-than-life bearing. For sure, he was beautiful; she couldn't help but notice. Everything, his entire package, made his presence difficult to ignore.

But he hated her and made her aware of that fact every chance he got. He always had. He'd seemed to take an instant dislike of her the very moment they'd met. Everyone else in the world knew him for his charisma and kindness, but those traits were never directed toward her. It made her acknowledgment of his attractiveness difficult to bear; it was almost embarrassing to recognize even to herself. Almost.

She was stronger than that, though; it was his loss that he was unable to see her. The real her. Never mind the fact that she hid her real self from him and everyone else. Self-preservation and all that.

Beatryce shook off her concerns with regards to him and forced herself to think of her future, or at least, what amounted to her future as it pertained to the next several days. She was a strong woman. She could ignore base attraction and focus on what was important.

Earlier, he had informed her that they would be posing as newlyweds—as Mr. and Mrs. Churchmouse.

Newlyweds? That didn't help ease her discomfort. And Churchmouse? What was he trying to say? *Keep your mouth shut, Lady Beatryce*, in all likelihood. She couldn't imagine anyone falling for that phony name. But he was supposed to be the expert. And she was too unhinged by his disrobing to argue the point at the moment. Even with herself.

After an eternity in her agitated state, the horses slowed as they pulled off the road. Finally. Her nerves were stretched thin. Their carriage rocked to a stop in front of an old, rundown inn; presumably their overnight accommodations were to be found within. She refused to acknowledge her distaste at the inn's state of disrepair; she'd rather be alive than comfortable.

Beatryce ducked her head and strained her eyes through misty night air as she tried to make out the sign above the door. In loud, gilded letters, the inn proclaimed itself "The Quiet Witch Pub and Inn".

Oh, he was definitely telling her something. She could just imagine him laughing at her expense.

It could be worse. At least the inn wasn't called "The Dead Witch Pub" or the "I'm Going to Strangle that Woman Inn". He'd probably tried to find one of those without success.

As he helped her out of the carriage, he leaned close and admitted, "Like the name of our inn, Lady Beatryce?"

She shivered and her skin tingled as his warm breath tickled her ear. He didn't wait for her to answer. He turned and brushed past, too close. Her breath caught as his arm grazed her breast. Her nipple stood to attention in response.

She nearly ran back to the carriage. Nearly. Instead she squared her shoulders, lifted her chin, and walked with confidence toward the inn.

Inside The Quiet Witch, dust coated every surface and cobwebs, every corner. Clearly, the proprietor had not heard John Wesley sermonize, "Slovenliness is no part of religion. Cleanliness is indeed next to Godliness." Beatryce silently thanked Dansbury for the over-sized dress now, for she would not be removing it to sleep. She'd probably awake with fleas in the morning. Or worse.

Despite the dirt, the inn boasted quite a few patrons in its main room. One particularly loud woman seemed to attract most of the attention. She was all smiles and quite vocal, talking to anyone who would listen, or so it seemed. Typical American. Beatryce sniffed and lifted her nose; then remembered the role she was to play.

Dansbury turned toward the main desk and the large mustachioed man sitting on a stool behind the counter. The main "lobby" of the inn was in reality a pub and the proprietor sat behind the bar.

Right, time for the show.

She grabbed Dansbury's arm with both hands and giggled like a schoolgirl as they crossed the room. Dansbury stumbled on a loose board. She was satisfied to have upset his equilibrium.

"What'd ye wont?" said the landlord, who'd obviously never been taught manners.

"Mr…and *Mrs.* Churchmouse," Dansbury smiled at her, and she giggled and scrunched her shoulders in response, her face beaming, "would like a room, please, sir."

"Aye and would Mr. and *Mrs.* Church*mouse* be wantin' a bath as well?"

"Mmmm…" Dansbury acted like a bath, with her, was his wildest fantasy come true. He touched her forehead with his and rubbed noses with her. "Perhaps another time, thank you very much."

"Right, then. Have a seat anywhere's ye like while we ready yer room. I'll send me wife, Bertha, to fetch ye when 'tis done. Let me barmaid, Ginny, know if ye want a pint or two ta wet yer whistle or a meal ta fill yer bellies."

*

Dansbury guided her to a table situated in a dimly lit back corner of the room. He acknowledged two men seated nearby with a simple nod of his head. One man was a giant, even larger than Dansbury, with dark, red hair. A Scot judging by the blue and brown kilt he wore. The Scot looked like he wore a scowl permanently etched on his rugged face. He threw a glare at the loud American woman on the other side of the room before turning back to contemplate his drink, which sat dwarfed on the table between his large, beefy hands.

The other man was lean and beautiful and dressed to the nines with midnight hair and bright eyes. He sprawled back in his chair with his legs outstretched and a grin that shouted 'I am a lothario, don't ye think me sexy?' Beatryce snorted to herself.

Just as Dansbury's arse touched his seat, she plopped herself in his lap. She laughed at his gaping mouth, her face radiating happiness, a show for their fellow patrons. Inside, she was all nerves. His arms had come up in reflex, caging her in. And he was so much larger than she, she was nearly overwhelmed. She curbed the instinct to flee like a coward.

Her upbringing demanded she act demure and composed. And she had to fight every notion she was raised to believe, for ladies were warned against public displays of affection. It was forbidden. Illicit. Bad. Only fast girls succumbed to the temptation. If anyone from the ton saw her, her reputation would be destroyed, such that it was. Truthfully, it hardly mattered anymore.

She ignored all those warnings and wrapped her arms around his neck. He stiffened in response, and she couldn't help but see the shock, backlit with loathing, in his eyes. She disregarded that look and leaned in to whisper in his ear.

She didn't actually say anything, just smiled and went "psst, psst, psst" in his ear, but the rest of their audience didn't know that. To them and judging by the expression on her face, she was whispering naughty nothings in his ear. Dansbury remained frozen beneath her, and she pulled back as a glower planted itself on his face. She smiled in return, a knowing smile.

She leaned forward again with a large grin fixed firmly on her face. "Don't blow our cover, you idiot. We're supposed to be happily married, remember?"

She leaned further down, her movements slow and seductive, and touched her nose to his neck. She inhaled his scent. *Mmm…*He smelled of sandalwood and leather and strong, virile man, her favorite scents.

La, that way lay danger.

She pulled back, taking her time to know him. She pressed her lips to his jaw and felt the scrape of his evening growth. She kissed the corner of his mouth, lingering for a moment, her eyes closed. His arms gripped her waist in response, his hands all but spanning her sides, his thumbs pressing in just beneath her breasts. She couldn't tell if he was pulling to bring her close or pushing to keep her away. Possibly both.

And she felt an altogether different sort of response stirring to life beneath her. *Hmm…*So, she aroused him, sexually. She filed that knowledge away for future use. For now, she needed to address the fact that he was failing miserably at acting the newlywed.

She pulled back and lifted her eyes as though reluctant to open them. His were dilated and hot. *Hmmm, better.* She responded in kind, despite herself, and all too soon, she began to wonder who was seducing whom. She studied his lips, both full and red, and the heat in the room notched up a few thousand degrees. She shivered and leaned forward, searching for another kiss.

"Mr. and Mrs. Churchmouse. Yer room be waitin'."

Dansbury practically threw her off his lap, but stood behind her, the proprietress's voice serving as a bucket of cold water and a dose of reality. Beatryce eyed the woman with not a little irritation. And Bertha looked back with a perceptive grin. She was as round and as clean as her husband and mustachioed just the same. She stood with arms the size of tree trunks crossed over a bosom the size of the highland Cullins, her foot tapping, and her beefy fist clutching a rusty old key.

It was clear she had no intention of leading them upstairs. "Here's yer key. Last room on the left's yers. We break fast at seven round here."

Dansbury cleared his throat. "Th-Thank you, we'll see ourselves settled, then."

* * * *

As soon as they reached the door to their room, Beatryce whirled on him. She looked angry, but only for an instant. Then, her look turned sultry and heavy-lidded; seduction emanating out of every pore. He was a little worried by that second look; it spelled trouble in absolute terms. She stepped closer.

He took it back. He was a lot worried, actually.

With another step, she moved into his personal space and looked up, her heated eyes capturing his undivided attention. And in that moment, he had no further thought but for her. In the here and now. No history, no future. He and she and no one else. His senses flew south for the summer, an evacuation that had started with her pretend seduction downstairs, leaving only a glimmer of awareness of their mutual dislike.

Her voice was low, an alto, and slow, sultry. "You are rude and always act as if you hate me…" She placed her hand against his aching, turgid cock and pressed in. Firm and tight. Just like he liked. "…but this says differently."

He hissed in a breath, and somehow managed to strangle the moan that threatened to give voice to the full depth of his desire.

He covered her hand with his, forcing her to press harder against him. He grunted and couldn't stop the shift of his hips as they surged forward, deeper into her cupped hand. She squeezed him in response. God, she squeezed him hard. And he closed his eyes as she began to rub her hand up and down his swollen length. Oh, it felt good. Mind-numbingly-forget-your-name-fuck-me-now good.

"And if you're not careful…" She gripped him even tighter and pressed that much harder "…you'll blow our damn cover, Dansbury." She all but hissed those last few words, snapping him back to reality.

She tried to pull away, but he held her in place. He searched deep, ignoring her warning. What did she expect? He'd hated her for too long to be able to easily act as if he adored her. But she had his attention now. Or at least his cock's devotion at any rate.

Right. Time to take control of the situation. He gripped the back of her neck and pulled her closer, cutting off her attempt to escape.

He leaned in close to her ear and whispered, "You are a beautiful, sensual woman…" He nuzzled her neck, then pulled back and glided his cheek against hers, caressing her with his opened lips, employing the barest touch, a whisper of feeling. "…and I would have to be dead not to notice."

He reached her lips and hesitated. He breathed in, a slow and steady breath, absorbing her scent—all woman and earthy. He touched his forehead to hers and took a moment to pull together the threads of his crumbling senses. He felt her trembling and it nearly undid him.

He opened his eyes and warned her with a hard look before he grabbed her with both hands and kissed her. Hard and fast and rough and inflexible. And on fire like he'd never been before. A one hundred and eighty degree contradiction to his soft caresses.

But this time he held on to his senses. Just. And in a flash, he pulled back the tiniest bit; though his lips remained close to hers, hovering and reluctant to leave.

"But you're still a bitch." Hard words spoken in a whisper with lust underlining the point. A contradiction all around.

He bent to kiss her again, but stopped short when she slapped him. Hard. His head jerked, and the sound shouted its anger as it echoed loudly in the vacant hall.

Ouch.

His cheek was on fire and stinging like nettles. He blinked in astonishment, surprised she had cuffed him so solidly. But she just smiled, wrapped her arms around his neck, and pulled him in for her own fiery kiss. Another fast and furious and passionate kiss, but one that this time, she had initiated. He could not suppress his moan of delight at her boldness. He discovered he liked bold. He liked bold quite a lot.

He was lost to her passion and he no longer cared. He forgot he hated her. He forgot his mission. But he didn't forget it was her. And all too soon it was over.

Beatryce pulled away this time. It was her kiss to end. She watched her hands as she drew them down his chest. She brushed away the wrinkles in his shirt. A domestic act. And he just watched her in return, slightly stunned. When she reached his waist, his abs clenched at her touch. This time, he held himself in check.

She tilted her head and looked him in the eye. She smiled, a knowing, confident smile, and said, "Yes. I am. And don't you forget it."

Then, she turned on her heel and slammed the door in his face.

CHAPTER 14

*"For every minute you remain angry, you give up sixty
seconds of peace of mind."*

— *Ralph Waldo Emerson*

Dansbury lumbered down the rickety stairs, one step at a time, stalling for time as he shook off the shattered remnants of his lust. Actually, all sorts of emotions fought for dominance in his head, but desire played the starring role. He paused midway down, turned, and banged his head against the wall. Christ, she was…Well, he didn't want to finish that thought. He still despised her, but now that he knew she kissed like…

No. No. No. No. And No.

He refused to go there.

He reined in his runaway thoughts. Still, he was reluctant to move. His friends, the Scot and the rogue, were waiting. And they were going to tease him unmercifully for what all and sundry had witnessed. Or at least Kelly would. What to do? He decided to embrace his anger, one of the many emotions twirling around inside his mind. Yes. Anger would protect him from the ribbing and deflect any barbs aimed his way. She was a trollop and bold as brass. And she was hard and cruel and unrepentant. His heart thundered in his chest and he clenched his fists. Yea, that did it. He was angry.

He jogged the rest of his way down the stairs.

He spotted his friends as soon as he stepped into the main room and headed for their table. He felt every patron watching him, remembering the scene with him and Lady Beatryce. In this very room. At that table. Right.

There.

He shook his head and looked at his friends. As expected, Ciarán Kelly, an Irish rake of the highest order, watched him with laughing eyes and a grin. Lord Alaistair MacLeod, the Scot, on the other hand, sported a look of concern and confusion. Definitely a change from his usual scowl.

"Stuff it. Do you hear? Don't say a word." He flung back his chair and sat with his legs sprawled out under table. He crossed his arms and dared them to say a word.

Kelly laughed. "Oh, but ye should see the look on yer face, my friend. Priceless. Got under your skin, has she?"

MacLeod, as usual, said nothing.

"That woman will be the death of me if I do not kill her first."

"Aye, if lusty sex can cause death, sure. It looked like she was about to kill ye with it. Nearly strangled ye with her tongue, did she?" Kelly retorted.

"It was all for show, and you know it. So shut. It. I despise that woman and you know it."

"Aye, ye've said as such before. Many times. Too many times. You know, this is the first time I've ever actually seen her. She is…"

"Don't. Say. It."

"All I'm saying, is that I wouldn't blame you, if you…"

Dansbury slammed his fist on the table, making their mugs of ale, and some of the nearby patrons, jump. He and MacLeod reached for their respective drinks; his friends had ordered him one in his absence.

Kelly just smirked, completely unruffled. "I don't understand why ye despise her so much. She nearly married Stonebridge, so she can't be all bad. And I hear tell yer uncommonly rude to her. She is…"

MacLeod dropped his mug to the table, just hard enough to gain their attention. "Och, he's rude because he wants to tup her, ye ken?"

Dansbury spewed his drink…all over his friends…the scarred table top…himself. He caught a bit of dribble with his hand using it as his handkerchief. Quite gentlemanly.

MacLeod wiped his face on his sleeve—his only acknowledgement to the mess.

"Now, cannae we just get doun to business?"

Dansbury fisted his hands, crumpling the soiled linen. "But I feel compelled to address your last point…"

"Deny it all ye want, my friend," Kelly interjected, "we all know the truth. The Scot is right. I'm telling you, the rest of the room fairly burned in the wake of yer lust, yer chemistry. Even I gave *Bertha* an extra look." Kelly shivered in disgust.

Dansbury barked out a laugh. They both did, him and Kelly. And just like that, his tension ebbed, and he was his usual easy self. How could one survive at life if you couldn't laugh at your own foibles? Besides, arguing just made their declarations look truthful. Which they weren't. They were so far off base, they…

He stifled that train of thought and turned to MacLeod, seeking him around the barmaid who'd come to wipe down the table. "How are you, my friend? Enjoyed your trip here with this here talkative rogue, I take it?" He knew Kelly was probably driving the Scot daft.

MacLeod just glared at him. He didn't take the bait. He never did.

Sigh.

"Right. Out with it then," said Dansbury.

MacLeod didn't waste another breath. "There were people here, asking aboot ye, before we arrived. It was a good thing ye changed yer clothes, they were asking aboot a pair of aristos."

MacLeod's eyes were fixed on him, though they flickered to something over his shoulder. Dansbury turned to look, but all he could see was the American woman laughing at a patron seated at the bar. The barmaid had finished cleaning up his mess and had moved on.

"Yea, what was Lady B wearing by the way, a tent?" Kelly laughed.

"Nearly. Who were they? Do you know? Did you find them?"

"Nae. But it doesna sit well that they looked fer ye here. This place isna easy to find and not the most obvious of places to search, ye ken?" The Scot's eyes flickered to the bar.

"You're right. It is a concern, though they could have gotten lucky. I'll be more vigilant, just in case. Any leads on who is pulling the strings?"

"Nae. Stonebridge has everyone in his command on it, though. Middlebury is the link." Again, MacLeod glanced at the bar. Dansbury peeked over his shoulder, but still, only the American and the anonymous patron were there.

"Well, it can't happen fast enough. Lady Beatryce is driving me mad," he added when he turned back around.

"Yea, it sure looked like it a little while ago," taunted Kelly. Dansbury ignored him.

"Aye, I hear ye. We'll be trailing ye for added protection, ye ken?" Kelly nodded his head in agreement with MacLeod.

"Thanks. Now, why do you keep looking over at the American, MacLeod?"

Alaistair didn't answer, but looked over again, then jumped to his feet. His chair scraped the wooden floor as he stood. Dansbury stood, too. Habit that. But Kelly continued to lounge, a shrewd grin covered his face. Speaking of rude.

"What's with all the brooding? You gentlemen look like you could use another drink," assumed the American as she approached their table.

Dansbury begged to differ. The American woman had it all wrong. Only the Scot brooded.

"I'm Mrs. Amelia Chase. From America. You know, the colonies?" She laughed at her own joke. "How are you gents this fine evening?"

"Clifford Churchmouse. It is a pleasure. This man is Lord Alaistair MacLeod and the man impolitely seated is Mr. Ciarán Kelly."

"Churchmouse? Are you the strong silent type then?" She laughed, again, and continued, "Lord MacLeod, Mr. Kelly. May I join you?"

"Nae." MacLeod shook his head no.

"Of course, allow me." Dansbury spoke over him and pulled out a chair for Mrs. Chase. She was bold and brassy, and he admired her spunk. She was a refreshing change from the usual timid English lady. Lady Beatryce didn't count among their number.

Kelly seemed to agree. He sat straighter and undressed her with his eyes. And she was indeed attractive, and quite young. MacLeod, however, just sneered as if she were some piece of offal he'd found on the bottom of his boot.

"What's wrong with him?" Mrs. Chase asked Dansbury as she jerked her head at MacLeod. Then, without waiting for a response, she turned to the red-faced Scot. "What's wrong with you? Got a burr up your kilt? You shouldn't scowl so much, it'll freeze your face that way." She lowered her voice like a man's, mimicking his Scot's accent. "Och, as you Scots say, too late for that!" She laughed again, almost a giggle, but not quite. Heartier. Happier. More real.

She nudged MacLeod. "Come on, laugh it up. Life's too short to be so angry." MacLeod didn't respond, of course, but continued to frown at Mrs. Chase.

"So, Mrs. Chase from America, are you traveling with your husband?" asked Dansbury.

"No," her voice cracked on the word. It was her first hint of any underlying sorrow in her otherwise bright personality. "Alas, I'm a widow." Mrs. Chase twisted her fingers and looked away, briefly, as she visibly pulled together her composure. Then she faced the men again, her cheery countenance restored.

"My apologies..." Dansbury began.

"No, please, no apology is necessary. You couldn't have known," she interrupted. She squeezed his arm and offered him a direct smile of reassurance. Still, a moment of awkward silence followed, until Kelly broke the silence.

"Dansbury, weren't you..." Kelly began. His voice trailed off when both Dansbury and MacLeod scowled at him for the obvious lapse. It was an odd mistake for someone of Kelly's experience to make. Dansbury was supposed to be Mr. Churchmouse. They'd just established that fact not two minutes before during the introductions. Fortunately, Mrs. Chase missed their twin expressions of ire as she was facing Kelly.

"D-Dansbury?" Mrs. Chase noticed the slip, of course. She turned to look at Dansbury, a curious expression on her face.

"Aye. We call him Dansbury because Churchmouse is just plain odd. And since he used to work fer the Dansbury estate, we took to calling him that." Kelly tried desperately to make up a story to explain away his gaffe.

Mrs. Chase acknowledged the reasoning with a slow nod of her head, but all the while, she stared at Dansbury as if he were some heretofore-unknown specimen of science.

After a few tense moments, Mrs. Chase finally asked, "You worked for the Dansbury estate? Do you know the marquess well then? Are they...are they nice...people?"

Mrs. Chase seemed oddly hesitant to ask her last question. Dansbury was more than a little curious over her interest in his family. He looked briefly at MacLeod over her shoulder. MacLeod was frowning...more than usual.

"Fairly well, I'd say." He tried not to chuckle at that understatement. "They are extremely nice people. Very giving. And you? Do you know the marquess?"

"I'm a...his...No..."

Interesting. Clearly she'd started to say something else, but changed her mind. Twice. He studied the woman before him. She was brown-haired with striking blonde and caramel streaks. She had wide brown eyes. And she did seem vaguely familiar, but he knew he hadn't met her. He'd remember. Who could forget such a vibrant personality? "...but I look forward to meeting him some time. I've heard great things."

"Asking about him, are you?" He turned on his infamous charm.

"The name's come up a time or two." She smiled in return and batted her lashes.

Ah, she was a master at the game, too.

"Really?" He smiled—a wide open tell-me-all-your-secrets-you-can-trust-me kind of smile. He thought he heard MacLeod growl from behind her.

Mrs. Chase didn't take the bait. Instead she turned back to MacLeod—perhaps he had growled—where she attempted to find some good humor in his dark depths.

After a few moments, she seemed to give up trying to pull MacLeod out of his foul mood. She asked questions about the country and about places to visit. General chit chat. Every once in a while, she tried again—with a surprising amount of frequency—to tease MacLeod into relaxing his guard, to no avail. After an hour, she gave that up to the lost cause it was and took her leave with a: "It's nice to meet you, Dansbury or Churchmouse, or whatever it is I should call you. It's been very informative."

Dansbury looked at MacLeod after she left. "I like her."

"As do I," Kelly chimed in.

MacLeod just chugged the remainder of his drink, his fifth since the American had joined them. His friend wasn't known to drink so heavily, must be Mrs. Chase. But he wouldn't call the man on it.

"Well, gentlemen. I'd best be headed upstairs." Dansbury knew it would look odd if he left Lady Beatryce waiting too long. She was supposed to be his new bride after all. He was not anticipating seeing her. In bed. Not at all.

"Aye, ye do that. I hope ye can find her beneath that tent." Kelly's laughed chased him up the stairs.

* * * *

Nearby...

A fire crackled in the hearth, the only light source in the small barren room. The bulk of the space remained hidden in the shadows, but there was only a table, a chair, and a small cot in the corner to be seen anyway. The table was covered with guns and steel. A veritable weapons cache.

The chimney leaked and smoke clouded and stunk up the tiny space, but the cloaked man paid it no mind. He tilted the note in his hand toward the flames and read.

They're staying at The Quiet Witch Pub and Inn. We'll take them tomorrow on the road.

He smiled. *Ah, yes. Excellent. Himself will be pleased.* The shrouded man threw the missive in the fire and returned to the nearby table. He took up his blade. He began to sharpen it, as if it were dull and unused. It wasn't. It was as sharp as the day it was made. It'd cut through flesh like butter.

He leered as he relished the thought of finally confronting his foe. Of seeing recognition dawn across his enemy's face. The sound of steel scraping steel echoed around the walls. The only other sound besides the crackling fire.

Soon. It would happen. Everything was falling into place as planned. And this time, he would not be denied his revenge.

CHAPTER 15

"The deepest feeling always shows itself in silence."
— *Marianne Moore*

He stood at the door to her room. Their room. It had a deep, dark scratch at eye level. And a reasonably sized crack. And dust. Lots of dust. A tiny spider worked its way in and out of the crack, busy and oblivious to his continued regard. Ten minutes must have passed as he watched that spider work—if not twenty.

Aw, hell. What was he waiting for? He turned the handle.

It was locked?

She'd locked him out. The idea was laughable.

He could slip in and out of anywhere undetected, despite his oversized shoulders and soaring height. He pulled a knife out of his boot. It was a matter of seconds before he was standing in the middle of their room. He hadn't made a sound to alert her to his presence.

And now he couldn't make a sound if his life depended on it.

She was mostly covered. Mostly being the key word here. The covers had shifted with her restless sleep…And she was naked.

One hundred percent naked-as-the-day-she-was-born naked.

He could tell because her side was exposed from her toes to the top of her ice-blonde head. Alabaster skin, looking as soft as newly spun silk glowed, uninterrupted, back at him.

He wished he'd been incapable of picking the damn lock.

He wanted to go to her; he wanted to stay utterly still. A dichotomy to be sure. He locked his knees to keep from moving. But he couldn't look away. It was as if he'd never seen a naked woman before now.

One long, trim leg was sprawled out from under the covers, seeking to cool her overheated body. The dim light cast by the fire settled over the contours of her leg, highlighting defined muscles. Her leg was athletic, slim, and strong, unusual for a woman.

Had he mentioned that he liked unusual before?

And she must be burning up under the covers, for the room was surely aflame.

He pulled at his cravat. Sweat beaded on his brow, and he wondered why the room was suddenly quite warm despite the chill outside. He wanted nothing more than to bury his head in a bucket of snow.

She shifted in her sleep. The covers slid a little more. And he grew envious of the bedclothes, draped so languidly over her naked curves.

But that wasn't what really captivated him. Held his attention as sure as chains tied to his eyeballs. Now. Oh, hell, now, one perfectly shaped breast was exposed to the air; one tight nipple puckered and pointing. At him. Begging him to sup.

His legs buckled. Thank God there was a chair behind him or he'd be sprawled on the floor. And how would he explain that? For the sound of his massive body hitting the floor would certainly wake her...and everyone else in the inn for that matter. He wiped a hand down his face.

She whimpered in her sleep. He couldn't tell if it was a whine of distress or a lusty moan. In his sex-addled brain, he went with the latter.

And before he knew what he was about, he was crawling on the bed, zeroed in on her nipple. He leaned in, and his tongue tingled, ready to flick the tip. What would one taste hurt? Or one quick suckle? He could feel it now, soft and pebbled on his tongue. Would she taste sweet like chocolate? Or earthy, like her natural scent.

Hell...He. Knew. Her. Scent.

He closed his eyes and froze. He was afraid to breathe lest he lose his remaining self-control. His shaft throbbed in his trousers. Pulsated and ached. He wanted more than anything to take himself in hand to relieve the pressure. It wouldn't take long. He'd been up and down in lust today, an emotional whirlwind. He opened his eyes and without conscious thought, homed in on her exposed breast. Hell, he wouldn't need to touch himself; he was going to explode just by staring at her nipple, tight and erect and begging for his attentions.

What the hell was he doing? He fisted the sheet and used every bit of his self-control to rein in his unwanted desire. It wasn't easy. *Ha, an understatement that.* He was on the edge. He fought and kicked his way back from the brink.

He searched his brain for a memory, any thought to put things in perspective. He found one, the memory of when he first saw her. The one where Middlebury had touched her intimately on the terrace for all the world to see. The one where she and Middlebury had discussed ruining an innocent woman as casually as if they were discussing the weather.

That did it. He reaffirmed his vow. He refused to be taken in by her. No matter how sexy…

He didn't finish the thought. He just backed off the bed with cautious intent. It wouldn't do to wake her now. He stood and embraced his disgust. It made him ill to know such an unconscionable person lived in such a beautiful package. What a load of rubbish, vile and smelly.

He turned on his heel and stormed out the door, slamming it behind him…no longer bothering to be silent.

Lady Beatryce opened her eyes and stared at the ceiling.

CHAPTER 16

"The web of our life is of a mingled yarn, good and ill
together. Our virtues would be proud if our faults
whipt them not; and our crimes would despair if they
were not cherish'd by our virtues."
                    — Shakespeare, All's Well That Ends Well

On the Road Again…
The Next Morning…

Beatryce looked over at her traveling companion. They had left behind The
Quiet Witch Inn early that morning, before the sun rose and the rooster
crowed. It was freezing out and she wrapped herself within the spacious
confines of her oversized dress. It actually provided a surprising measure of
warmth. It was cozy, once her nose got used to the smell. She didn't think
she'd ever forget the memory of the stench for as long as she lived.

Dansbury glared out the window as she considered his profile, their
roles reversed from their journey the day before. His arms were folded across
his chest and his legs were stretched out and crossed at his booted feet. He
was angry, that much was obvious, and contemplative. His blond hair was
disheveled and partially covering his face, enhancing his agitated look.

"You're angry," she said. It wasn't a question, but an observation. And
she didn't understand her reasoning behind why she felt the need to say it
out loud which was quite unlike her.

"I'm not used to being around the same person, day in and day out, twenty-four hours a day. And it's you. Of course, I'm irritated. Why aren't you?" He wasted no time responding. As if he'd been waiting for her to break the silence. As if he was eager to inform her of how much she annoyed him.

She ignored his question, braced herself as their carriage dipped over another pothole, and asked one of her own. "Where is the charming man everyone raves about? I never see him."

The coach windows rattled their panes.

He snorted. "I lock him away when you're around. It's called self-preservation."

"Self-preservation? Ha. You, my friend, are afraid. What are you afraid of, Dansbury?"

"You…" He winced. It looked as if he meant to say more, but chose not to. Clearly, he hadn't wanted to admit that much.

She was surprised by his confession. Her heart picked up its pace, and she felt anxious of a sudden, but she hid it well. She twisted her hands in the folds of her overgrown dress, a nervous gesture that wasn't hers by habit.

She attempted to sound light-hearted and unconcerned when she teased, "La, Dansbury, that is the most honest thing you've said to me since we started out on this misbegotten adventure. I'm flattered."

She didn't think he noticed the slight tremble to her voice. For some unknown reason, she was on the verge of laughing like a nervous bedlamite. A strange quagmire of emotions entangled her mind and her normally well-ordered thoughts.

"Yea, and what happened to the silent ice queen I started out with—I want her back."

"Why? Scared I'll make you confess your darkest secrets…your innermost desires?" She added a sultry twist to the end of that question. God, she was discovering just how much she loved to bait him. She relished it.

"No. I just don't like the man I am when I'm with you."

"Charmer." She emphasized sarcasm while she suppressed a sudden pang of hurt. Following on the heels of nervous anticipation, the change in emotion was jarring. It was not like she hadn't worked hard for his animosity—she knew she'd earned it. And she still didn't regret it. Much.

"You keeping quiet helps. Less chance of you making me angry. Less chance of me doing something I—you'll regret."

Beatryce considered his admission. It didn't escape her notice that he had started to say "I" before he switched to "You". How could she use this knowledge to her advantage? He wasn't the only one with a heightened instinct for self-preservation.

Sure, she'd been aloof and contemplative before—her father had just been murdered. It would have been odd not to be somewhat respectful to his memory. No matter that he was a bastard of the worst kind and everyone knew it. No matter that she was pleased he was dead. Did that make her a bad person? She didn't think so; he was the devil's own.

And her silence worked as a way for her to analyze her situation with Dansbury and determine how to handle their enforced proximity. It was a calculated move on her part.

Not to mention that she'd been angry and bitter—life wasn't fair, especially for her, it seemed.

After a moment's consideration, she decided to change tactics. "How do you see this all playing out? Are we going to just travel merrily along to our destination, and then remain hidden until someone tells us it is safe to come out? Are you just going to leave me?"

Their eyes locked as she choked out those last words. Her throat tightened and cut off her remaining words, at the thought of him leaving her alone. She couldn't even swallow. It was an unexpected feeling coming from her. She was stronger than that. She did not need anyone.

His gaze softened for a moment. "I don't know. Surprisingly, I don't have all the answers. I only know that justice will prevail in the end."

"La, how do you know? Sometimes bad guys win." She looked at her white-knuckled hands, afraid he'd see the sudden fear in her eyes she couldn't easily hide. Her experiences told her that the bad guys quite often won.

He leaned across and lifted her chin, forcing her to meet his gaze. "No. They can't. I won't allow it. Might makes right. Surely, you of all people hold with that sentiment. You were prepared to do anything to get away from your father. Well. I will do whatever it takes to make sure justice is served. Even…"

He didn't finish that thought. Beatryce was glad. She didn't like the sudden look in his eye, and thus, she did not want to know what he was prepared to do to see justice served.

It wasn't like him. Sure, he looked at her that way, but he wasn't really thinking of her at the moment, that much was obvious. For the first time, she considered just how formidable a man he could be. He had the potential to be dark. Ferocious. Dangerous.

Though she didn't think he realized it. And she knew nobody else saw it, either. But then, she remembered the cloaked man's written taunt. *PS: Tell Dansbury, I know his secrets.*

What could this man be hiding?

Whatever it was, she suspected it haunted him.

She ignored the voice that screamed how much she might like dark. And she made a mental note not to push him past his limits. She decided to pull him back to the light, out of his shadowy mental hole. Otherwise, he'd make the day long and miserable, and she just wasn't up to another day like that.

She leaned toward him and placed her hand on his thigh. A well-muscled, surprisingly hot and hard appendage that. "Cliff."

"Don't you *dare* call me Cliff!" He swiped her hand away on an unexpected growl. She nearly fell face first into his lap as her support was knocked from beneath her. His voice was a roaring bellow. Gone was the caring, empathetic demeanor from just a moment before.

He rose and reached for her as if he intended to shake her or worse, when the glass of the carriage's rear window shattered.

"Bea. Get down. Now!" he yelled.

Several more shots were fired into the wooden walls of the carriage as Dansbury dropped to the floor and flipped up the cushion of his seat. Good God, they had a small armory inside that seat.

He grabbed two pistols and peeked out the rear window. Both guns were already primed and ready to fire. Within the trunk lay all manner of additional weapons, including prepared shells and the tools to prime the remaining guns.

Beatryce didn't think, she grabbed two and readied them, tamping them down so they'd fire correctly. As soon as Dansbury fired his, he dropped them to the floor. She immediately replaced them with her two.

He never once looked down. Somehow, someway, she anticipated his needs without direction from him. They worked in concert as if they'd done so for years. As if she read his mind. As if he had confidence in her ability to do so.

Dansbury ducked as a shot nearly clipped his ear and imbedded itself in the front wall of the coach.

Beatryce's heart leapt in response.

Three more shots followed before Dansbury peeked up, aimed, and let fly his next two. He dropped his guns and grabbed the next two she'd prepped while he took aim. He started to duck down, jerked back up for one last look, and ducked down again.

More shots rang out in rapid succession.

There must be more than one man shooting. Four, if Beatryce had to guess. She didn't dare look to be sure. Besides, she had a job to do there on the floor.

They continued on this way, shots volleying, guns dropped and replaced, for what felt like hours, but was only a handful of minutes, before Dansbury leaned back against her seat, hands dangling over his raised knees. Finished.

Guns littered the floor; they'd run through half their store.

Dansbury released a breath of relief. "They're gone. We got one. But the others, three more of them, fled into the woods."

"Why aren't we stopping?"

"My man knows not to stop for any reason short of death. It's too dangerous. We carry on until we reach safety." He suddenly looked at her. "Are you all right? You're not hurt?"

"Yes. No. I'm fine."

He searched her face, for what she didn't know. She didn't break the connection.

He smiled then and her gut twisted. He'd never smiled at her before, happy with whatever he'd found in her eyes. Not like that.

"You did well, Lady Beatryce. Thank you." He reached out as if he were going to caress her cheek, but then jerked his hand back, fist clenched.

No. No. No. No.

She wouldn't let him back away from that. She launched herself across his lap, straddling his legs. She grabbed his head and kissed him for all she was worth, her adrenaline firing her passion and making her reckless.

He kissed her back. But his hands remained steady and gripping her sides. He nearly hurt her, he was clutching her so fiercely about the waist.

Her dress billowed all around, hiding them from the world. She scrambled for his trousers, intending to unbutton them and free his erection. He wanted her; she wanted him. The danger had passed. They were free to indulge.

But he grabbed her wrists and broke away. "Beatryce, I never become intimate with someone under my protection. I'm funny that way."

"I can protect myself." She kissed his face between words.

"Sure, love, then let me put it another way. I don't fuck people I don't like."

That got her attention. She was quick to change strides. "Such language. Seems out of character for you, at least that's what I hear. Must have touched a sore spot," she said between kisses.

She was confident in her charms. She nipped at his lips.

He kissed her back despite words to the contrary. "No. Just speaking the truth."

They continued to kiss. She wanted to climb inside his skin. She would consider the consequences later.

Then he capitulated, for after a moment he said, "Ah, hell," and he wrapped his arms around her and proceeded to kiss her relentlessly.

Thank God! Her body all but screamed its agreement with their unspoken plans. She reached for his trousers again, but he stalled her. Again.

"Not here. I'll not take you on the ground of a cramped and dirty carriage with glass and guns strewn about the place." He smiled as he touched his forehead to hers. "I have a reputation to consider..."

They burst out laughing.

CHAPTER 17

"What loneliness is more lonely than distrust?"
— George Eliot, Middlemarch

The Sorceress and the Lusty Hound Inn...

Dansbury slammed the door to their shabby room and began tearing at Beatryce's clothes before the pictures finished rattling on the wall. He refused to think on the wisdom, or not, of their actions. Right now, intelligence and forethought was overrated.

She only wore the oversized dress he had given her. Thank God. He only needed to open a few buttons, and then he was able to pull it over her head and throw it to the floor. He stood back and admired the vision she presented.

She did not hide from him, though her hands were clenched into fists and her pulse beat nervously at her neck. He was pleased, and nearly dropped to his knees and begged his thanks.

Damn. She was striking. Perfect. Firm, high breasts with nipples standing erect and ready to be suckled. She was toned, athletic, unusual for a lady. And he discovered that he no longer like soft and voluptuous. Thick, blonde hair down below hid her treasures from his gaze. God, he was more excited than he'd ever been in his life. His cock twitched and throbbed in anticipation. He wanted her everywhere. In every way. He felt the evidence of pre-cum cooling on his pants. He was beyond ready. He might not last long. This time.

He reached for her and all but tossed her on the bed. She leaned back on her elbows and watched him as he tore off his clothes.

Once naked, he nearly strutted with pride as he noticed her eyes widen as she stared at his cock. His prick bobbed its head in greeting. Yes, he knew he was over-endowed, and he could see that she was pleased with that fact. He all but crowed with delight, and he was thrilled she wasn't cowed by the sight.

He crawled up the bed toward her, his body temperature climbing with each passing second. He could feel moisture collecting on his back from the heat. She rolled over onto her hands and knees and his mouth turned dry at the sight. If possible, his cock swelled further. She was gorgeous, her ass smooth and firm and high in the air. Begging for him. Inviting him to touch, to dine. Her legs widened in invitation, and her back arched. He could see the moisture coating her woman's hair. God, he could even smell her excitement. All he had to do was surge forward, and he would be buried to the hilt in her hot, willing sheath.

Mmm...

He moaned at the thought. He couldn't control the outburst. And he wanted her in this way, on her knees in submission. But not this time. Not their first time. And so despite his cock's complaints about the delay, he reached out to nudge her back over.

She resisted and spoke over her shoulder. "If you want to fuck me, you'll have to accept me this way. I don't do it face to face."

He was surprised and couldn't control his lustful response to her vulgar words. *Shite.*

He was beginning to like bold over demure, as well. He didn't think when he asked, "You mean, you've never?"

Pain flickered across her face before she shut it down. "Are you going to keep talking?"

The hurt he glimpsed bothered him. She had done it the other way before, that much was plain, but somewhere deep down burned an unpleasant memory. Inexplicable rage surged to the surface. He fought it down.

Fine. He'd do it her way. This time. But he vowed she would never forget the experience. He would claim her and teach her about what sex ought to be, replacing her upsetting remembrance in the process.

He stood on his knees, his cock leading the way and straining toward her wet and waiting core. She was ready. Her woman's hair was absolutely coated with her moisture, glistening and winking at him in the candlelight. He drew in a slow, deep breath, and her womanly fragrance set every inch of his body to nigh bursting with need.

He lost the last of his control. And without using his hands or his tongue to prepare the way, he gripped his cock and guided it to…

Knock. Knock. Knock.

"Mr. Churchmouse?" came the muffled voice.

Shite.

Dansbury leaned back on his heels, knees spread, and dragged his hand down his face. His throbbing cock stood out erect in front of him, rigid and purple and proud.

Beatryce flattened herself to the bed, her face buried in the crook of one arm.

"Yes, what is it?" His voice practically growled though he tried to play his role.

"A message for you has arrived downstairs. The runner said it was urgent and that he was to give it only to you. Directly."

Beatryce crawled out of bed. Dansbury followed her with his eyes.

"I'll be right down. Thank. You." He all but bit out the last, not even attempting to hide his irritation.

*

Dansbury pulled on his trousers, his movement jerky in his agitated state. Beatryce watched him through the mirror before her. And as he pulled them over his hips, she caught sight of his cock, semi-hard and not quite relaxed, before he tucked it away.

He hadn't even put on his drawers.

He left without another word, slamming the door on his way out. Just like earlier, the pictures shook the walls and remained askew.

Beatryce thrust aside her frustration and turned her attention to practical matters: to the fire, or where a fire should be burning bright. In their haste to have at each other, they hadn't spared the time to light one. And despite their heated passion, the room had turned cool as night fell.

So, she set herself to the task of lighting a fire. She'd seen maids and footmen perform this chore numerous times before, and she understood the mechanics of fire making. How hard could it really be?

Hands on her hips and jaw set with confidence, Bea checked the

91

battered coalscuttle next to the hearth. It was half full, but the lumps within didn't look quite like the coal she was used to. She reached in and picked one at random; it was lighter in color than coal.

Dark, yes, but not quite as black.

She took a sniff.

And immediately dropped the foul thing.

Ack. Horse dung. Erg, figures.

She wiped her hands on her dress, pulled back her sleeves, and picked up the scuttle. She poured what she thought to be a reasonable amount of dried manure into the coal grate, then searched for a tinderbox. An abused and beaten circular tin container lay on the mantle. That must be it.

She sat down before the hearth and took everything out except the tinder and began the process of striking steel to flint over the shredded kindling.

Or should it be flint to steel?

Both felt awkward in her unpracticed hands. She'd always gone out of her way to avoid learning how to light a simple match.

Ten minutes later, Beatryce had a newfound respect for the servants.

Actually, for anyone who could light a fire.

Twenty minutes later and she was ready to scream in frustration.

The tinder would not win, dammit. She would build a fire if it were the last thing she ever did.

Twenty-five minutes later, she gave her hands a break while she paced the cold room, mumbling to herself and cursing the laughing tinderbox. She was going to have to ask Dansbury to up his staff's wages after this, for surely he couldn't be paying them enough to perform a task such as this.

Eventually, she dropped to her knees before the hearth once again.

Another five minutes more and the tinder finally caught.

Yes! Such sweet success.

She lit her match and managed to transfer flame to the dung in the hearth.

Right, nearly there.

She turned to snuff out the tinder and put everything away again, but when she stood to place the box on the mantle, she noticed…that the fire had gone out.

Argh.

Bea sucked in a deep breath and started the process all over again. She was far too stubborn to lose to horseshit.

After another ten minutes and much coaxing and blowing and not turning her back for a second, a respectable fire burned in the grate. At last!

She held her hands out to warm them as the flames worked to erase the chill on the air. She was still there, bent toward the hearth, when Dansbury returned a few minutes later.

She jumped and spun around and caught him standing in the doorway, staring where her ass had been. The look in his eyes made it clear the direction his thoughts had gone. But only for a moment.

His mouth turned down in a glower as he marched into the room. Clearly, they weren't going to address the large white elephant in the room— the fact that they'd almost had sex.

"You've started a fire, I see. I'm surprised."

She nearly rolled her eyes. "Some of us women are more useful than you men give us credit for." She decided not to tell him what an arduous task it had been.

He barked out a cynical laugh as he joined her at the hearth. "I doubt I'll ever underestimate you again."

She wasn't sure whether or not to take that as a compliment. She decided to ignore it. He seemed to be finished anyway. He fed his missive to the fire and turned contemplative as he stared off into the flickering flames.

"Wait! What did it say?"

He disregarded her; his focus lost in the blaze. His posture screamed inward reflection; his mind buried deep. She sat down before the hearth, tucked her knees beneath her dress, and crossed her arms. She would wait him out. He'd speak when he was ready. She needed to know what that missive said and pushing him when he wasn't ready was the surest way to keep him from telling her what she wanted to know.

After a moment, he blinked as he came back to the present. "The men following us seem to know our every move. Though I don't want to admit it, I'm beginning to suspect we have a traitor in our midst."

He looked weary, grave, and aged beyond his years by that thought. He was only about thirty if she had to guess, and from what she knew of him, he had lived a life of ease despite the fact that his parents and brother were killed some years ago.

Certainly, his life had to have been better than hers. Again, the thought that he had hidden secrets just begged her to ask him of it. But he wasn't ready…they weren't ready…to divulge such confidences.

Her life had been filled with lies, hatred, and abuse. From her own father—a man she was supposed to be able to trust. She swallowed the lump in her throat and it made her angry. After all these years, the thought of the earl's abuse still managed to upset her. He was supposed to love her, instead he abused her. And she hated that she still wished she could have won his regard. It was mad and wrong. Insane, like him. Would she ever stop seeking his approval?

Father made her bitter and unable to trust. Anyone. Save herself. Dansbury, on the other hand, seemed to trust everyone. Well, except her. And she was surprised when she thought about it. He was a spy for the Crown. He should be used to betrayal and corruption. It didn't make sense.

She didn't think it through before she queried him on it. "How can you be in your line of work and still trust anyone?"

He turned on her in a flash. "How can you live in a world where you don't?" His flash of anger caught her off guard.

He continued on. "There are beautiful things and there are ugly things, Lady Beatryce. Everywhere. You will always find whichever you seek."

She thought on that for a moment. Perhaps it was true. She was a poor judge for she only ever experienced the ugly side of life. Or so it seemed. And then she thought on it further, as she regarded him in the flickering light of the fire.

Here is something beautiful. Right before my eyes. I can see that much even though he is only ever hostile to me…well, mostly hostile.

The thought gave her pause. Was it true? Did she only see the viciousness in life because she chose to? That was difficult to accept.

Father abused her. Abused. Her. Beat her to the point where she had to take to her bed. For days. Her own father!

Why me? Why not someone else? Would anyone blame me for having a cynical view of the world with a father like that?

No. She shut down the memories; she'd had years of practice at it. "So what do you see when you look at me then?"

Where had that come from?

And apparently, she wasn't finished. She didn't give him a chance to respond to her first query. "How come you are kind to everyone but me?"

"Because I'm too afraid of finding out I like you after all." He didn't look at her as he admitted it.

Coward.

But what could she say to that?

Nothing.

She stood and turned to tidy the bed, an action born of nerves stretched tight. She was just plumping the last pillow when he broke the strained silence. "We should do something."

"I am." She liked to use sarcasm when she was angry.

He chuckled. "Not that. I mean, about this case. I don't want to sit around and wait for someone to tell us to come out of hiding. I want to do something. Take action. You seem as if you are capable."

Beatryce beamed inside but hid it well. If she wanted anyone to notice anything about her, anything at all, it was her capabilities. Her father's old taunts threatened to ruin the moment. They told her Dansbury lied to gain her compliance. She thrust those unproductive thoughts aside.

"Thank you."

"Don't thank me yet. You know, you're going to have to trust me. If you don't, you die."

She analyzed his words, turning them over in her mind. "I noticed you didn't say 'we' die."

"Of course not, I trust myself."

"I couldn't even trust my own father. How am I supposed to trust you?"

"That is up to you, Lady Beatryce. I cannot make it happen. But you know what I think? I think you trust me already and it scares you. I think it is why you chose me to protect you. Your request for my protection implies a certain measure of trust, does it not?"

It made sense, but she would never own up to it. No. She could only believe in herself. "Just tell me what you want to do."

"For now, we proceed to our next stop as planned."

"That's all?"

"For now..."

* * * *

Nearby, Outside an Abandoned Shack...
That Same Night...

The cloaked man pulled out his gun and shot the messenger. A small flock of birds took flight at the sound. "I do not accept failure, nor excuses for it."

He looked up from the victim, his eyes shadowed by his hood, and glared at his remaining men. He waved his still smoking gun in the air as he spoke. "Anyone else care to explain how four of you, now two, managed to let a lone woman and one man escape?

We had every advantage. My dog could have managed this simple task better."

The men standing before him shifted their feet and all but wet their trousers, but no one volunteered a response. They had seen what happened to the last guy after all. Perhaps they weren't entirely foolish.

Ha. The both of them were utter idiots. Not an ounce of sense to be shared between the two.

Mist drifted in and out of the woods surrounding them, snaking around the trees and swirling around the men's legs. Silence blanketed the scene save for a few brave crickets. As if the woodland creatures held their breath, hoping not to draw his notice.

He nearly growled his frustration at his men's incompetence. Now, he would be forced to explain matters to Himself. He wasn't afraid of that. He just hated that he had to cozy up to the man for he only allowed the man to think he was in charge. All the groveling and posturing cut into the time he could be spent dreaming about and plotting his revenge…and training for the moment he would seize it. Alas, he needed the man's power and money to see the job through. And that fact never failed to make him bitter.

He would do it though. Beg and plead and serve…do whatever was required to make this happen. At least until Himself outlived his own usefulness.

The cloaked man sighed. "Very well. It seems I'll have to take care of this myself. In the meantime, I have another task for the pair of you. This one even you two should be able to handle. I need you to fetch something for me."

It was only a matter of time before he would revel in his victory. He was confident of that; it was the only acceptable outcome.

CHAPTER 18

"Three things cannot long stay hidden: the sun, the moon and the truth."

—Buddha

The next morning, Dansbury and Beatryce headed downstairs with the rising sun. As usual. They hadn't spoken a word, and he was glad of it. He'd slept on the floor after yesterday…played the gentleman…though it chafed. Why should he be the one to suffer while she slept on…or snored on as it were?

He was exhausted now, and surly, for he hadn't slept a wink. Discomfort combined with too many tortured thoughts and even more torturous sights clattered about in his mind throughout the night. And all of it centered on her; when he should be thinking about their traitor. Or at the very least, sleeping so he could be clear-headed and well-rested. It was another gripe to lay at her feet.

They reached the ground floor without exchanging more than a glance. He turned the corner and was surprised to see MacLeod in the dining area. And the man wasn't alone, but it wasn't Kelly who graced his table as might be expected. It was the American, Mrs. Chase. She didn't appear to be happy about that fact either. She wasn't at all acting like the ebullient woman from yesterday. The one who had every man in the room, and some women, too, hanging on her every word. Well, everyone except MacLeod.

MacLeod looked like he always did. Kilted and angry.

Oh, he couldn't wait to hear this.

Dansbury nearly rubbed his hands with glee as he suddenly rediscovered his normal amiable manner, albeit this time, his manner held a touch of mischievousness. His friends always managed to bring him back to himself.

Dansbury slapped on an extra wide grin for good measure. "Good morning, my friend."

"Churchmouse," came the brusque reply. As usual, no smile came from that quarter.

"I see you have company. Why?" He didn't beat around the bush.

"Doona ask…"

Dansbury grinned wider. "But…"

"Doona. Ask."

He tried to keep a straight face. "You nev…"

"I said Doona. Fooking. Ask."

"Right…I won't ask." He held up a finger. "But you know…"

MacLeod took a swing and Dansbury only just managed to duck out of the way of the man's ham-sized fist.

Hmm. A might touchy today, aren't we?

He laughed at his friend. It's how they usually related to one another. He laughed, MacLeod scowled. Never mind that his own laugh was a touch strained today, an unusual occurrence to be sure.

He let go his teasing and turned to introduce Mrs. Chase to Lady Beatryce. "Mrs. Chase? This is my wife, Mrs. Betty Churchmouse."

"How do you do, Mrs. Churchmouse?" came the downcast reply.

"MacLeod, may I present my wife, Mrs. Churchmouse? Darling, this is my friend, Lord Alaistair MacLeod."

Mrs. Chase jerked her head up, her eyes wide with curiosity, and Dansbury winced as he realized his mistake. Another to fuel Mrs. Chase's curiosity. Based on their conversation at the last inn, Mrs. Chase would surely find it odd that his wife and his friend were not acquainted. And clearly, she'd noticed the blunder. Or suspected that something was off. But what could he say now? Nothing, really. In the end, he didn't offer an excuse, and as expected, she was too polite to query him on it.

Predictably, MacLeod snarled over Dansbury's use of "Lord". He was quite touchy on the subject of his own nobility.

In all, the tension around the table was so thick as to be almost visible.

Beatryce took charge to diffuse the situation.

Dansbury couldn't help but admire her as she spoke to MacLeod and Mrs. Chase. She stepped into the role of Mrs. Churchmouse as if she was born to it. Damn, but she was a surprise. At least, she put on a good show. She was lively and quick and quite swiftly put Mrs. Chase at ease. Not so MacLeod, but then Dansbury didn't think anyone was that capable. That man was born angry. But he was faithful.

Wasn't he?

Dansbury hated that he doubted the man, even for a moment. He owed that man many things, his faith among them.

MacLeod abruptly stood. "I need to check on my horse. She was acting verra strange on the way over." Then, he walked away without another word.

Right. That was his cue. Dansbury, too, made his excuses and followed after MacLeod to the stables.

* * * *

Dansbury entered the stables and was immediately awash with the scent of fresh hay and horses. It was a comforting smell. Normal.

MacLeod was leaning against a stall, stroking his horse's nose. He murmured softly and his mare visibly relaxed over his shoulder. She nudged his hand and whinnied in response.

And Dansbury witnessed the rarest of all things—a smile on Alaistair MacLeod's face.

It was brief and strange and no one would believe him if he told of it. But he saw it and it was an odd sight to behold. It almost looked wrong on the man, for it completely altered his usual appearance. Or at least, recently normal appearance. Five years, thirty-two days normal to be precise. Dansbury shook off dark memories that threatened to surface.

Here was a man who never offered an unnecessary word to a human. He'd always been that way. Polite conversation completely escaped the gruff man. More so since... He didn't complete the thought.

Yet MacLeod was as gentle as a lamb with his cattle, and clearly had much to say. He allowed few, if any, to ever see this side of him. Dansbury almost felt like an intruder, despite the fact that he probably knew this man better than anyone else in the world.

"I got your note." He got right to the point. The infamous note he'd received while he and Beatryce were...nearly...engaged in physical congress had been from MacLeod.

Alaistair didn't answer, but continued to stroke his mare's nose and murmur quietly.

The ritual seemed to soothe the man as much as the beast. Many would claim it was the mare as much as the beast.

"A traitor?" He prodded his friend.

"Aye. It's the only explanation that makes sense, ye ken?"

Dansbury shuffled the straw at his feet. He didn't want to face this truth. Every part of him rebelled against the idea of one of their own betraying them.

MacLeod must have noticed his demeanor though he never once looked at Dansbury.

"Och, I doona like it either."

They were certainly in agreement on that. "Do you suspect anyone?"

"Aye and nae. I doona have proof, mind, but I have my suspicions, and I doona like them. I doona want them to be truth, ye ken?" MacLeod continued to stroke his mare's nose. He looked off into space.

"Where is Kelly?" Dansbury asked the question he assumed was really on both their minds.

MacLeod turned to look at him then, his gaze hard and cold. His look conveyed much that would remain unspoken. For now. "Och. He's not here, aye? He's off chasing doun a lead, ye ken?"

Dansbury looked down and dug up a stone at his feet with the toe of his boot. "Yes. I believe we understand each other perfectly."

* * * *

"So, Mrs. Chase. MacLeod seems an ill-tempered sort. What dire event has placed you in his keeping? I did see you at the Quiet Witch Inn, did I not?"

Mrs. Chase nodded and smiled and every man in the room seemed to turn as one in her direction. She was quite stunning when she smiled—for she did so with her entire face. Here was a woman who would find it impossible to be dishonest. It had been some time since Beatryce had met the like. Had she ever?

She is quite the opposite of me to be sure.

"It's a long story, Mrs. Churchmouse. You wouldn't believe me if I told you." She answered with a wave of her hand.

Beatryce threw on her biggest smile. "La, try me. And call me Bea...um

Betty. I believe we are going to be seeing a lot of each other in the future, Mrs. Chase."

Mrs. Chase widened her eyes in surprise before adopting a more thoughtful mien. Beatryce waited patiently and assumed her most innocent expression—the one guaranteed to make anyone spill their secrets. Especially the open, friendly type like Mrs. Chase.

It worked. It wasn't a moment before Mrs. Chase nodded her head as she came to a decision. She folded her hands on the table. "Well," she said, "you know I'm from America, but did you know that I was born an orphan?"

CHAPTER 19

"Tempt not a desperate man."
— Shakespeare, Romeo and Juliet

On the Road Again...

Dansbury was in a mood. Again. He sat with his boots propped up on the seat before him, his arms resting on his knees as he all but glared at the walking stick he held between his legs. Every once in a while he pulled at his worn cravat with a worried expression, and then scowled at the trees passing outside his window before returning his attention to the offensive cane. Eventually he tossed his cravat and his cane on the seat before him.

At one point, Beatryce thought he might toss both items out the window. It would probably be a good idea. If anyone were to see his walking stick they'd wonder why a man of his standing would own such a costly thing. It would blow away their cover. At least he'd had the sense to leave it in the carriage each night so it wouldn't be seen by the patrons at the inns.

His mercurial expressions were so obvious, she nearly laughed at the sight of him brooding in the corner. She refrained. Just. Instead, she watched it all from her side of the carriage with only a twitch or two of her lips to betray her inner thoughts.

She didn't try to hide her perusal, but if he noticed, and Beatryce had no doubt that he did, he did not show it. Which was fine. She was quite content to simply observe, catalogue, and then reach her own conclusions about what conflicting thoughts were running through his mind.

And then there was Mrs. Chase and her monumental revelations. Monumental might even be regarded an understatement. Mrs. Chase had revealed far more than Beatryce could have ever imagined. In fact, she was still trying to come to terms with it all. Mrs. Chase's story had far reaching implications...for Dansbury. For Stonebridge's team...

La, but what to do with this information?

She didn't know at the moment. But the knowledge was important and Dansbury needed to know...when the time was right.

Now was not that time. He was clearly distraught over one possible traitor...but this? This might very well push him over the edge and into a rage that made his tying-her-to-the-chair-and-gagging-her tirade look like child's play. Not to mention the pain and confusion that would soon follow. Though possibly some joy, too.

No. For now it was best she still her tongue and go along with the current plan, which wasn't really much of a plan at all. Certainly not a new one. They were simply going to proceed with the original scheme—at least until the next stop. Which meant they were off to another ratty inn in the middle of nowhere.

Ha! Men and their schemes.

Unbeknownst to Dansbury and MacLeod, Mrs. Chase had agreed to stay within sight of MacLeod. For now. Beatryce rather thought Mrs. Chase would not find that task too much of a hardship. And MacLeod, though dark and brusque, appeared incapable of keeping his eyes from following Mrs. Chase's every move in return. Considering Mrs. Chase was normally quite animated, the effect was amusing on such a brooding man.

Beatryce returned her thoughts to Dansbury and soon noticed that Dansbury's mood had continued to deteriorate with every mile they traveled. She decided to redirect his ire. "You've led quite a charmed life, haven't you?"

That should do it.

"What is that supposed to mean?" He all but bit off every word.

Yea, that did it.

"You have wealth, power, excessive good looks, friends who care, friends with money, family who supports your every move...I say you with your 'life-is-what-you-make-of-it, look-for-the-positive-and-ye-shall-find-it, holier-than-thou' attitude, you have never had your ideals truly tested..."

"Love, my values are challenged every single minute I'm around you, and they've survived intact thus far."

"Yes, you proved that well last night. I seem to recall you telling me you never fuck anyone under your protection…"

"We didn't."

"Only due to the damn missive. Deny it all you want. It would have happened if someone hadn't knocked on the door."

Judging by the thunderous expression that stampeded across his face, he was downright furious. And despite the fact that he was still angry, at least now, his irate countenance lost some of the bleakness she saw hovering around the edges before.

But she wasn't finished. Because now she was irritated over his attempted denial of their obvious attraction. She kept her composure though. Even when she realized that it was the first time she had acknowledged their mutual attraction, even to herself.

And it was true. The attraction was real. On both sides.

"I think you've grown tired of being good. I think there is a part of you lurking inside that wants to be just a little bit bad and it is making you crazy."

"Ha! You see me through tinted eyes. I love being good. In fact, I excel at it. But what about you, *Dr. Beckett*? Are you tired of being bad? What do you want? What makes you tick? You don't act like a normal lady…"

"I am not a normal lady."

When had he drawn so close? He had crossed to her side of the carriage and was in her face now. She smelled his earthy scent, his minty breath. He was breathing hard and she responded in kind.

Were they even talking about the same thing anymore?

He bent to kiss her; she read the intent in his eyes as he learned forward. And she nearly allowed it.

But instead, she put her hand up to stop him. She'd given this a lot of thought during her sleepless night. "I will not do this."

He leaned forward and touched his forehead to hers instead. Then rubbed her nose with his and whispered, "You seemed to manage just fine yesterday." His voice had quieted, barely above a whisper now.

"Yes, well I can't now. Don't ask me why."

It was called self-preservation.

He leaned back and looked at her. If anything, his lust seemed to flame hotter rather than diminish with her rejection of his advances. And an answering call swelled inside her.

She tamped it down and lifted her chin. "Go back to your side of the carriage, Dansbury. You were good, what I had of you, but I've moved on."

For a moment, there was a challenge to his gaze. She'd impugned his virility with her words. His male nature would require him to accept the challenge. To prove her wrong. But all too soon, his challenging look was replaced with a knowing one shaded with a large portion of confidence.

That look was frightening.

He braced his arms on either side of her, effectively caging her to the seat. He leaned close, his breath tickling her ear as he said, "Oh, I'll have you, never doubt it. And you'll be begging for it when I do…"

La, he wanted to be bad. With her. Ha!

He brushed his lips against the side of her face, a caress she felt down to her toes. But then he pulled away and moved back to his side of the carriage as per her request…

No. Demand. Dammit.

Despite the distance that now separated them, the carriage still felt like it had shrunk. To the size of a rabbit hole. That was on fire.

He smiled again. A mischievous, knowing sort of grin. Then crossed his arms and let his eyes roam her figure before returning to look at her. She saw the heat in them and wanted her fan. Or a bucket of ice.

He leaned forward and braced his hands on his thighs. "Ah, Bea. You have no idea of the things I want to do to you…The things I've dreamt…The things we will do…"

He lost his smile then, his face turned serious. "And Bea? You had better be ready…"

CHAPTER 20

"Et tu, Brute?"
— *William Shakespeare, Julius Caesar*

*"If his lips are silent, he chatters with his fingertips;
betrayal oozes out of him at every pore."*
— *Sigmund Freud*

*The Queen and the Horny Toad Inn…
That Night…*

He wanted to jump into the stream running alongside the inn. His body all but demanded he douse the burning in his loins. He could hear the trickle of water and smell its clean scent. And it beckoned him closer. Enticed him to dive in, clothes and all.

Damn, but she touched something inside of him that set his blood on fire. Whether it be anger or lust, it all seemed to amount to the same thing with her…his blood burning through his veins.

Who was this depraved monster that suddenly craved sex? With her. All of the damn time.

Yet he couldn't resist taunting her as he helped her out of the carriage. "Like the name of the Inn? Appropriate, don't you think?"

Despite the taunt, what the name implied was all too true. Unfortunately.

She didn't respond and he was glad. He'd disconcerted the impossible-to-disconcert Ice Queen. Finally. Though somehow his success felt hollow.

They rushed inside and once again he was caught off guard by her complete change in demeanor the minute they walked through the door and introduced themselves as Mr. & Mrs. Churchmouse to all and sundry. She unnerved him with her ability to change on demand, to cloak her personality in a believable façade. It was all he could do to maintain his own pretense as they waited for their room to finish being readied...in front of twenty-five other patrons enjoying themselves in the inn's taproom. He felt like he was on stage.

More than an hour later, two hours after they had disembarked from their entirely too small conveyance, lust still made his skin sensitive to the touch. His shirt grazed his prickled flesh with every step. He wanted to rip his clothes off.

More concerning, he wanted to rip off hers.

Alas, he was on his way to the public room. This time to meet with Kelly, who was awaiting him downstairs. Like last time, Beatryce remained upstairs in their room. And like last time, he tried not to dwell on that fact. Or remember what he'd found awaiting him when he'd returned to their room.

"Kelly..."

"D...Churchmouse?"

"Another near slip? You're getting lax, old man." Dansbury tried to keep the accusation from his tone.

"Though, I shan't like to admit it, ye're right. I'm feeling my age, fer sure."

Kelly seemed different. Unsettled. Dansbury tried to decide whether or not he was simply projecting his own distrust on his friend. Or was his friend finding it tough to hide his guilt?

"Where were you this morning? Imagine my surprise to find MacLeod with Mrs. Chase instead of you. Though, I must say she is a damn sight better to look at." Dansbury tried to make his question humorous, to put his friend at ease...loosen the tongue a bit.

They laughed, but Kelly's was clearly strained. "I had to check on something," was all he said. Vague and noncommittal.

Dansbury waited while Kelly fiddled with his mug of ale. It hadn't escaped his notice that Kelly seemed surprised to learn of Mrs. Chase's presence at the last inn. After a while, he prompted, "Something..."

"I can't say. I don't want to believe in my suspicions. Aye?"

"You have suspicions?" Well, this was unexpected.

"That's just it. I don't even want to admit them, aye? We've all worked together for too long. Trusted each other, aye?"

"Yes," he said with more than a little hesitation.

"I just want to know fer sure. And I don't want to believe what I suspect. But it cannot possibly be a coincidence that those assassins found your trail so quickly..." Kelly was bringing up the possibility of a traitor?

"Where is MacLeod?" He wanted to shake Kelly, demand he tell the truth because right now he didn't know who was playing false. One man he didn't want to believe would betray him; the other he couldn't believe...his mind shied away from the very thought of it.

"That is the question isn't it, ye know?"

"Yes, I believe we do..."

And just like that Dansbury knew that the only person he could trust right now was himself. And it made him ill to know it. Was Kelly trying to throw him off the scent by framing MacLeod? Or was MacLeod truly the traitorous one?

He ended their 'meeting' quite quickly after that, knowing that he and Beatryce were on their own now and that he wouldn't learn the truth this night.

But he was a damn good spy; he would finish this on his own terms. When the time was right.

Dansbury proceeded upstairs and picked the lock to their room. Again. But this time, he crossed the room in silent strides, without once looking or even so much as glancing at the bed and her lying in it. Possibly unclothed. Damn, he was proud of his self-control.

Instead, he walked straight through to the window, and with all the innate grace of a large cat, climbed out it and into the inky night. Their plans had just changed.

* * * *

At Sunrise…

Birds sung their morning song outside the cloaked man's window. It seemed like there were a hundred of them all projecting their twittering, chirpy melody straight into his brain through the back of his head. God, they were a damned nuisance and distracting to his task. He wanted to run from the room screaming with his hands blocking his ears against the noise. It was a crazy thought. He knew it. So he pushed the random thought away and read through the missive he'd just penned to Himself:

> *My Lord Master,*
>
> *I regret to inform you that there has been a slight wrinkle in our plans. My men failed to capture Lord D and Lady B at the appointed time.*
>
> *Not to worry, for our useful traitor has proved his worth quite convincingly by providing us with invaluable, timely, and accurate information on our quarry's whereabouts. To our advantage, we remain close on Lord D's trail. The man has proven a trusting fool…as you suspected he would.*

I am still on point to bring Lord D before you as planned. For now, I have adapted my plans and have chosen to taunt him from afar as we follow his every move. He will grow paranoid and angry as I toy with him—which will only serve you well in the future...the better to convince Lord D to join us in our righteous cause in the end.

I have every faith you will be most victorious in this endeavor, as always. I long for the day when we can publicly celebrate our victory.

I will be at the rendezvous point in a fortnight as planned...with our reluctant, but soon to be subservient, guests.

Respectfully, your most loyal servant,

-D

He had to force himself to steady his hands lest he crumple the missive in ire. He despised groveling. But, alas, it was sometimes required. Fortunately, it would not be necessary for much longer.

The cloaked man sanded his note and folded it, relishing the fact that Himself could not know that when he brought Dansbury before Him, it would only be Dansbury's heart he would be throwing at His feet—not the man himself as implied. Nor did He realize that Lady Beatryce would remain his own personal bed toy, indefinitely—certainly not His.

For why would a dead man have need of a bed slave?

Aaah, it was such a sweet dream to imagine...He savored the image, the look of surprise he imagined on the old man's face when he plunged his dagger through the old bastard's heart. Oh, after all these years...It would finally...finally...happen.

A heavy tread sounded in the hallway outside his rented room. Ah good, so good. It was time to torment the mouse with a gift... *Knock. Knock. Knock.*

Yes. Just in time.

"Enter..."

The cloaked man was pleased to see their traitorous spy enter the room as expected. He made the younger man wait as he returned his attention to the task of sealing the missive to Himself rather than greet his visitor. The traitor certainly had proven his worth, though. That part of the note was no lie.

He looked up to see if his turncoat was annoyed by the delay. He didn't appear to be, which was damn irritating. Alas, the appropriate level of frustration would come in time. Followed closely by doubt and indecision. It worked that way every single time. Oh, how easily people were maneuvered. Like sheep.

For now, he would send the man on another errand, but not with the charge of dispatching the missive. No. That he would do himself.

Finally, he gifted the man with his full attention, "Ah, good. You're right on schedule. I have a task for you. A present, of sorts, I need you to deliver to our mutual friend. Though I suspect Dansbury doesn't realize you're not much of a friend to him, does he?"

CHAPTER 21

"The earth laughs in flowers."

— *Ralph Waldo Emerson*

On the Road Again…

They rode in a wagon. Yea. A wagon. Not a traveling carriage as before, but a wagon that was little more than a cart with an old donkey that looked like he'd been put to pasture some ten years prior. And some blankets. And possibly a basket with day old bread for a meal…Hopefully with some cheese and ale to wash it down. Beatryce hadn't bothered to check its contents.

Oh, and their small armory from the rented carriage filled the back. Dansbury had covered most of it up with some of their new moth-worn blankets that reeked of cows and other things she'd rather not name.

A traveling carriage, even one as rundown as the one they'd arrived in, would have been preferable. But alas, beggars do not have the luxury of being choosy. And they were pretending to be little more than beggars. Hence, the cart.

They'd awoken even earlier than on their previous days. Before the rooster outside had even thought about crowing, Dansbury had shaken her awake without a word more than "Let's go." No innuendoes. No smile of greeting. Not even a scowl as was his usual manner in her presence. Just fierce determination with a sharp edge of impatience.

She had no idea where he'd spent the night. All she remembered was him picking the lock to their room. The thought had made her smile. Then, he walked straight through and out the window. She'd laughed out loud when he was gone and then wondered if one would have to get used to such behavior in order to live with a man like Dansbury. She didn't think about that for long...drove that thought right out of her mind lest she spend another night without a wink of sleep to show for it.

Beatryce presumed this, the cart, was arranged by him, and she knew by his demeanor that now was not the time to question him on it. So she went along with it. For now. She knew their position was precarious what with the idea of a traitor or two and deadly assassins trailing them.

La, it sounded like something out of a poorly-written gothic novel.

Oh, and she was driving the cart.

Dansbury was in the back prepping their small armory. Ensuring everything was dry.

And ready should they need it. She wished she could be back there with him. Helping. But all he had said to her since he woke her was, "You're driving," as he helped her up into her seat. Then he walked away and climbed onto the back. Someone had to drive the cart.

She supposed she should be pleased that he didn't question her capabilities.

But that was hours ago, and it was impossible to converse with him when she was up front driving while he was in the back playing spy. She was going to start conversing with the donkey soon. She'd already named him Dansbury the Younger.

"Oh, Dansbury, you are a fine ass," she whispered to the ass...er, donkey. Loudly.

La, she was losing her mind.

"Did you say something?" yelled a masculine voice from behind.

"Wasn't talking to you," she threw back. With a secret smile she didn't dare reveal.

The cart began rocking as Dansbury climbed over his little caches of weaponry. Before she knew it, he was practically breathing down her neck.

She tightened her grip on the reins. Dansbury the Younger shook his head in protest. And brayed his displeasure.

Haaaaw Heeee

"Sorry..." she pleaded to the donkey in a feigned whisper she meant for Dansbury to hear.

He rested his arm on the backrest behind her and leaned over her shoulder. "You're doing remarkably well, Bea. How are you holding up?"

His breath tickled and raised goose bumps on her arms. She nearly giggled. Giggled! Like a naïve little debutante. Something she'd never had the luxury to be. She swallowed the impulse and ignored the smile her soul delivered over his acknowledgement.

"Thank you. I'm fine. The donkey here is a wonderful conversationalist."

He laughed over her shoulder and she felt it all the way to her toes where it bounced around for a while before it settled in her gut.

"Lady Bea, I'm sure you could hold an interesting conversation with anyone, be it man or beast."

Her soul beamed brighter. She ignored the fool. Both of them. She knew she should thank him for the compliment, but she didn't trust her voice just now.

And he didn't seem to mind. "There is a cart path to the right just past that bend up ahead. It is easy to miss, so beware. Why don't we pull off for a spell and have a rest?"

He didn't wait for her to answer, and his continued faith in her abilities further astounded her. He simply made the statement, and then she felt the cart shake again as he climbed back to his former position.

Her neck felt cool with the loss of his body heat, and her eyes began to water. The wind was particularly sharp today, and cold, causing her eyes to tear up from the dryness.

No one had ever had faith in her. No one.

And she didn't cry. Ever. Thus, it was clearly the wind.

As was becoming the norm, she had to suppress her father's voice as he screamed in her mind that Dansbury was only saying these things to bend her to his will. Would she ever be free of the agony of her father's torment?

She slowed the cart as they neared the bend and only just managed to turn off onto the little trail to the side. She had no idea where they were, but she was relieved for the respite.

The path they were on was short, and before too long, it ended in a grassy field filled with wildflowers. A small stream ran nearby. She couldn't see it; she could only just hear it. It must be lower down where the field sloped down up ahead and fell from view.

Her hands were cramped from hours of holding on to the reins and her bottom was sore from sitting on the hard bench. She stood and stretched, her muscles protesting yet sighing with relief. Before she could take her first step down from the cart, Dansbury was reaching up to help her down.

He simply gripped her by the waist and hoisted her off the cart.

She locked eyes with his. He smiled at her with a smile so warm, his eyes seemed to sparkle. He had never looked at her that way before, and she knew, then and there, that she would never forget that look for the rest of her miserable life.

Damn him for planting that memory!

She wanted to rail at him for it, though she knew it was unfair. She held her tongue, though not for that reason. As was her nature, she remained silent and simply smiled in return because she needed information from him and making him angry was not the way to get it. She knew that. It was a conscious decision on her part.

See, she was always self-centered. Always thinking of number one. It was ingrained in the fabric of her being…she couldn't be any other way. Even now. Even with him.

Whether or not the behavior was hers by nature or by nurture (ha!)—as a victim of circumstance developed through self-preservation from a lifetime of abuse from her father—was irrelevant. This was her. Now. Probably forever as she was too old to change her ways.

The thought depressed her somewhat.

Dansbury tilted her chin. His eyes were questions that begged to know what was on her mind.

Had she been so transparent? Huh. That was new.

She tried to look away, but he wouldn't allow it.

"Bea, what is the matter? You look…lost."

For a moment she considered revealing it all, and she knew he could see that in her eyes. But her survival instinct was far too strong. She collected herself, and she felt him stiffen in response at the sight of her composure.

"La, I'm fine, Dansbury. Just sore. And trying hard not to blame you for it."

He looked like he would say more, but she stopped the question hanging on the tip of his tongue. "Leave it, Dansbury."

Then she turned on her heal, leaving him to retrieve their basket from the back of the wagon.

*

"So what are our plans now?"

They'd finished eating and were both lying on their backs on one of their ratty blankets, staring up at the clear, blue sky. The air was crisp and fresh, despite the foul blanket beneath them. She didn't know what he was thinking about, but she was imagining shapes in the clouds passing overhead while she waited for the opportune time to approach the subject of their plans to end all this.

It started with a sigh, a deep, drawn out sigh. She took it as a sign that he was concerned she wasn't going to like what he had to say. She braced herself for bad news.

He turned on his side to face her and propped his head up with one arm. He was fiddling with a dandelion, but he looked her in the eye when he spoke. "We're going to be traveling in this wagon for a week...sleeping wherever we can find shelter. *Wherever.*

They'll be no more high class inns for Mr. and Mrs. Churchmouse."

They both laughed at the idea that their previous nights' accommodations were more than what they were. High-class, indeed.

"I mean it, Bea. We cannot afford the risk. I don't know who to trust besides myself. So I plan to keep traveling by wagon until we reach my Aunt's house. It should take about three to five days, depending on the weather, our skill, and our luck. I have no doubt of our skill."

Beatryce raised her brow at this. "Isn't it risky to travel to a family member's house?"

"Usually, yes. But I don't think anyone will suspect that to be our plan; that is the beauty of it. I'm not kidding myself into believing that the men following us are unaware of my occupation with the Crown...or of my reputation in that capacity." He seemed to beam with pride at his vaunted reputation.

Sigh. Men.

"But honestly, even if they knew that is where we're hiding, I'm not worried. It's being out in the open, exposed, that is more of a danger to us. Being in a place I'm familiar with is preferable. I'm confident in my own capabilities and my ability to protect you, especially at home in a well-known environment." She was lost at "protect you." Damn his eyes.

And he knew it. His eyes darkened; his hand stopped absentmindedly twirling his dandelion. A cloud passed overhead, blocking the sun, shading his face even further and enhancing the effect, the sign of his desire. For her.

And before she knew what either of them were about, he'd dropped the flower, leaned over, and kissed her.

Slowly.

Gently.

Not the passionate attack she was expecting.

And she was completely undone by it. By his gentleness, his reverence, for she'd never experienced the like.

His lips slid back and forth across hers, a light flutter and barely there. Yes, there was desire, but the gesture also spoke of tenderness. Tenderness was foreign to her, so she brushed it away by deliberately inciting his passion.

She pushed up, pushed him over, and kissed him for all she was worth. He needn't know she'd put her heart and soul into it. That in her kiss, she was saying thanks for her first taste of tender compassion.

He needed no further convincing. He responded in kind.

His hands searched her body, rubbing her back, her sides, her arse. At one point, his hands came up her sides, his thumbs pressing in just beneath her breasts.

She simply held on to his head, one hand on each side, her fingers buried in thick, golden locks as she attacked his mouth with her own.

Crack!

A loud sound in the distance startled them apart. A flock of birds took flight several hundred yards to her left. It sounded like the thick branch of a tree falling to the ground.

Whatever, it was enough to bring them both to their senses.

She was wading into dangerous territory.

Dansbury had turned to look at the sound. Now, he looked back at her, his eyes still heavy with passion. Like hers. Both of them were breathing erratically.

He reached for her, but she stayed him with her hand.

"Enough, Dansbury."

He backed away immediately, and she nearly laughed at the disappointment she felt flutter around her heart. It was another sign she was growing soft. And soft was dangerous.

She was soiled goods; her heart was dark. And mean. He was a good man; even she knew that. And he was not for her. She wouldn't taint him with her problems, her humble future. And she would never trust him enough to make it work. They'd be miserable. She laughed at the thought—as if he was thinking of anything more permanent than a few nights of sex. Not likely.

"That was fun, Dansbury, but la, I've had enough. We really need to get moving so we can find some place to settle down before it grows dark."

He smiled, which was unnerving in that it was unexpected.

"Sure, Bea. You speak some truth; we'll go." He stood, but she remained rooted to the ground. She knew he wasn't finished.

"But, Bea…" He was standing, but he leaned down and over her, face to face. She could smell his breath. "I never took you for a coward." And he walked off.

CHAPTER 22

"Curiosity is the lust of the mind."

— *Thomas Hobbes*

The Barn...

They were sleeping in an abandoned barn. La, a barn. Had someone told her she'd one day be sleeping in the hayloft of a derelict barn, Beatryce would have laughed until her sides split. Then called upon the warden at Bedlam.

Yet here she was. In a barn that looked as if it hadn't been used in a century or more. A hole in the roof offered her a clear view of the night sky above her head. The air around her was damp and chilly, making her nose cold despite the mound of blankets covering her from her chin on down.

She'd been wrapped up in Dansbury's arms when she went to sleep, cocooned and cozy beneath a hundred blankets.

For warmth. Simply warmth. Honest.

And she'd slept more deeply than she ever had in her life, despite lying on a thin bed of musty hay. Yet now she was wide awake and shivering. Dansbury was gone and based on the feel of his side of their 'bed', he'd been away for some time.

She knew better than to think anything was wrong. Dansbury was a big boy and could take care of himself. But now that she was awake, she realized she needed to find the ladies' retiring room. She chuckled to herself as she imagined a fancy room, complete with maids and toiletries, hidden amidst the trees outside.

Luckily, the moon was out and she was able to make out the top of the ladder to their loft. She crawled toward it trying not to stumble over her voluminous dress in the process.

She failed. At one point, she placed her left knee too far forward, stepped on her dress with it, and planted her face into the rank hay as she tried to move her right leg. She inhaled a breath full of musty straw and came up sputtering.

She sniggered at her clumsiness and pulled a few stray pieces of hay from her hair. Then, she pulled her dress free and tried again. This time she made it to the ladder without trouble. Though as she swung her leg over to the first rung, she managed to knock a heap of hay over the edge of the loft and to the floor below. *Oops.* Based on the weight and feel of the pile, she might have tossed over a few blankets as well. Guess they'd find out what was lost in the morning. It was too dark below to see anything, making it pointless to bother searching now.

She picked her way down the ladder with light feet, desperate to be as quiet as possible. It seemed to take forever, but before long, she was on the ground. Beatryce stepped cautiously across the dirt-covered floor, occasionally turning her ankle on churned earth. Other spots were wet and mushy causing her feet to slip and slide, but with no light to see, all she could do was tread carefully. Clouds had temporarily covered the moon making everything as dark as pitch. Fortunately, she knew there was nothing in the barn to bar her way. She simply walked with arms outstretched until she felt the rough wood of the wall on the opposite side from the loft. Then felt her way along it until she found the door to the outside.

She pushed the door open and stepped out. She could just make out some ambiguous shapes, but only enough to give her a vague sense of direction.

Still no sign of Dansbury.

He's probably out on patrol.

She laughed at the image of him marching the perimeter, eyes alert, playing soldier. She shook off the ridiculous image and headed toward the trees and the general direction of a small pool of water Dansbury had told her about yesterday. It would be the perfect place to clean up after seeing to her personal needs.

A few minutes into the woods and Bea wished the clouds would break apart and reveal the moon so she could see. She could feel a slight breeze blowing through the trees, and she hoped that higher up, the wind would finally move the clouds along. As it was, she progressed slowly from tree to tree, arms outstretched, trying to ignore what she couldn't see beneath her feet.

Sometimes the ground was squishy, and she cursed herself for not taking the time to put on her shoes. Other times, she could hear the crunch of sticks and fallen leaves below her feet. She hoped that the ground remained reasonably level, but she had no way of knowing for sure. For that reason, she proceeded with extra care.

After a few more minutes, though it felt like hours, Bea could tell she had almost reached her destination. She could just make out the smell and sound of water as it lapped upon its rocky shore. She was just about to take another step when a break finally opened up in the clouds, revealing an almost-full moon.

Ahead of her, the moonlight glinted off a small body of water just visible through a gap framed by two large boulders. She was near the edge of the woods; there were only a few more trees to pass and a short open area to cross before she reached the entrance to the pool.

At last.

Now that she could see, Bea picked up her pace. She left the woods behind, crossed the gap, and peered cautiously around the boulders.

And realized that she wasn't alone.

Dansbury...was at the pool.

He looked odd there, lying amongst the rocks. She nearly stepped out and made some quip about it, but her voice died in her throat when she realized he was... Stark. Naked.

Bare as the day he was born naked.

He lay sprawled across one large boulder, one knee bent and chin tilted to the moon as if offering himself upon some alter to the Gods.

She wanted to be the goddess who worshiped his sacrifice.

She could see the long length of him—from head to toe—as she approached, slowly and quietly, from his side. She could not help but take full advantage of the view...to look upon him in secret...to fill her eyes with the sight of him, without his knowledge and the frequent look of condescension he threw her way.

Goodness. He was a man in his prime, and she had never seen the like. Light and shadows played off the muscles in his arms and thighs as they rippled with his movement. One foot was planted firmly on a lower rock, his foot wide and long...masculine.

He groaned, and she almost fell to her knees right there on the rocks. She subconsciously took another step and he groaned again. Now that she was closer, she could see why.

Oh, God she knew why…

He was pleasuring himself.

One large hand was wrapped firmly around his turgid manhood as he stroked, slow and steady.

Up and down.

Up and down.

The head of his cock peeked out, then disappeared in his firm, sure grip.

She was close enough now to see the muscles in his abdomen clench with each stroke. She longed to go to him, to be the one to ease him. Yet she couldn't move. She was frozen as she watched, transfixed, at the obvious pleasure written plain across his face and in every inch of his lean, taut body.

Again, his hand stroked up, and she squeezed her legs together in response, an echo of pleasure pulsed in her core.

He stroked down, and she could feel wetness release between her legs.

Lord, he was beautiful. Painfully beautiful. Like a god himself. Untouchable and unreal. At least for her.

He gritted his teeth in pleasure-pain as he continued to plunge and pull his long, hard cock, the muscles of his arm flexing and bulging with every stroke.

Her nipples stood erect and tingled. She wanted his lips on her breasts, his tongue tweaking and circling the buds before he sucked one nipple into his mouth while he caressed the other…while she stroked his manhood with her hands; not him.

Or licked the head with her mouth.

She'd never performed fellatio before, but he looked so desirable there before her, his manhood so large and firm, she suddenly longed to experience the act.

As if he was in harmony with her thoughts, he began to move faster and faster, and Bea could tell his crisis drew near. She could see the obvious signs of desire ripple across his face as he gritted his teeth, and her heart beat faster and in time with his every stroke.

Then, he went taught and for a moment everything froze. Even the earth seemed to stop spinning on its axis and the wind appeared to hold its breath.

Then with a shout, he yelled, "God, Bea!" as he found his release.

Beatryce's heart fell to her knees with those words. Impossible, glorious words.

And unlike the strong woman she knew herself to be, she ran. Ran from those words. From him. From them. Unmindful and uncaring of the noises she made with her hasty retreat.

CHAPTER 23

"If we couldn't laugh we would all go insane."

— Robert Frost

The Next Morning…

"Bea, wake up. We have a problem."

Beatryce didn't even move, much less acknowledge him. He squatted down beside her. It wasn't easy for he was wrapped in a large blanket with two corners loosely tied together over his shoulder to hold it in place.

He nudged her again, but all she did was emit a soft snore and carry on in blissful slumber. He hated to wake her; he knew she hadn't slept well last night.

A ray of sunshine burst through the hole in the ceiling illuminating the loft and bathing her face in light making her hair and skin appear to glow. She scrunched her nose, probably at the sudden warmth, but carried on sleeping. He turned his head just so and caught a glimpse of tiny dust motes dancing in the light's rays. For a moment, he imagined they were little fairies coming down from the heavens to view the sleeping Fae princess.

He shook his head. What nonsense was this? He didn't have time to wax poetic about her beauty. They had a real problem to address.

He reached out and shook her again. This time, he raised his voice, speaking just shy of a shout. "Bea, wake up!"

Beatryce blinked open her eyes. He knew she'd had little sleep last night.

Especially after the eyeful she'd gotten of him pleasuring himself.

Oh, yes. He knew she'd seen it all. And he knew she'd tossed and turned the night through because of it. Or, at least, that was his possibly arrogant assumption.

He shoved aside such thoughts with a promise to address them later. Right now, they, or at least he, had bigger problems.

Beatryce sat up and rubbed the sleep from her eyes. Eyes that were so beautiful to behold, and probably gritty from a lack of sleep. She blinked again and looked up at him a moment. Her eyes automatically lowered to the general vicinity of his groin. He was completely covered, but she blushed and turned away anyway. It was ludicrous; she was no innocent, and she'd already seen all he had to offer. Twice now.

He'd explore her odd behavior later.

"Bea, we have a problem. My clothes are gone."

That got her attention. She turned back around to face him, her eyes wide. "What do you mean gone?"

"I mean gone. They were in the loft and now they're not." He still couldn't believe it.

"Did you check the floor below? I may have knocked them off last night." She blushed again as she likely thought of what she'd seen because she'd ventured outside the hayloft last night.

Yea, they'd definitely address that later.

"I checked every inch of this barn from top to bottom. Three times. They are not here."

Her eyes widened again and then she burst out laughing. Not a titter or a giggle. No, not Beatryce. No, she let loose a hard belly-aching-side-splitting laugh that almost made him laugh, too. Despite the seriousness of his predicament.

"Bea, it's not funny," he said with a smile. He couldn't help it.

"Oh, it is funny…*ha ha ha*…all right. It's very…*tee hee*…funny. It is absolutely…*snort*…unbelievably hysterical, it's so funny." She managed between large, wailing guffaws and the odd snort or two. He could not believe she was laughing about this.

"Bea. Seriously."

She laughed that much harder.

"Fine, it might be a little funny, but it's still a problem. So if you don't mind, I'd appreciate it if you could pull yourself together and give me a hand with this."

She just doubled over and laughed some more and it made him want to gather her up in his arms and kiss her senseless. Which was absurd. Apparently, taking the edge off last night hadn't helped. God, he was in a bad way.

But she just looked so carefree when she laughed, with her head tilted back and her arms wrapped around her waist. Her laughter was the thing that had attracted him the first time he'd seen her on that darkened terrace so long ago. Her laugh; it held the power to captivate him.

Every time her amusement began to subside, she'd look at him and start howling and snorting all over again.

"Don't look at me if it's going to make you laugh," he said with a bit of a chuckle himself.

It seemed like ten minutes passed before her laughter began to trail off for good. He'd long since given up squatting and was sitting on his bottom with his back against the wall.

Her laughter was only coming in fits and giggles now. When her breathing finally returned to some semblance of normalcy, she said, "All right. I'll help you look around and see what we can find," as she wiped the remains of tears from her eyes.

Half an hour later they knew exactly what had happened. He, with a scratchy blanket wrapped around him like an ill-fitting toga, and she, with her perfectly functional oversized dress (he was actually a touch jealous now) managed to find the remains of his clothes hanging from the mouths of a pair of goats.

Goats.

And there was nothing left to salvage, damned beasties.

The sight of his shredded clothes started Beatryce's hysterics all over again. He crossed his arms and tapped his fingers impatiently, but with a small smile, as he waited for her to calm down. Again.

"Are you finished?"

"Perhaps," she said with more than a little cheek. She was in a damn fine mood this morning, all things considered.

"Good, then let's move on and see if we can find an abandoned house to go with this barn. Perhaps we'll get lucky and find me some more appropriate clothing."

"Fine," she chuckled again, "I'll go to the left, and you head out to the right. We'll meet back here in an hour." *Snort.*

He shook his head. "Bea, I cannot have you wandering off on your own."

"Please, don't be ridiculous. I'll be fine. There is no one here for miles. And I know what I'm about. Worry about yourself. That blanket offers scant protection for your backside." And she left, laughing again as she walked away.

He reluctantly let her go.

*

An hour later, he returned to the barn with nothing to show for his search save a few scratches on his exposed arms and legs and a new tear in his blanket-dress. He refused to acknowledge the thorns he'd had to pull out of his arse. Stupid briars.

He hoped to God Bea'd had better luck. He tried not to worry over the fact that she wasn't back.

Ten minutes later, though, and he was prepared to go searching for her. It was with relief when he heard her call out. "Dansbury?"

"Here…" He stood away from the barn wall.

She stepped out of the woods with her arms behind her back and a wide smile on her face. "Well, I've got some good news and some bad news."

"All right…" he said with some hesitation.

"The good news is I found some clothes, but…"

"But…"

"Weeelll, they're not exactly what you had in mind."

"All right…"

Slowly, she pulled one arm from behind her back and with a face devoid of any trace of humor, held out an over-sized…

…dress…

A large, multi-flowered, grease-splattered, heavily-patched, tent-sized dress. One that made hers look like it was custom-made from the pages of *La Belle Assemble.*

"Are you crazy?" Was she crazy?

"Well, it is better than what you've got on now." She nodded at his toga blanket. "At least this will stay…up."

He stared her down and tried to determine whether or not she was serious.

127

Her mouth didn't even twitch.

Damn. She was. She was honest to God serious, and he could scarcely believe it. He shook his head in disbelief when he realized she was right. He had no choice. Damn.

He turned to go inside the barn. "Fine. Bring it." He turned and pointed a finger at her. "But turn your back."

Yea. His request was ridiculous. She's seen him completely naked. Twice. But for some reason it felt wrong to let her see him put on a dress. A dress!

Once inside, he took the frock and waited for her to turn her back before he threw the dress over his head and gathered up his blanket.

The dress sagged in the front. And he could smell smoke and bacon. Among other unmentionable things. Well, at least they'd be outside. And it was only temporary. God, his friends would never let him live it down; he'd earn himself a nickname for sure if they could see him.

But he would manage; he was no coward.

Though he didn't even look in Bea's direction as he marched past and said, "Come on, let's go."

She didn't follow. Instead, she started laughing all over again. He stopped and beseeched the heavens. Then he turned to look back at her.

Tears streamed down her face, she was laughing so hard. Yea, he looked ludicrous.

He knew it. And he couldn't help but start laughing, too. Laughter truly was contagious. It was all so unbelievably preposterous; he couldn't invent such a ridiculous situation even if he tried.

Oddly enough, she started shaking her head no. Strange.

"No? Why are you shaking your head no?" he said between his own fits of laughter.

"B-b-b-because. You d-didn't let me f-finish."

"Finish? Finish what?" He was no longer laughing. He had a sinking feeling in his gut.

"Showing you…*snort*…my…er…your…other option."

Then, she pulled her other arm from behind her back and held out a pair of men's trousers and a shirt.

She shrieked as he hiked up his day dress and charged.

CHAPTER 24

*"The only way to get rid of a temptation is to
yield to it."*

— *Oscar Wilde*

He caught her just as she made it to the door. His arms wrapped around her waist as he lifted her from behind and pulled her to his chest. She shrieked in protest, but only a token shout for she laughed as well.

He walked a few steps, then turned her and pushed her up against a nearby wall. His hands slid up her sides, then up her arms as he caught both her wrists together in one hand. Her breath caught when she opened her laughing eyes and looked at him. Really looked.

She froze.

Yea, he knew what she saw. He was lust filled and crazed with desire. And he knew...right at that moment...without a single inkling of a doubt...that she would not deny him this time.

He didn't waste her gift as he claimed her lips with his own.

Oh, God, sweet heaven was to be found in her arms.

No tenderness. No preliminaries. Pure raw need had taken over. He nipped at her lips and turned his head this way and that. He couldn't seem to get close enough; he wanted to crawl inside her skin and synchronize his racing heart with hers.

She tasted of honey and spring and warmth and home. All rolled into one.

God, his desire for her was an ache that grew in strength with each passing day. A fire that burned hot and out of control. Her lips, her taste only fanned the flames. He needed more.

He picked her up and turned in the direction of the ladder. She wrapped her legs around his waist, her voluminous dress was so large, if offered no impediment, and proceeded to kiss him all over every inch of his face as he made his way across the barn.

He placed one hand on the first rung; she still within his arms, holding on, and kissing him in any place she could reach. Hell. He nearly rutted with her on the ground right there at the base of the ladder, he could scarcely concentrate to make the climb.

Once at the top, he set her down in the loft and whipped her dress off and over his head. It fluttered to the ground below. He nearly fell off the ladder at the sight. She was beautiful and it took his breath away every single time. She smiled and started to slide backward. He crawled forward, mimicking her every move. She leaned back on her elbows and watched as he tore off his own dress and tossed it over the edge to join the other.

His prick bobbed a few times as it was freed from the confines of his frock. Again, her eyes flared wide at the sight of his desire. He all but howled as a wolf to the moon he was so pleased. He felt like an animal, crazed with lust.

He crept toward her; heat enflaming his body with every move. Like last time, she rolled over onto her hands and knees and his mouth, yet again, turned dry at the sight. Would he ever tire of looking at her? She was sensual, sex incarnate. And inviting. He wanted to devour her whole.

Despite her previous claims, he thought they'd been through enough that she would accept him in the more traditional way. Face to face. He wanted to feel her breasts sliding against his chest as they found their pleasure. He reached out to turn her over.

Again, she resisted. She looked back at him. "No. You know my rules, Dansbury."

Fine. She could have it her way. For the moment. He moved forward, his cock straining to be inside her. He clasped his manhood, it was harder than it had ever been in his life.

He nudged forward and guided it into...

...Heaven

Ah, God. Pure, sweet bliss.

He could scarcely believe the sensation. Had he ever had sex before?

He pulled back, slowly, until the flared edge of his crown peeked out. And he watched, captivated, as her channel clenched, sucking at him, desperate to hold him inside. His urge was to plow into her. Hard and Fast. Over and over. Until they both came, screaming their release. But he held back and took it slow despite every instinct to simply take. Take. Take. Take.

He set a steady rhythm, slow and sensual, but when he was nearly all the way to her womb, he flicked his hips that last little bit. Every. Time. And every time, his hips slapped her ass, his cods thumped her cunt, the sound erotic amidst their moans of pleasure.

And he was not alone in his bliss. She thrashed her head and chanted his name every time he drove home. Her perfect composure was shattered, and he relished seeing her in the raw. Uninhibited and melting in his hands.

All too soon he was nearing his crisis, but he refused to tumble over the edge alone. He leaned forward and reached around her to find her clitoris, hidden in her folds. She seemed to startle, but quickly she began to moan, words no longer able to form on her lips. He knew just the feeling. He felt it himself.

He was close, the end just within reach and he already hated that fact. But experience told him she was there, nearly. She was taut like a bow about to release its arrow when he said, "Let go, Bea, let it go."

She screamed his name and began to convulse on his cock. He pistoned his hips in response for a moment, then without warning, flipped her over. She was too insensate with pleasure to complain. Right away, he dove back in and picked up his previous rhythm.

"Bea. Oh, Bea. That's it. I can't. I can't. Ah God, I can't take it anymore."

His hips moved out of his control now, he couldn't stop. He rammed home, again and again, and again once more. Then one more time and he shouted as he came and came and came. Copious amounts of his juice filled her still clenching sheath. He ground his hips dragging out every last inch of pleasure. He'd never come so hard in his life. Shite.

He collapsed at last. He didn't even try to stop from crushing her. He was spent and boneless and ready to sleep. Ah, yes. The little death.

She squirmed beneath him, interrupting his descent to oblivion, and he rolled off her, but pulled her with him into the crook of his arms.

She pushed back and sat up, her hands braced on his chest. She looked at him a moment, anger writ plain across her face. Then, she reached back and slapped him, hard, across the face.

"Damn you, Dansbury. Damn you!"

"What was that for? And don't pretend you didn't enjoy every minute of what we just did. You certainly weren't complaining two minutes ago."

"I had my reasons. I gave you one rule. One! No face to face. But you refused to respect my wishes on that! How dare you?"

"Tell me then. Tell me why."

"It's none of your damn business why. As a gentleman you should respect a lady's wishes." She reached for one of their numerous blankets and covered her chest.

"Ha! Lady? We just fucked, Beatryce. And you're not like any normal lady I've ever known."

"You're right. I'm not a normal lady and glad of it. And you know nothing. Nothing!"

She rolled away and began to climb down the ladder.

A thought nagged at him, and he spoke before he could decide if it was wise. As if what he'd just said and done wasn't bad enough. "You acted as if you've never had an orgasm before."

She paused in the act of climbing down the ladder, her head just visible above the loft floor. She chuckled, a contradiction, and said, "Inconceivable, isn't it?"

He couldn't believe it. "Are you telling me that was your first? Despite…"

He shouldn't have said that. It just popped out. He was an idiot for sure. Never mind his firsts at Eton. But he needed to know. He was stubborn when he wanted answers. It was what made him a good agent. And how he justified saying whatever came to mind to have his answers.

Her anger nigh rolled off her in waves. "You mean despite the number of times I've whored myself out? Charming, Dansbury. Charming. It's a wonder you've ever had sex."

He rode on her anger. "Don't brush me off with your sarcasm. You're avoiding the question. Was that your first time?"

"It's none of your business!"

He looked at her, but didn't say a word. She was glaring at him in return. He waited, his arms crossed. He could wait all day. He didn't know why he was mad now as well. In truth, only she had that right.

She gave in. "Yes! Damn you! Yes! Satisfied now?"

He was a bastard. Yes, he wanted to be satisfied with her answer. And a part of him crowed with delight over the idea that he was the first to ever truly pleasure her. But sorrow for her situation dominated his thoughts. Her life, so much of it he didn't really know, was a mystery to him. And complex. And he couldn't help but wonder: What more was she hiding?

CHAPTER 25

"My heart was fashioned to be susceptible of love and sympathy, and when wrenched by misery to vice and hatred, it did not endure the violence of the change without torture such as you cannot even imagine."

— Mary Shelley, Frankenstein

"We dance round in a ring and suppose, but the secret sits in the middle and knows."

—Robert Frost, The Secret Sits

On the Road Again…
The Longest Road in Existence…
Will They Ever Get Off?

Beatryce was still fuming four hours later as their wagon rumbled down yet another winding, country lane. The roads were all starting to look alike. Even the fields of wildflowers were blurring together. And that made her angrier still, for she was too upset to enjoy the breathtaking view. Or the fragrance of the multitude of blossoms blooming at the side of the lane. La, she couldn't even enjoy the fact that she had enjoyed her very first orgasm this morning.

Ooooh. It was a good thing he was driving. She might've taken it in her mind to run their wagon right off the road. She was still tempted to push him off. Let him walk for a while in his worn out boots.

Sometimes she wondered why men even bothered to open their mouths—there was always a boot in it. Or food. One or the other.

The truly infuriating part was that she knew she was in danger of falling for this man. Of caring about what he thought of her. Despite his occasional tendency to say the dumbest things.

That was a man for you. Oh sure, he was often brooding and irritable on this misbegotten adventure, but she didn't blame him for it. It wasn't his normal mien, and she'd be just as grumpy if she had to travel with someone like herself as well.

Ha! What a thing to know about oneself.

And she was no good for him. Despite his normally charming ways, and she was confident she could bring him back around to his easy-going self if she'd wanted to, she would never trust him. Ever. Thus, in the end, it would ruin whatever…thing…they might have for each other.

So she decided to pick a fight. Besides, there was no sense in her being the only one to steep in righteous anger. But first she stretched and adopted a pleasant mien. As planned, he noticed and she nearly chuckled out loud when his shoulders stiffened in response. The man wasn't a dunce. And he was right to be worried when an angry woman suddenly brightens.

"La, Dansbury, it was so good of you to introduce me to the joys of orgasm. The knowledge should prove useful in the future. But tell me, were you really planning to do that with my cousin?"

Dansbury pulled on the brake so hard their wheels actually slid across the ground for a few feet before they came to a stop. The handle creaked in protest as it nearly snapped in two, he'd pulled on it so hard. Dansbury the Younger brayed in protest. Dansbury the Elder dropped the reins and turned to face her. He was so furious he was shaking, his face as red as a poppy.

Ah, the beast awakens.

"For the sake of your life, I am going to pretend you didn't just ask me that question." His eyes narrowed. "But I'm thinking you're doing it on purpose?" He looked deep and peeked into her soul. He was the only one who might be capable. The only one who'd ever tried.

"Are you, Beatryce? Are you intentionally being disgusting and low simply to infuriate me?"

"Oh, Dansbury," she laughed in an attempt to distract him from looking too close, "you do think highly of yourself, don't you? Besides, I can't imagine why I would want to do a silly thing like that."

If anything, he leaned closer. "Can't you, Lady Beatryce?" He placed one hand at the base of her neck and slid up until he cupped her chin in the palm of his hand. "Truly, Bea? Perhaps…Hmmm…" He closed his eyes and inhaled a long, drawn-out breath, and when he opened his eyes, she nearly drowned in their brown and gold-flecked depths. She unconsciously leaned into him. "Perhaps it's you who is scared." His voice was a whisper now. "Perhaps you yearn…to trust…me…"

He was far too close to the truth, damn his perceptive eyes. She shook off whatever magic spell he wove over her analytical mind. It wasn't easy.

"Dansbury, I couldn't even trust my own father. My. Own. Father! The one person in the world I should have been able to trust. Everyone else was…dead. So, no. I will never be able to trust you, or anyone else for that matter. Because when it comes down to it, we're all just looking out for ourselves."

His eyes softened, a response she could not have predicted.

"Can you not see that your past is coloring your perceptions of everything and everyone around you?"

"Of course it does, I am my past. I cannot divorce myself from it."

"Sure, sure, but you can choose to not let it define your future. You can choose to look for the good in others."

"That's easy for you to say."

"This isn't about me. Somehow, someway you are going to have to learn to put your past behind you if you ever want to have a future with any remote chance of happiness."

"But I don't know how to be any other way! My father abused me. Abused. Me." She slammed her fist into her chest to drive home the point. "His own daughter. And he allowed others to do so as well. How in the hell could I possibly trust anyone besides myself?"

"Oh, Bea…"

"No! Don't 'Oh, Bea' me. Don't pity me. And you sure as hell better not trust me."

"Oh, I definitely don't pity you. But I am frustrated to see the pain reflected in your eyes. To see the hint of doubt in yourself."

"I will never doubt myself."

He didn't swallow the lie. "You say you are strong. You act like you are strong.

Now, you must believe it too! What is this if not doubt in yourself?"

"I never doubted myself before I met you!"

"Never?"

Slap.

He didn't even flinch when she struck him. He didn't even look angry. Just continued to search her face for the truth. Probably looking for some way past her defenses. He'd never see his way through. She wouldn't allow it. She would never allow it.

"Just drive, Dansbury. And stop trying to analyze me."

"But it's so much fun." He said it with a smile, before turning serious once again. "And I just want to understand you…your behavior. Your reasoning, if you will. You've tried to ruin people, with success at times. Why? Why be so deliberately cruel? Just to get your way?"

She laughed, but not in jest. "Just to get my way? You have no idea what it is like to be desperate. Do you even have an inkling? I had to get away. I had to make it happen. On my own."

"Surely, there were other options available to you…"

"As a woman? Ha! Maybe now, just maybe. But when my father was alive? No. Nothing. Tell me what would you have done? He wouldn't allow me to entertain a paid position. He wouldn't allow me to remain a spinster forever living in his home, upon his largesse—besides the fact that the thought was too distasteful to contemplate. Then, what would you have me do? Run away? Or marry a duke…What would you do in those circumstances? To me, the choice was obvious."

"Sure, but…"

"But nothing. I did whatever I could to see that happen. Marrying Stonebridge was my escape. My freedom. The only choice I saw available to me. I would have done anything to see that happen. So how about you? Have you ever wanted something so desperately, you would have done anything to have it?"

He didn't answer, but his eyes flared wide. His pupils dilated, and for a moment, she kidded herself into believing his answer to be "Yes", and that it was she he wanted so desperately. But she never could fool herself for long.

The sound of a pin falling to the floor would have sounded like thunder for how quiet they sat, each deep in their own thoughts.

Haaaaw Heeee

Dansbury the Younger chose that opportune moment to make his displeasure known. He, at least, wanted to press on. And with that, their silence was shattered.

Dansbury looked shaken. She'd disturbed him with her insight. Good. He'd led too charmed a life. He should see behind the scenes of the darker side of life. It was surprising he hadn't before, considering his line of work. Or did he see it and just choose to walk away with blinders on?

"Here. Take the reins," he said. "I've got to finish up back here." Then he jumped over the seat and into the wagon bed. Running away.

Beatryce sat in silence for a moment, loath to move on. She was just about to take up the reins, when she decided to take one last look back at Dansbury. To her surprise, his face was pale and drawn.

She didn't hesitate; she dropped the reins, climbed over the seat, and raced to him as fast as she could whilst stepping over piles of munitions. When she reached him, she straddled his lap and grabbed his face. "Dansbury, what's wrong? Tell me."

He opened his hand. Upon his palm lay a ring. It was a man's ring with a large jade stone. In the stone, a tree was carved with an intertwining P and E. She'd seen that symbol before in her father's secret papers. It was the symbol for the Secret Society for the Purification of England—bad men who had murdered twice and were following them across the countryside.

"This shouldn't be here…" he said.

"I know. They must have found us…"

Dansbury stared at the ring in his hand, turning it over and over in his hands. "No. I mean…I had forgotten this ring; it was so long ago, and I was so young when I last saw it…It was…God, I hate to even admit it…I can't believe I never made the connection before now. It was…my brother's. He wore it always. He would have been wearing it when he died."

He looked up at Beatryce, his face still pale. "This ring shouldn't be here. My brother drowned…"

"Maybe it's not his. Maybe it's another's…" She stopped as he started shaking his head. Never mind the implications that his brother wore a ring belonging to the society. He looked away, staring off into the distance.

"It's his all right."

"But…"

He looked at her directly now. "Bea, I know it's his. His initials are carved inside."

CHAPTER 26

"It is easier to forgive an enemy than to forgive a friend."

— *William Blake*

In the Woods Nearby...
Entirely Too Close to Dansbury and Beatryce...

"Did you leave them my little present?"

"Aye."

"Good. Very good." The cloaked man closed his eyes as he tried to imagine the scene.

He was quite certain Cliff would remember the ring. But would his heart start racing with fear? Would he confess everything to the little whore he traveled with? Would he even understand the significance of the ring? Would his memories be...painful to recall?

The cloaked man took a deep breath to subdue the excitement he felt at the thought, but he couldn't resist adding, "God, I would have loved to see the look on his face when he found it." *Sigh.* "But it's enough to know the torment he must be feeling. So it'll do. For now."

The cloaked man opened his eyes and looked down his nose at the younger man before him...the traitor so willing to betray his own friends. And so typical of someone who was not English by blood or birth. He wanted to make this man uncomfortable, too. To make him squirm. God, the thought was thrilling.

It was a rare stroke of genius for Himself to enlist this man's assistance. To convince him to betray his own friends. He wondered if the turncoat realized that traitors always lose in the end. Alas, now was not the time to make the man aware of this fact. Not while he was still of some use.

And it was really quite frustrating that the man did not appear to cower under his powerful glare.

So be it. He would still delight in revealing this man's identity to Dansbury...right before he killed Dansbury once and for all. For now, he would bide his time and send this latest henchman, this puppet, on his way.

"Excellent, my friend. You've been very useful to the Society. In future, you will be rewarded quite handsomely for your service. But for now, keep on their trail and report back to me when you can."

He continued, "I'm sure I don't have to remind you not to get caught. Dansbury can be quite lethal when he wants to be, you know."

The traitor crossed his arms, but didn't speak, frustrating the cloaked man to no end. He loved tormenting others. Loved to see fear and pain in another man's eyes. It was how he kept his sanity through all his years of hiding. Damn this man's eyes. What was it going to take to break him? Whatever it was, he would find out before it was over. Before the deceiver's life was forfeited for the cause.

"By the way, I have another little present for our friends. This time I want you to stay and take note of Dansbury's reaction to my little gift. I want to know every detail when you return with your report."

"Aye..."

* * * *

An Abandoned Tenant Hut...

Beatryce looked around their lodgings for the night with a practical eye. The one-roomed place was drafty and isolated, and that was an understatement to be sure. But at least this time, there was a fireplace with a blazing fire to keep them warm...er. The hole in the roof certainly hindered the effect. And the gaps in the walls that even a rather large bird could fit through didn't help matters either.

There wasn't a bed, not even a rickety old table. Just a couple of rocking chairs, one on the verge of collapse, the fireplace, and the floor. In fact, there weren't even any hinges to hold up the door. Just some crude lengths of wood that would be nailed in place by Dansbury to keep the door from falling in. Or out.

He'd found a hammer on the floor just inside the open doorway when they'd arrived—as if he'd known it would be there waiting. Certainly it was odd. La, this entire journey was bizarre.

The hut must have been abandoned sometime in the last century—at the latest. Despite that, the place smelled fresh—thanks to all of the built in ventilation and a lack of any linens to speak of. For that, the place was infinitely better than their stay at the barn. Possibly even better than the last Inn for that matter. And they'd stay reasonably dry if it rained in the night. La, she could care less about sleeping on the floor so long as she stayed dry and the bed—er, pallet on the floor—was lice and odor-free.

While Dansbury tended to his namesake outside, Bea made up two pallets on the floor with their surfeit of blankets. She really did wonder where Dansbury had found them all and why he'd thought they'd need so many. She wouldn't complain, for they were certainly coming in useful tonight.

And there she went, answering her own question.

Her pallet was likely to be reasonably soft and warm for a makeshift bed on a hard-packed, earthen floor.

Dansbury returned just as she was settling in on her crude pallet. He didn't acknowledge her presence, simply set to work 'locking' them in. His color had returned to normal; his demeanor now only 'slightly angry', if she were any judge. It was better than his earlier desolate look of despair and horror. Like he'd seen a ghost, if one believed in such things.

He'd been lost in his thoughts the entire day. In fact, they hadn't spoken at all throughout the rest of their drive save for him to give her directions for when and where to stop or where to turn. Though there was the one time she pulled off of her own volition for lunch and a rest. He didn't even question her decision; he just took care of his own needs, and after a small rest, returned with her to the wagon to resume their trek.

Well, she was finished with his silent brooding. He needed to talk about it, though she doubted he'd agree. He was a man after all.

"All right, Dansbury, what have you come up with?"

He looked up at her, startled. As if he'd forgotten she was present. Forgotten even where they were. He was sitting on his own pallet, his arms resting on raised knees. He only stared at her a moment before he leaned back against the wall behind him and sought the ceiling. The moon shone through one of the many gaps in the roof, making his golden locks sparkle. The sight was distracting.

Surprisingly, he spoke his thoughts. "I remember Father giving my brother the ring now. I was very young, possibly six, and the bulk of the memory is somewhat vague. I remember watching them from beneath a sofa in my father's library. I'd been hiding in there for some time with my toy soldiers. They didn't know I was there. I remember wanting desperately not to get caught though I don't remember why exactly. And I remember nothing of what was said.

"The worst of it all is that I do recall, now, my brother's face as he looked up from admiring his new ring. I remember him rubbing the stone with his thumb while he grinned up at Father. I remember thinking it was an odd sort of smile. One I didn't fully understand at the time. But after that, I never gave it much thought, though I must have just buried the memory deep in my mind because now, I can see his face, and it is as clear as if I were still in that library looking at the both of them now. His grin is quite vividly imprinted there. And as an adult, I see it, and I know that what I didn't recognize then was the look of…greed."

Was this one of the secrets the assassin referred to in his note? She doubted it; it wasn't haunting enough, though a terrible memory to be sure.

Dansbury banged his head once against the wall in frustration. "I am somewhat saddened to know this."

He said 'know this' and Bea understood that he did not doubt his recollection at all. She also understood that 'somewhat saddened' was the perfect example of an understatement. He was torn apart inside. She leaned back on her elbows and watched him from beneath her lashes. Her relaxed pose all but inviting him to continue.

He looked over at her then, "It gets worse, though I hope I am wrong. You see, I cannot help but wonder what else is known about my family's involvement with the Society?"

He appeared to be getting angry now. He balled his hands into fists on his knees, and continued, "How could the Home Office not know of my family's connection to the
Society? How could Stonebridge not know it?"

There. That was the crux of the matter, she could see it as plain as day. It wasn't ire at his brother's possible deceptions that brought forth his anger;

he was just a boy when his brother died…thus, any brotherly feelings toward him would have diminished with the passage of time.

But Stonebridge? The duke was another matter altogether. Could Stonebridge have known about his family's involvement with the society and kept this information from his friend all these years? His best friend? And it couldn't have been simply a lie of omission. Stonebridge would have had to actively cover up Dansbury's familial connection to the society in order to keep this information secret.

She sat up and began to chew her nails. Something she hadn't done in years. She felt cold at the thought of what all this might do to Dansbury. How it might change him. Would it break him?

To lead a life of relative ease. To trust so easily and completely, only to have it all come raining down on your head in a matter of days…

Deception—from a fellow agent? From your best friend? Treason. Learning your family might have significant skeletons in their closet. Knowing someone knows and is clearly taunting you about it.

Not to mention having to travel across the country with a woman you generally despise. Or did. Perhaps, not any longer.

La, Dansbury's world seemed to be crashing down around his ears. He was on a straight path to hell.

And he didn't even know the half of it. How was she ever going to tell him the rest?

She didn't know, but yet again, now was not the time. She looked at him, and said, "Well, we can't know for sure until you talk to Stonebridge. And quite frankly, your family's past is irrelevant to the matter at hand."

"Ah, but that's where you're wrong, Bea. Someone knows something about my family, and that gives them an advantage."

Every time he called her Bea, it lit a flame inside her she desperately wanted—no, needed—to ignore. Unfortunately, she could recall the exact moment, in detail, he'd first called her that. It was when they'd been shot at on their second day out of London. She'd done her best to chalk the event up to the stress of the situation. But then he'd called her Bea again. And again. With increasing frequency. And, now, it was impossible to ignore. She liked it. Perhaps more than liked it. No one had ever given her a pet name before. Or at least not one that wasn't crass or rude.

She shook off her fanciful thoughts and returned to the matter at hand. "So what is your plan, then?"

"Our plan is to go to the place we're most likely to find answers. And from there, I will send a message to Stonebridge, inviting him to join us…"

CHAPTER 27

*"Sometimes in life we find comfort in people we
least expect it from."*

—*Unknown*

The Next Morning...

He'd managed to keep his hands off her the entire night. It hadn't been easy. She was so near, yet so far away. Oh, but he'd wanted to both hold her for comfort and bury himself so deeply inside her they'd not know where one began and the other ended. It was a sobering thought. His friends had been right. He wanted to tup her; he admitted it freely now.

He hadn't allowed himself to analyze any further feelings toward her. But, he realized, it wasn't so long ago that he abhorred the very thought of being attracted to her at all. But he could confess, now, that the attraction was there. And strong. Had never gone away, really. And the thought no longer bothered him like it had. She was a beautiful and inherently sexual woman. He'd have to be dead not to notice and respond to her appeal.

But he was starting to realize that Lady Beatryce was so much more than she seemed on the surface. He was starting to understand her, even if he didn't always agree with her actions. He'd caught a glimpse of her past and could see the demons that drove her behavior. And he was starting to admire her strength, and her practical nature.

They'd been on the road for days now, sleeping in extreme and remote locations. Not once had she complained about it. And she did everything he asked without question. It wasn't blind obedience, that, but her understanding of the seriousness of the situation and, though she'd rather die than admit it, her trust. In him.

That knowledge was far more disturbing because he understood the significance of it for a woman like Beatryce. And he shied away from the thought of its importance to him.

He looked up and inhaled the crisp morning air. The sun had just made its presence known above the horizon. Dew still coated the ground and made the toes of his boots darken with the dampness.

He approached their carriage with his pallet of blankets, but was halted in his steps by the sight that greeted him. For there, on one side wall of the wagon's bed, stood a child's toy soldier.

And right away, he knew it was his.

Anger surged. He dropped the pile of blankets and grabbed the toy. Then, he spun around and scanned the trees around him. Of course, there was no sign of the traitor lurking nearby.

"Damn you, you traitorous bastard! You were supposed to be my friend! My friend! How could you?" He bellowed his questions to the trees, hoping that the turncoat was still nearby to hear his curse. He didn't know if the man following them was MacLeod or Kelly. But it was one of them, without a doubt. Not many people had the skill.

And he'd counted them both as friends. His eyes watered with emotion at the thought. It tore at him. Ate at his soul. Never mind, the significance of the toy soldier.

The one he'd thought he lost after that fateful day under the sofa in Father's library.

He spun at the sound of footsteps behind him. It was Beatryce, wrapped in an oversized blanket with her hair sticking out in all directions. She was a mess, dirty and disheveled. She'd never looked more beautiful.

"What is it? What's the matter?" she asked, concern darkening her brow.

He broke the trance brought on by her beauty. "What's the matter? A fool has dared to play a terrible, dangerous trick on me. A dupe who will pay with his life." He looked to the trees again. "Do you hear me, you bastard? You will pay with your damn life!"

He was so angry his hands shook. His heart raced, and his mouth went dry. His thoughts were wild; he couldn't focus on any one thing. And the things around him looked off, sharper and off-color. He was so angry…and destroyed…by the thought of betrayal.

A warm hand began rubbing his back in slow, smooth circles. It eased him, somewhat—took the edge off his racing thoughts. He turned and without a second thought, enveloped Bea in his arms.

He buried his face in the crook of her neck and inhaled her scent through a deep breath. She smelled of the outdoors. Of pine and grass. Crisp. With a trace of smoke from the fire that'd burned in the hearth.

They stood there that way for what might have been hours, embracing and sharing their strength. He didn't care that the turncoat might be watching. He didn't care that not long ago, he'd despised this woman. She offered her strength, which he knew was formidable, and he took it.

Eventually he pulled back and looked at her. He couldn't resist running his hands through her hair in an attempt to straighten it. He watched his hands as they disappeared into her thick blonde tresses. His fingers caught in a particularly tangled knot. He tugged and picked at it a moment, then he caught her smile out of the corner of his eye.

He looked down, into her eyes, and they both burst out laughing.

"Don't even bother trying to fix it. I know I'm a mess. Always have been. Always will be. My father always claimed nothing could help."

"I hope you didn't believe him." She looked somewhat bothered by his remark, and he was both astonished and angry to see it. He never would have believed this strong, beautiful woman could doubt herself. Even for a minute. Ah, but she was a complex woman…with hidden vulnerabilities and insecurities. They made her real even though he didn't like the thought of her feeling that way.

He wanted to kill her father all over again for making her doubt herself, thus he didn't think before he blurted out, "How can you think that when you're the most beautiful woman I've ever laid eyes on?"

Her mouth fell open. It would have been funny, if he wasn't red-faced with sudden embarrassment. "You think…"

"Ah, hell, I didn't mean to say that."

* * * *

In a Nearby Village…

The cloaked man paced the floor of his room, desperate to hear news of Dansbury's reaction to his latest gift. He'd spent all night dreaming of the many possible outcomes— vivid, fantastic dreams. Dreams that made him excited to the point that he'd spent himself in bed. The idea of his foe in fear was indescribably titillating. A fantasy come true, one he'd harbored for years.

He paused by the room's lone table. It was scarred and wobbled persistently. His finger traced a particularly deep groove, carved by a small knife. Just that light touch was enough to cause the table to rock, the far leg hit the wooden floor with a clunk.

He clenched his fists in anger at the thought that he had to stoop to sleeping in such low class accommodations. Such squalor. Hell, he would hardly classify the room as an accommodation; it wasn't fit to house rats.

He should be living in gilded splendor. And it was all Dansbury's fault that he wasn't, damn the man. It was comforting to know that their roles would be reversed soon enough. He would have it all. As he should. As he deserved. Soon.

One wooden chair sat behind the table, facing the door. He decided it would be best if he were sitting when the traitor arrived. It wouldn't do to have the man see him pacing the floor, as if he were anxious. Or concerned. No, that wouldn't do at all.

He sat in the chair and clasped his hands together on the table. He forced his body into perfect alignment, to exude calm confidence. Manly poise. Both feet firmly on the floor. Head lifted…

Knock. Knock. Knock.

His hands tightened in reflex, and his cock hardened in his breeches. This was it. This was the news he'd been eager to hear.

"Enter."

He was proud his voice conveyed patience and self-assurance. He knew it was so. He was nothing if not confident in himself.

The turncoat entered the room and stood before the table, his hat in his hands. A sign of respect. Good.

The cloaked man forced his hands to relax and not clench in anticipation of the news this man carried. He studied the man before him. Took time to note his stance and appearance. He'd always considered himself good at reading people. And he knew making his hirelings wait worked to increase their anxiety. It was a calculated trick.

The traitor had a peculiar smirk on his face. One the cloaked man did not like at all. It caused him to lose a bit of his self-control. That was his excuse for blurting out, "Out with it. What happened? Spare no detail." He rubbed his hands together in eager anticipation, losing all sense of his need to demonstrate patience.

"Aye, well. He saw it, and he was angry," the conspirator replied.

The cloaked man stopped rubbing his hands. That was it? "Just angry?"

"Weel, irate, then. Er, absolutely crazed with anger."

"But just angry? Not worried? Scared? Or better yet, terrified?" He tried desperately not to sound too fervent, but he was quite quickly growing alarmingly frustrated. Yet at the same time, he still salivated over the idea of causing Dansbury fear. He'd dreamt of it.

It must have happened that way. It couldn't be any other way.

"Oh, aye. He was most definitely terrified."

The cloaked man grinned. Ah yes. Of course. It was exactly as he'd imagined. He practically drooled over the thought. He nearly allowed himself to get caught up in his fantasy of how Dansbury must have looked, drowning in his fear. He cleared his mind. Later, he'd allow his mind its freedom to imagine the scene. Over and over again. When he was alone.

He narrowed his eyes on the man before him.

Was there a touch of humor in his eyes? Was the man playing with him?

He looked harder, but the man blanked his face, hiding his thoughts. A skill he also employed when needed.

"So where are they headed now? Do you know?"

"Aye. I do."

"Of course. Excellent. So? Out with it."

"They're headed to his aunt's estate. Lady Harriett. Just outside Bath."

"You know this, how?"

"I know Clifford Ross."

CHAPTER 28

"Nothing weighs on us so heavily as a secret."
— *Jean de La Fontaine*

Bloomfield Place
Country Home of Lady Harriett Ross, Dansbury's Aunt
Near Bath, England
One Day Later…

Lady Harriett Ross, Dansbury's aunt, was a delightful, loveable…dragon. Indeed, she was colorful and wiry and altogether far too outspoken. Yea, candid was her middle name and today was no exception. In fact, Dansbury entered her drawing room with more than a little hesitation about what to expect from her unpredictable tongue. He traveled with a notorious woman. Without chaperone. Surely, she'd have something to say about that.

"Well, you fool, it's about time you bothered to come see me. I didn't think you'd simply run off and hide, but I was beginning to wonder."

Ah. He was delighted to know he wouldn't be disappointed.

He bent to kiss her cheek. "And how do you know we were running anywhere?" He said it with a smile in his eyes and laughter in his voice despite the seriousness of his question. Between their assumed traitor and Aunt Harriett, did everyone know what they were about? It was an alarming thought to contemplate.

"Um, well, I don't know…let me see." She held up her hands to tick off her points, sarcasm all but dripping from her lips. "One. You send me an urgent missive telling me to retire to Bloomfield Place with all haste. In the middle of the season, no less." She took a moment to lean forward and adjust the pillow behind her, then sat back and continued reciting her list. "Two. Lady Beatryce and Stonebridge disappointed more than a thousand guests waiting at St. George's to witness THE wedding of the season. A grand, ducal wedding...those don't happen often, you know. And without so much as a single, reasonable or even gossip-inducing explanation for calling it all off. I was there, you know, though I can't say I was disappointed. Stonebridge isn't the man for our gel; his heart belongs to someone else, as we all know."

She threw him a knowing look, while Beatryce sat across from him and chuckled lightly. Aunt Harriett looked over at Bea and winked. Winked!?

And what was her meaningful look supposed to imply? And for that matter, what did she mean by "our gel"? Had Aunt Harriett finally lost her wits? Since when was Beatryce "our gel"? He ignored the traitorous voice that shouted *she's my gel* in the deepest recess of his mind.

"Third." She continued, as if she hadn't just been sending odd and confusing signals with her eyes. "Lady Beatryce all but disappears from society and does not attend her own father's funeral." She looked over at Bea again and added, "Not that I blame you, mind. In fact, I applaud your strength. I wouldn't have gone either, were I you. Why your stepmother even bothered to attend was beyond me. She could barely keep a straight face the entire time, or so I'm told...I didn't go either, I must admit. But from what I have heard, she kept having to stifle her laughter. I can only imagine why." Bea looked stunned.

"Anyway, I can only assume..." Aunt Harriett paused then and took a sip of her coffee. She cleared her throat. "Now, then, need I say more?"

Dansbury shook his head as he said, "No ma'am." He wasn't surprised at her conclusions for she was a clever and precocious woman. More to the point, he was curious to know what she had intended to say, but didn't. What did she assume? He would normally question her on it. They were used to being frank with each other. But this time...

He looked over at Bea, who was still sitting there, stunned, likely over Aunt Harriett's praise of her strength. Which was spot on, though she probably didn't realize it. Or, more likely, didn't expect others to realize it. He was ashamed to note that he'd never noticed. Perhaps that had been her intention?

And why should he have noticed? She had more than a few character flaws that overshadowed that strength.

Aunt Harriett cleared her throat again, then sighed a definite sigh of resignation. Her tone was far more subdued when she spoke. He'd never heard her speak with such a tone; it prompted him to sit up and take note. This was important.

"I suppose I knew this day would come. Though I dare say, I had hoped it would not." She stared into her coffee cup while she spoke. As if the darkened liquid would offer some sort of assistance or guidance. He grew alarmed at her unusual, pensive behavior.

"Auntie…perhaps we should speak of this in private." He wasn't sure he wanted to know what she was going to say. The child in him didn't want to lose his ignorance. And he knew whatever she had to say would change his life forever. Did he want Bea to be here to witness such an event?

Aunt Harriett looked up, surprised. Her voice held its usual strength. "Pshaw. That gel deserves to know. You need her to know. She can handle it. The question is, can you?"

He stood on impulse. Surprised she would question his fortitude. Never mind his own earlier doubts.

"Oh, sit down, boy. You know I don't really doubt you for a moment. I was just trying to make a point."

Aunt Harriett placed her coffee cup back on the table before her, then sat back and gathered the edges of her colorful shawl. Her wrap was bright orange, and crocheted; she didn't care for knitting. It was so her, and he smiled a moment with fondness despite the seriousness of their conversation. She certainly was a colorful lady. Her orange shawl complemented her ginger hair. And her green and violet dress was most…uncommon. She had a turban on her head, in pink. He shook his head with fondness.

Yea. Aunt Harriett certainly liked to make a statement. And it fit her personality to perfection. It felt like home, seeing her dressed with her usual flair. And he allowed that thought to ease his mind somewhat.

He retook his seat as she began talking.

"First, I want you to know that your mother was everything that was kind. I loved her like a daughter. Like a best friend. Like a sister. All of them rolled up in one. Her death brought me more grief than I could ever have imagined. You, dear boy, and your need of someone, was the only thing that kept me from wallowing away in my own sorrow. You needed me. Hmmm. We needed each other."

She put a hand on his knee and squeezed before pulling a handkerchief out of her sleeve and dabbling at her eyes. "Forgive me."

There was nothing to forgive. He knew she knew that. He waited while she composed herself once again. He felt his own eyes burning, but he ignored the sensation. And he couldn't speak; his throat was closed up tight. He held a taut leash on his control as he braced himself to hear this story. His family's story. His history.

It wasn't long before she continued; she was the perfect example of a woman with superior inner strength. It was no wonder she'd recognized the like in Lady Beatryce.

"M-my brother, on the other hand, was…" She sighed as she seemed to search for the right words to use. "…misguided. He was a man of strong, moral character…else your mother would never have married him…but sometimes…" She struggled with her words, and he was amazed. Aunt Harriett was never tongue-tied. "Well, sometimes things happen. Conflict. Horrible things that should never be, but happen anyway…God only knows why."

Aunt Harriett reached for her reticule on the seat beside her and pulled out a miniature painting, faded and worn. She handed it to him with obvious hesitation. He looked down to see an infant with a thick crop of wavy, blond hair. The hairs on his arms stood on end.

"You see, your father and mother had a son. Born a few years before you. His name was George."

He stood at the news, stunned, still holding the likeness of the brother he'd never met. He'd never known. He'd never heard an inkling of this news. He began to pace the floor. This time, Aunt Harriett didn't ask him to sit, as if she knew he needed to walk this off. His emotions were churning…dread being the predominate mood that now flooded his veins.

"Your mother hired a nursemaid for him, a girl she knew from the nearby village. An Irish girl…"

Beatryce gasped while trepidation churned within him. The Society was against anyone not born of England…especially the Irish. Oh, he now knew where this was headed, as did Bea. And it was awful.

"I don't know if we'll ever know what really happened. But your brother was killed. He was only t-two."

Aunt Harriett took a deep breath.

"Your father blamed this young Irish woman. I don't know if she was guilty—if his accusations were true. Perhaps she was. Or maybe he was led to believe she was through the poisoned words of others. For sure, George was in her care when the accident occurred…" Aunt Harriett sighed again. Words were difficult to speak. She would have mourned his loss as well; George was her nephew, after all. She swallowed and continued on, "She'd seemed such a sweet soul, but then she fled, making her guilt seem obvious to those who wanted to believe it."

"You sound like you don't believe it." He couldn't believe he'd found his voice.

"I honestly don't know. But what matters is that your father did. It broke him. Made him act out of character. The next thing we knew, he was involved with this group of men who seemed to fuel that hatred toward all things Irish. Her family was run out of town; their house was burned to the ground, their belongings with it. And months later, we heard that they had all been murdered. Among them, your brother's nurse.

"No one tried very hard to investigate the matter, and your mother was heartbroken all over again. You see, she never doubted the nurse's innocence, but there was no convincing your father once his friends had got ahold of him."

Aunt Harriett paused to take another sip of her coffee. The silence in the air was thick with tension. Dansbury struggled to come to terms with his own chaotic thoughts.

Aunt Harriett placed her cup back on the table, and started again. He had no more words.

"I'm sure you realize this was the beginning of our family's involvement in the Secret Society for the Purification of England, though I didn't know it at the time. And I didn't know the extent of their hatred towards other nationalities. I thought it was all political posturing. There were whispers, of course, but I was still naïve and didn't think men were capable of such atrocities.

"Your mother never condoned his behavior from that moment on. But your father was determined and all but blind to reason. And I'm ashamed to say, it greatly influenced your brother, Edward…He was at the perfect age for it."

God. Edward. It all made sense, and he hated that it did.

"By the time you came along, your father was deeply involved and as angry as ever. Angrier even. And your mother was well aware of the influence his behavior was having on Edward, but by the time she realized it, it was too late. Besides, he was the heir. Your father was particularly involved in Edward's upbringing. Grooming him to one day take his place. As one might expect, of course. But you mother…she was determined not to let the same thing happen to you, so she shielded you as best she could from it all."

Aunt Harriett paused a moment to collect her thoughts again. He didn't know how much more he wanted to hear. Eventually she continued, smiling softly now, "Around the time you turned seven, your father started to show signs of softening. A comment here. A kindness there. It could have been his age. Maybe your mother's kindness had finally gotten through to him." She looked directly at him. "Or maybe it was you—you were such a charming boy, even then."

She smiled at him with watery eyes. Lost for a moment in more pleasant memories.

It didn't last.

She frowned as she continued, "But your brother, Edward, he was at that age. Not a boy. Not quite a man, but believing he was…that he knew it all. He was fully indoctrinated in his hatred toward the Irish. It was too late, by then, to turn him around. At least, not at his age.

"Then, your father began acting strange. Paranoid. This is when I started to believe all the dirty rumors about the Society. I believe your father was prepared to talk about it to the authorities. To tell them all he knew.

"They left you with me, when they began their fateful trip. I still don't even know why. Nor where they were going. Or even why they were going. It made no sense to me, but what was I to say?

"And of course, they never returned. They all died on that boat crossing the channel. I didn't even know they were planning to go to France. It was all so very peculiar."

Dansbury's shoulders sagged as she reached the end of her tale. It was a lot to take in. It was almost unreal, like they were discussing someone else's family. Not his. All his beliefs about his family were shattered, though in hindsight, the cracks were always there.

He heard Aunt Harriett shuffle about, but he had his back to her. He couldn't look at either her or Bea while he digested all he'd learned. Aunt Harriett sighed again, and the hairs on the back of his neck lifted in warning. He turned and started walking back toward his seat. Toward Aunt Harriett, a warning beating in his heart with every step.

What could be worse than all she'd revealed so far?

"But that's not all. When you were two, your mother bore another child. A girl." That.

He collapsed in his chair. Grateful he'd been standing in front of it. He knew there was more to come. Something monumental. He rested his head in his hands, but listened carefully.

"Your father thought she was stillborn. Everyone thought so.

"But...she wasn't. Your m-mother..." Aunt Harriett let out a gasped cry then. She quickly caught her breath, and in a rush added, "...f-found a way to secret her away to an orphanage in America. F-Forever. Without any way to ever s-see her again..."

Aunt Harriett sobbed then, great heaving sobs. Dansbury fell to his knees at her feet and enveloped her in his arms. She buried her face in his cravat and wailed between gasps for air. She shuddered and he squeezed her tighter.

"I'm s-sorry," she managed, "I thought I could say it and remain composed..."

He rubbed her back as he held her tight. "Nonsense, Auntie. Don't ever apologize."

She shuddered some more and he felt powerless. Never mind his own emotions, churning just beneath the surface. He was near to the breaking point himself. He looked over her shoulder to Bea.

Bea was sitting straight and tall. Regal, as any Queen. Her chin was tilted up, just slightly, and her hands were gripped tightly together in her lap, making her knuckles turn white.

But what made his breath catch was the sight of her tears streaming down her face. It broke him.

CHAPTER 29

"I have no other but a woman's reason; I think him
so, because I think him so."
                    —*Shakespeare, The Two Gentlemen of Verona*

Bloomfield Park...
Beatryce's Room...
The Next Day...

She would never forget the sight of Dansbury crying. She knew as sure as she knew her own name that the sight would be forever emblazoned in her mind. After yesterday's revelations, she, too, felt heavy and emotional. Lethargic even. And drained. Her throat was sore and her jaw ached from clenching it for far too long. She imagined Dansbury felt much worse.

This. This was the aftermath of grief.

To think of that poor, young woman, for Dansbury's sister was a woman now. Growing up orphaned, possibly feeling unloved. And his mother. Oh, how she must have grieved, yet at the same time, she had to have had the strength of ten normal men to go through with what she had to do.

Even though she'd never felt the motherly type, Beatryce could imagine how difficult it must have been for his mother to give up her child, her only daughter. It was heartbreaking to ponder, for it was all both a blessing and a curse, wasn't it? For everyone involved.

How did one come to terms with all that was lost? Even if Dansbury and his sister were reunited tomorrow, they would never be able to make up for those years apart. Missed birthdays. Growing up. A first tooth. A first step. A first love. A first fall.

Beatryce laughed. It was all ironic coming from her. As if she knew what it was like. Ha. To share birthdays with people you love? To miss your family? Who was she to know? She was on her own herself. Always had been, but worse, for her father had actually been around. She would gladly give anything to trade places with Dansbury's sister. No question.

And she was beginning to know Dansbury. She knew he would have been a wonderful older brother. Protective. Honorable. God, she envied his sister, because even though they didn't yet know each other, they would. One day they would. And wasn't that the ultimate in self-centeredness? To envy them the happiness denied them so long through the machinations of evil men.

She hadn't seen Dansbury since yesterday afternoon's monumental revelations. They'd all retired to their rooms soon after, and by unspoken agreement, took dinner in their own chambers that night.

Now, it was passing noon of the next day. She'd awoken several hours earlier, still tired, but hungry. She'd been pleased to see a simple morning gown, with all the accompanying feminine garments, lying at the foot of her bed. She'd wondered if they'd burned the dress she'd arrived in. She didn't think even the best maid could see it properly cleaned. She certainly hadn't slept in it—it would have soiled the sheets irreparably.

She'd been the only one to come down to breakfast, and she hadn't seen a soul save for the servants since. And who'd want to see the servants?

Bea immediately chastised herself for the thought. It was an unkind sentiment, even unspoken, and a carryover from a lifetime of influence from her father. It shamed her, that habit. She needed to break it. Dansbury had been right; servants were people too. She hated the fact that she'd been indoctrinated into believing they were inferior. She'd never given a thought of it before Dansbury had pointed out the error of her ways.

And those types of mean thoughts had been ingrained in her for so long, they were now a bad habit…something she would have to work to change. And she would. She didn't want to be cruel. It would take time, but she was up to the task.

In the meantime, she was beginning to worry about Dansbury and Lady Harriett. She decided to seek out Lady Harriett first.

* * * *

"He's been hiding in the library, writing missives since early this morning. I think he's determined to find his sister."

"Oh." Lady Harriett had answered her unspoken question the moment Bea walked through the door to her private parlor. They were now comfortably ensconced in two wing back chairs in front of the fire taking tea. And by tea, she meant coffee. Lady Harriett adored coffee, and Bea found she preferred it as well. Father had never allowed the Beckett family to partake. The childish girl inside her silently stuck her tongue out at his memory as she enjoyed another sip.

Take that, you bastard.

"I've watched you, you know. From afar." Beatryce nearly choked on her coffee.

Well, what did one say to that?

"I've noticed what others haven't—or refused—to see. You are strong. And determined."

Bea wanted to beam with pride despite the dour mood permeating the air in the house.

"...I realize you were quite, quite desperate."

Yes. She was. Or had been.

But it was one thing to know it yourself. And something else to know someone else had noticed it, too. As if their witness to your desperation made it all more real.

When you are the only one to know it, you can embrace a touch of denial during the times when circumstances threaten to drown you in your inner turmoil.

"I don't blame you, gel. Not one bit."

Bea felt silent tears sliding down her cheeks. Until yesterday, she hadn't cried since she was fourteen. She didn't like it. It made her feel vulnerable when she should be spending every minute rejoicing over her newfound freedom. She'd waited an eternity to be so free.

"Lady H..."

"Pshaw. Call me Auntie Harriett." Lady Harriett looked at her, considering. It was a thoughtful look, though sad as her eyes were still puffy and tinged with red. She handed over a handkerchief. "I like you."

Now, that was a surprise.

But even more surprising was her sudden desperate need to unburden herself to this woman. To expose her weaknesses and her greatest fears. It was a novel feeling. Beatryce took the proffered cloth and dabbed at her eyes.

"Lady…Aunt Harriett. I-I don't know what to say. I don't de…"

"Stop right there, young lady. Don't you dare, for one minute, think that I'm going to let you suggest you don't deserve my admiration. I have half a mind to take you over my knee…see if I can't."

Beatryce nearly laughed, inappropriate as that would have been. She knew her own worth. She just never expected others to know it. She all but handed Aunt Harriett an excuse to find her lacking, "But with my past…"

"To hell with your past. Maybe I don't know the extent of your history. But I can make a fairly accurate guess. If I were you, I'd have gone to the same lengths as you to see myself married to Stonebridge and out from under my father's thumb. Perhaps I'd have taken it even further. I'm sure I would have sent Grace away the moment I met her. Just in case, mind, for that gel is a great beauty to be sure. Knowing I'd have sent her away though? That is saying something because I love that gel.

"But you see, after what I've lived through, I know good and evil can be cloaked by complicated masks. I've learned the hard way to look beneath the surface. Most don't." She looked at Beatryce now. "Pity that. For I'm sure your desperate measures have overshadowed recognition of your true spirit and your determination."

Aunt Harriett shook her head. "Your father's mask covered a barbaric, hateful man.

Gracious, even his mask was unpleasant, he didn't even try to hide that."

"The man was a monster." Bea agreed.

"Indeed." Aunt Harriett reached over and squeezed her hand. It was a touching gesture. Then, she carried on. "Now, pull yourself together and find that inner strength I know is in there. And never doubt yourself again, or I'll be disappointed in you. Might take it in my head to beat you with my Umbrella. Ask Stonebridge. He's felt the end of The Umbrella on more than one occasion in the past.

"Besides," she continued, "Dansbury's going to need you…"

This time, Bea did choke on her coffee. It was bad timing to take a sip just at that precise moment. Did Aunt Harriett refer to Dansbury's own secrets?

And Dansbury? Need her? "La, I appreciate your confidence, but Dansbury is a strong man."

"Well, I'm glad you've noticed. I'm sure you've figured out by now that Dansbury has led a reasonably charmed life. Yes, he lost his parents and his brother quite young, but he was never alone. He had me. He had good friends. Other than that, he's never had to work hard to succeed; it comes naturally to him.

"But by now, he'll have realized that Stonebridge has known all about his family's connection to the Society for some time. And Dansbury, for all his charm and easygoing manner believes quite strongly in trust. He trusts openly and completely. So this, betrayal, will be hard on him. I wouldn't be surprised if he feels a bit of resentment toward me this morning as well..."

"Nonsense, I..."

"Oh, don't try to placate me. I don't like it. I prefer to call things like I see them. If you think otherwise, then I might be forced to reassess my good opinion of you."

Beatryce smiled, duly chastised. "It won't happen again."

"Good." Aunt Harriett all but snorted; she certainly lifted her chin. "See that it doesn't." Then, they both laughed.

For a moment, they were content to sip their coffee quietly and ponder everything that'd happened to lead them to this moment. Beatryce thought about the things Aunt Harriett didn't know. Bea suspected Aunt Harriett didn't know about the secrets the assassin implied he would reveal.

And she didn't know the secret Beatryce had yet to disclose either; the one that would affect them both—Harriett and Dansbury.

Bea came to a decision; she decided to tell her. Aunt Harriett would know what to do.

Beatryce set down her cup, clenched her hands together, and sat tall in order to drop her bomb with dignity.

"Aunt Harriett. I know how to find his sister, your niece..."

CHAPTER 30

"Silence is one of the great arts of conversation."
—Marcus Tullius Cicero

After her third knock on the library door, Bea called out, "Dansbury. It's Beatryce."

Still no answer, blast the man.

Well, she had tried. Clearly, the courteous route was not going to get her very far this afternoon. So it wasn't really her fault she would have to be rude and enter the room uninvited.

Bea opened the door and walked in despite the fact that Dansbury had not given her leave to enter. She caught a quick glimpse of him—quill midair, shirt sleeves rolled up, no jacket, no cravat, and mouth practically hanging open—before she averted her eyes and studied the room. She didn't bother to clarify why she'd entered the room without his permission. And he didn't ask her for an explanation.

The room was warm but cavernous, with walnut shelves from floor to ceiling covering most available wall space save for the window in front of her, overlooking the back garden, and a fireplace on the wall to her left. Every shelf was filled with books. Lots and lots of books. Bea inhaled a deep breath. She could smell old leather and lemon oil. The smell was divine. She'd escaped reality many times between the pages of a good book. She was a closet bluestocking.

She stepped forward onto a plush, ornate area rug. The pile, thick and lush. It begged to be touched. She toed off her shoes and then stood there, wiggling her toes into the soft fibers. She heard a strangled cough come from somewhere in Dansbury's direction. She could imagine him staring at her toes. It almost startled a chuckle out of her. She chose to ignore him and began walking around the room.

Two club chairs made for a comfortable seating area before the hearth. And two more were situated in front of the desk behind which Dansbury was sitting, his back to the window. She ignored the chairs—and Dansbury—and continued to explore the room.

After a few minutes, she heard Dansbury resume writing. Neither of them had said a word. Eventually, after circumnavigating the entire room, she sat in a chair before the desk and picked up a book that was lying on the table beside her. *The Mysteries of Udolpho* by Ann Radcliffe.

Hmmm. An interesting choice to be left out on the table. Gothic romance? The women of the ton unanimously frowned upon Ms. Radcliffe's novels as sensational nonsense. It figures Aunt Harriett would disregard popular opinion.

Bea had secretly loved and read every one of Ms. Radcliffe's novels. She'd read this one a dozen times at the very least.

She opened the book and proceeded to thumb through the pages while Dansbury continued to write.

They carried on that way in companionable silence for half an hour at least. Bea jumped straight to her favorite passages while D played spy.

After a while, she set the book aside and drummed her fingers on the arms of her chair as she looked around the room once more. Dansbury had stopped writing. He was looking at her. She could feel his regard. She pretended to ignore him.

He was the first to break the silence. "I sent a missive to Stonebridge, summoning him here. I suspect he'll arrive in a few days."

She looked at him now and laced her arms in front of her, elbows resting on the arms of her chair. "That sounds wise. Are you sure he'll..." He raised one brow at her and offered her a boyish, almost charming grin. As if to say, *Are you really questioning my capabilities*, but in a teasing manner.

"Oh. Of course, my mistake." She couldn't help but smile in return, a sort of half smile, and lower her eyes. He was ridiculously charming when he wanted to be. They shared a few more silent looks between them, exchanging entire thoughts without saying a single word. It was uncanny. Yet it felt good to share a smile or two after yesterday. "Tomorrow, I'm taking you to Bath. To the Pump Room." She heard a small amount of hesitation in his voice.

"Oh my. The Pump Room. La, how grand. Well, that should definitely cause quite a stir if that is your aim."

"I am depending on it."

"…especially wearing my lovely oversized sack dress." She grinned at the imagery. "Perhaps you could wear yours as well, and then we'll really set the old ladies on fire." Now, she was ready to laugh. The images playing out in her mind were simply hilarious.

Dansbury chuckled. It helped to penetrate some of the pall that still clung to the air. "Perhaps another time. I've sent a maid and a footman to a friend's house in town. They'll bring back something appropriate for you to wear by tonight. The maids can make any alterations necessary by tomorrow."

"My. How enterprising. A friend you say?"

"A friend." He didn't explain. She didn't push for a more descriptive answer.

"Well, I can't wait to see what they uncover." She shook her head at him, amazed at his ability to get whatever he wanted. To make things happen the way he wanted them to, no matter how far-fetched his plan. He truly did lead a charmed life. Or had. She forced away the frown that threatened. "So, I assume our goal is to stir up gossip. Let the bad guys, so to speak, know where we are."

"Yes. Though I have no doubt they already know where we are. Our traitor has followed us. I'm quite sure he knew where we were headed long before we left our humble abode yesterday.

"No, my point is to send them a stronger message than that. I want them to know that we are here and that we are not going to hide away in fear."

She looked at him carefully for a moment, then shook her head. She looked at her hands, now clasped in her lap, and said, "No. That's not quite it, is it?" She looked back up at Dansbury and waved one of her hands in the air, as if what she was about to say was a trifling, superficial thing, and said, "La, Dansbury, you must think I'm bottle-headed." She straightened, looked him in the eye, and poked her finger into the arm of her chair as she spoke— the better to emphasize her point. "You're putting us out there as bait."

It wasn't a question.

CHAPTER 31

"All human actions have one or more of these seven causes: chance, nature, compulsions, habit, reason, passion, desire."

—Aristotle

The Pump Room...
Bath, England...

It wasn't quite a London ball. But it was the place to see and be seen in Bath. Everyone who was anyone in high society—or at least visiting Bath at the time—was present and accounted for. Yes, there was even a Subscription Book one could peruse which listed all who were present in town at the time.

Oh, the nobility and their quest for tribute and distinction.

How ironic that in doing so, they achieved the opposite effect. Bea brushed aside the sudden image of dancing sheep dressed in the latest fashions. Her lips twitched in amusement at the thought.

Baa.

Beatryce entered the Pump Room on Dansbury's arm via the North Colonnade. She was nervous despite her colorful imaginings. People would talk. And stare. Sure, she and Cliff were counting on it, but it didn't mean she looked forward to facing that prospect in reality.

As anticipated, as soon as they stepped out of the anteroom and into the great room, the people around them paused to stare. And like a ripple across water, silence descended down and across the length and breadth of the room, which was significant as the room was well over sixty feet long and more than forty feet wide. The undulation rapidly spread until every corner and nearly everyone in between was silent and homed in on them. Just them. As if they had taken center stage. Naked.

She almost chuckled again at her fanciful imagery. Almost.

The only sound at all was the music from the orchestra who, surprisingly, continued playing in the musician's gallery as if nothing at all was amiss. Everyone else had stopped as if frozen in time, living statues of curiosity and grace with mouths practically agape in shock and awe. Some held glasses aloft as if about to take their next sip. Others held on to each other, immobilized mid-dance.

Of course they were surprised.

*Hmmm, let's see…*She had all but disappeared from society. She and the groom skipped out on their own wedding—on their wedding day. Father had died, and she hadn't attended the funeral. Oh, and now, she was out socializing, in azure silk, no less, and not at home, wearing black. In mourning. La, if she'd had any desire to ever return to society in the future, that possibility had just been destroyed. She would be lucky if the lot of them didn't snub her completely right here and now.

And funnily enough, she didn't care. But she didn't want to witness it firsthand, either.

The air inside the Pump Room was thick and hot. From the hot spring water as much as the overcrowded room, which was swarming with people. Or would be swarming, if they'd quit gawking and move.

Beatryce felt vertigo pressing in on all sides, regardless of the fact that the room was light and bright thanks to huge windows running down the north side of the room. She looked about, searching for anything that might steady her resolve, and only just stopped from fanning herself. She couldn't help but squirm as she felt a trickle of sweat slide down her back. How could they all stand this heat? Or endure the smell of mineral and sulfur for more than a moment? Bea wanted desperately to pull out her handkerchief and cover her nose. Which was saying something considering the state of the dress she'd been wearing only days before.

Oh, the things one did to be fashionable.

Together, Bea and Dansbury stepped further into the room, maneuvering around living effigies and nodding to everyone they knew. Many returned the sentiment, but with obvious reservation.

Midway up the length of the room and to their right, stood the infamous fountain, flanked by two fireplaces, where women filled glasses from the fountain and gave them to the young or old and infirm, which appeared to be everyone here save for the people who'd been dancing prior to their arrival.

La, even the women working had paused in the midst of carrying out their duties in order to watch the Bea and Dansbury taproom concert. Again, she felt her lips twitch with mirth.

It was no matter, the men and women accepting the proffered glasses weren't paying any attention either, their gazes all narrowed in on her.

Zounds.

By unspoken agreement, she and Dansbury turned toward each other, blocking out their audience, and like a switch, everyone resumed talking at once.

Ah. Let the gossiping begin.

Beatryce pasted on a smile and led Dansbury over to the Dowager Duchess of Lyme who was sitting midway down the room between two massive windows.

Beatryce curtsied. "Your Grace."

The dowager raised her lorgnette and looked Bea over from head to toe. "Ah, Lady Beatryce. What a surprise to see you here. Why are you here? And where are you staying?"

"La, I'm staying with Lady Harriett Ross at Bloomfield Park. I believe you are friends?" She risked absolute banishment and ignored the dowager's first question.

The dowager simply harrumphed and turned to acknowledge Dansbury. He took her hand and bowed over it. "Your Grace."

"Dansbury. You've looked better. How is your aunt?"

"Well. She's doing quite well, thank you for asking. Fine weather we're experiencing for this time of year, I daresay?"

Her reply could not be heard above the sound of clapping as the orchestra played the last notes of their piece. Beatryce was just stunned that the old gal hadn't forced the issue of her aborted wedding, or her father's murder. Not that she wanted to see these topics raised. Maybe she should count her blessings instead of worrying over negative outcomes that hadn't materialized.

After dispensing with the social niceties, Dansbury leaned over and whispered, "Let's dance," just as the orchestra began playing the first bars of a waltz.

Beatryce swore a muffled gasp could be heard across the room as they made their way out onto the dance floor. But for some reason, the sound didn't bother her. For the first time in her life, she felt an inkling of what it was like to be free. Free to do as she would. The feeling was good.

No, the feeling was liberating. She started her dance with Dansbury, walking on air.

She'd danced the waltz over a thousand times or more. Yet today felt like the first. Better, actually. Maybe it was her newfound sense of freedom. Or maybe it was the man holding her in his arms. She looked up and watched him. For the first time ever, she didn't look about her while she danced, wondering who was watching or what they were thinking. She didn't check to see whether or not they were going to run into another couple. She practiced trust. In him.

He was keeping an eye out for them, and she took the opportunity to study his face. She knew his eyes were brown, but now, she could see that his irises were peppered with gold and green streaks, and that the entire thing was ringed in black. Startling. Complex. Like the man.

His forehead was high and wide, with a telltale round scar, probably from a childhood case of the chickenpox. His lips were full, his jaw squared. He was a broad, strong man. It was amazing how smoothly he danced. She glanced down at his large feet, and she inexplicably wondered what his bare feet looked like. Would his toes be perfectly formed, like the man? Of course, she'd seen him naked more than once, but she'd been focused on other more interesting parts of his anatomy...ahem...or it was simply too dark to see them properly. Bea laughed out loud at her odd, ridiculous thoughts. Dansbury jerked his eyes down to her and smiled. "What's so funny?"

She felt his smile to her toes. "Nothing. Let's just say I have an overactive imagination and leave it at that."

"Whatever the lady wishes." And he twirled her in a circle. Fast. So fast, she couldn't help but laugh at his antics. It was marvelous. Too much so. Thus, she was disappointed when the dance was over. Like waking up from a delicious dream before you are ready.

They walked the perimeter of the room now, making sure to be seen. Beatryce looked ahead, and then jerked to a stop. Ugh. Lady Esther Weatherby. She nearly groaned out loud at the sight. Oh Lord, this girl was vicious. Made *her* behavior seem saint-like.

In London, they had pretended to be the best of friends. Now, Beatryce just wanted to crawl beneath the floor. She did not want to speak to her old "friend" at all. This woman was a part of her past. A past she was desperately attempting to leave behind.

Alas, any thought of escaping undetected died before she could take action. "Lady Beatryce! What a surprise? I had no idea you were in Bath. Have you been here long?" Beatryce could only assume that either they weren't being snubbed because Dansbury carried too much clout, or society was too eager to find out what was going on to want to snub her...yet. Probably a bit of both.

"No. Not long. You know how much I detest anything that isn't London. La, this is a short stay, if you must know. I hope to return home very, very soon. Yesterday would not be soon enough." Beatryce adopted a put upon air. A look she had perfected in crowds much like this one.

She felt Dansbury stiffen beside her and studiously tried to ignore it.

"Don't I know what you mean. I wouldn't be here if it weren't for Father. He made us take a break from London. Thought it would do our standing good to appear in high demand and unavailable for a spell." Lady Weatherby tittered behind her fan like a juvenile making Beatryce wonder how she'd ever put up with this woman for as long as she had without slapping her at least once. Every day.

"Now. I simply must ask. Is it true your cousin married the Duke of Stonebridge?" Beatryce could only nod her head in reply. Rude, yes. But she was dreading what she knew this girl would say next.

"Well, I declare I am surprised. And after all the trouble you went through to have her discredited. What a pity. To lose a man like that to the likes of her."

"La, tell me truly. Isn't that just..."

She never got to finish that thought. Dansbury grabbed her by the arm and effectively dragged her back out of the room and into the street. No goodbyes. No explanations. No see you next times.

Well, they'd certainly created a stir. An understatement to be sure. And what was one more nail in her social coffin? It's not like she'd had plans to be a part of society in the future, anyway.

But Dansbury was clearly furious. He'd dropped her hand the moment they stepped outside and stood stiff next to her; his hands clenched into fists.

They stood in silence while a footman went to fetch the driver and carriage. Dansbury all but radiating his wrath in great heaping waves.

Humph. C'est la vie. She was who she was, and if he didn't like it, he could go hang. She held onto that attitude as she tried to ignore her thundering heart and the sunken feeling in her gut.

*

Just when he'd started to like her. Damn her eyes. Now, he just wanted to kill her.

Again.

All right, maybe he didn't quite want to kill her anymore, just throttle her.

Or at least rage at her in a stern manner.

He simply couldn't make sense of her snide remarks in the Pump Room, so reminiscent of the Beatryce of old, the witch he'd hated with righteous fury for the past year and a half.

He thought she'd changed, that it had all been an act to get away from her father. But her father was gone now, yet she'd reverted to form the minute they stepped out in society. It infuriated him. Not only because she was speaking against Grace, her cousin, whom he respected a great deal. But also because he'd begun to like her, dammit. Or at least admire her strength.

Their coach pulled up just in time. Thank, God. He didn't know how much longer he could stand there in silence before he snapped and started yelling at her. Right there on the public pavement. Or throttling her. Something. But he really didn't want to do it in public, more than he had already.

He helped her inside without saying a word.

Why?

He just wanted to make sense of it all, but she refused to fit into any specific mold he'd formed in his mind of how a lady should behave. Of how she should behave.

Once he was seated, he decided to ask her. To put it all out there and damn the consequences. "Why? Why did you say those absurd things?"

She didn't respond at first.

"Bea..."

"I don't know," she snapped. "I couldn't seem to stop myself. As soon as the words passed my lips, I regretted saying them." She shook her head and looked out the window.

"That's not good enough. You have no reason to be that way anymore."

"Maybe I don't know how to be any other way..."

"No. That's not an acceptable answer. Bea, look at me. Think about it. Why say things you don't mean? What purpose do such words serve? Especially now."

"I don't know! All right? Old habits? I just don't know. Maybe I'm just made that way...Maybe it's just too late for me." She looked at him earnestly then, tears glistening in her eyes. Her voice softened, a tenor in which he'd never heard her speak. "Before, I'd always justified my actions to myself. Every waking thought, everything I said or did, was by design toward self-preservation. Now, the reason behind such a need is gone, yet my thoughts still seem to run in the same direction, like a bad habit I cannot seem to change. One minute I'm feeling happy and carefree, and I think, 'I can do this. I can let it all go and just be me.' And the next minute I'm worried and angry and all my old thoughts reappear like a crutch. Plans to ensure I'm safe. Bad thoughts, even though they're geared toward self-preservation, to ensure my future. Maybe I just lean toward being wicked."

"Aw, love." He touched her cheek and wiped away a lone tear. "We all have a bit of both churning around inside. Good and bad. You have to choose which side to embrace. It's all a matter of choice."

She laughed at that, and he hated the way it sounded. A sort of self-deprecating humor. But not funny in the least. She looked up at him again, a resigned smile graced her face. "Even you?"

He closed his eyes and said, "Especially me. Can you imagine, for just a moment, the things I've seen? The things I've had to do? I would not pollute your mind with the details, but I'm sure you can imagine. If I let them, those things would tear me down. I beat it by feeding the good in me."

He opened his eyes and looked at her, expecting to see shock written on her face. Instead, she looked thoughtful.

"Do you know, I wake up every single day with the fear that my father is still alive and going to hurt me for all of this?" She waved her hands around as if to encompass everything around them, the entire world even. "For running away. For ruining my wedding. Not to mention ruining the family name." She laughed again, and again it didn't sound the least bit humorous. "My every day starts off in a state of panic until I recall what's happened, until I can get my emotions back under control. And this madman chasing after us doesn't help matters. I don't know how long this will last. How long will it be before I can finally wake up and not be afraid...to finally feel well and truly safe?"

"Actually, you have to admit, the madman, as you appropriately call him, seems more interested in me than you at the moment."

"That really doesn't help."

He laughed. "I know; it was a stupid thing to say." He reached for her then. "Aw, love, would that I could take that fear away…"

She pushed against his chest, not to push him away but to make him pause a moment. "But you can't. And I know that. This change has to come from within me. It's just not going to be so easy. Or quick. But I do realize it will come. Eventually."

"Now, that's my girl."

"Ha! Your girl, Dansbury?"

* * * *

Meanwhile…

Crack. Nearby, a flock of birds took flight.

Crack. A squirrel barked its displeasure.

Crack.

Three shots, three different guns. Three targets destroyed. Dead center. The cloaked man didn't need to go look to know this. He never missed. Still, he practiced every single day. Luckily, Himself enabled him to do so. It was the one thing Himself was useful for, he kept his best assassin loaded with pistols and shot. Too bad he was too frugal to provide enough money for better accommodations while carrying out the man's dirtier deeds. The man would understand the consequences of that oversight all too soon. He smiled with pleasure. Oh yes, all too soon.

The cloaked man set his third gun on the tree stump before him. Then rolled his head to stretch out the knots in his neck. He'd slept in a hayloft last night. It was most uncomfortable. He'd burned two marks on his arm as part of a growing tally of things to hold Dansbury and Himself responsible for…his arm was now littered with little scars, a dozen at least. The new burns still itched this afternoon.

Thankfully, he would be exacting payment from them both soon enough. Now, to practice his swordsmanship.

Snap.

The cloaked man pulled his sword out of its sheath and turned to look where someone had stepped on a fallen branch. His useful traitor stepped out of the shadows and into the clearing. This was most unexpected.

"What is it?" He snapped at the newcomer.

"I thought you should know that Dansbury and Lady Beatryce were seen at the Pump Room in Bath today."

"What!?"

"I said…"

"I don't actually need you to repeat it. Give me a moment."

He turned his back on the man. To think. He rubbed at one of the burn marks on his arm to direct his thoughts and set a target for his ire.

The nerve of Dansbury. Taunting him that way. Making him look foolish, for Himself would surely hear of this as well. Damn Dansbury for having the money to attend a place like the Pump Room in the first place. It wasn't fair!

It was time this ended, to hell with waiting. Yes. It was time. He couldn't go another day living in haunted shadows. Dansbury's end would bring him back out into the light. Into society's welcoming embrace. He knew it. His mind told him it was true; thus, it was.

He turned back around to face his unwanted assistant and the bearer of frustrating news. "Follow me. I've a note for you to deliver. You will need to make sure Dansbury sees it. Today."

So Dansbury thought he could show his face without fear, did he? Well, it was time to end all this. For good.

CHAPTER 32

"True friendship can afford true knowledge. It does not
depend on darkness and ignorance."

—*Henry David Thoreau*

The Library at Bloomfield Place...

"My first instinct is to throttle you, but due to our long history together, I'm prepared to give you the benefit of the doubt. Now talk."

It was all the warning Dansbury gave Ambrose as he walked through the library door. According to the butler, Grace and Ambrose had arrived just after he and Beatryce had left for the Pump Room earlier that morning.

Now, the duke was comfortably relaxed on a sofa in the library. Reading. Seemingly at ease without a care in the world, while Dansbury's world was upended.

And the man wore spectacles. He didn't even know Ambrose wore glasses. God, did he even know this man at all?

Ambrose marked his spot in his book with his finger and looked up at Dansbury, his infernal brow raised in silent query. At the moment, Dansbury hated that particular habit of his.

Dammit. Ambrose had a lot of explaining to do. He had every right to be angry with the duke, his so-called best friend. Dansbury walked over to a side table, which held all manner of liquid fortification. He poured himself a whisky. He was sure he would need it to survive this conversation.

Particularly if he wanted to get to the end without punching Ambrose in his face.

Ambrose set his book on a nearby table, rubbed the bridge of his nose and let out a long sigh. "I suppose I deserved that."

Cliff didn't answer, just glared at the man he called a friend. Even though the man wasn't looking and couldn't appreciate the full effect of his scowl. He tossed his head back and drank the entire contents of his glass in one swallow. Then refilled his glass with more whisky.

"Yes. I knew about your family's connection with the Society, as I'm sure you've figured out. At least, I assume that's what this is about." He turned to look at Dansbury then.

Cliff kept his frown firmly in place. Though he set down his untouched second drink and began to pace. "Go on."

"You're a good man, Dansbury."

He stopped and slashed his hand at the duke. "Oh spare me the 'You're a good man' bullshit. Let's get to the point. Did you not think I could handle it? Did you doubt me?" He continued his frustrated stroll about the room as he spoke.

"No! It wasn't like that at all. First of all…Hold. Could you stop circling the room?

I'm getting a crick in my neck."

"No. Stand if you don't like it, but keep talking."

Ambrose stood. He walked over to the window and leaned against the sill. He crossed his arms, his posture somewhat defensive. Understandable. "I wasn't at liberty to tell you all. Then. And whether you want to hear it or not…whether you like it or not…then, yes, I admit that a part of my decision was me not wanting to disillusion you. What was the point? Your family, those that were involved, were, as far as we knew at the time, dead."

Dansbury nearly pulled his hair out in frustration. He gripped the back of a nearby chair, his knuckles turning white. It was that or throttle his friend. "What was the point? What was the point!? How about my ability to do my job. Knowing all the facts so I know where to look." He threw up his hands. "And what about my sister? I could have been looking for her! All this time." He ran his hands through his hair and down his face.

"Christ, Ambrose, I might have found her. I might have known her."

"That's exactly one of the reasons I didn't want to tell you. It was safer for her to remain in hiding."

Dansbury shook his head. "I might understand that as my boss. But as my friend? As my brother by choice? How could you deny me that option? Besides, why should it have mattered once my family was gone?"

"Perhaps you are right. Perhaps I chose poorly. But I cannot undo that now. Right or wrong, it was a decision I made. And I admit that in hindsight, knowing what I know now and because of the man I've become thanks to my wife, I would have made a different choice had I been the same man then. But I cannot undo it, and though it pains me, I do have to live with the consequences of my actions."

"We both do."

"Yes."

"I'm going to find her."

"I'll help you."

Dansbury stopped his aimless pacing and looked up at Ambrose then. Surprised. Ambrose had always been a man to follow the rules to the letter. This. All of it. Was bending the rules a bit.

Though he was still angry, he offered Ambrose a small smile. "Thanks."

Stonebridge smiled in return, briefly. But then his look turned serious. The hair on Dansbury's arm stood on end in warning.

"There's more…"

"Tell me."

Knock. Knock. Knock.

"Enter," he called out. The staff knew he was not to be disturbed while he spoke with Stonebridge unless it was important.

"My lord, this was just delivered for you. The footman said it was urgent."

"Thank you. That will be all."

Dansbury tore open the oddly shaped letter. It was clunky for there was an object inside the envelope besides the note, which read:

Dansbury,

Midnight. The abandoned mill. Bring Lady Beatryce.

The note wasn't signed, but enclosed was another toy soldier.

So, that cloaked bastard wanted to meet? Could this be the end? Finally?

He handed the note to Stonebridge to read while he resumed pacing, lost in thought.

Stonebridge moved across the room to toss the missive into the fireplace. "What do you intend to do?"

"I'll meet him, of course."

"And Lady Beatryce?"

"She'll go."

"Cliff, you cannot possibly think to actually take her?"

"Of course I can. She can handle it. I have faith in that, at least."

The look that came across Stonebridge's face was comical. Ambrose looked at him as if he'd suddenly sprouted two heads. Admittedly, it was probably odd to see him saying something positive about Lady Beatryce, of all people.

"I suspect we have more to talk about than I realized."

"No. We don't. Talk about Lady Beatryce is off limits with you."

Ambrose raised that infernal brow. Again. He thought of sneaking into the man's room tonight to pluck the hairs of his brow out. Then he wouldn't have to see it lift in query all the time. It must drive Grace mad at times.

"Now. Let's get back to what you were about to tell me before the interruption."

Ambrose dropped his hands to his sides and stood taller, his fists clenched. "Your brother, Edward, is alive."

* * * *

Grace Stonebridge's Guest Room at Bloomfield House...

Knock. Knock. Knock.

"Come in." came a muffled voice through the bedroom door.

Beatryce took a deep breath, lifted her chin, and entered Grace's room. Grace, who was sitting in a chair by the fire, stood upon her entry.

"Beatryce."

"Grace."

For a moment, neither of them spoke another word. Beatryce clasped her hands together, and entered the room. Her hands were clammy with her anxious nerves; she wiped them on her dress. "Thank you for seeing me." As if she'd given Grace much of a choice. "Um. How was your trip?"

Ugh. She was a coward, after all. Beating around the bush like that.

Hadn't she always thought she was strong? Hadn't Aunt Harriett just proclaimed it so only yesterday? Right now she didn't feel it at all.

"Fine. Thank you." Grace crossed her arms and raised her brow—something Stonebridge often did that had always irritated Bea to no end. Grace must have picked up his bad habit. Beatryce offered up a thankful prayer that she'd been spared having to see it day after day for the rest of her life.

"Beatryce," Grace continued. "I assume you're not here to talk about the weather and my trip. Is there some purpose to this visit?"

Beatryce smiled at her cousin. The woman was still kind, but stronger than she'd been. Marriage to Stonebridge clearly agreed with her.

"Right. Yes. I—uh—I just wanted to apologize. For my behavior toward you. I was unkind to you. Many times. And for that, I am sorry. Truly sorry."

"I see."

"Yes, well."

They both stood in uncomfortable silence. For once, Bea did not know what to say. Beatryce could see the struggle on Grace's face, the woman never could hide her thoughts and feelings. Clearly, Grace wanted to know more. To understand why, but manners dictated she not press Beatryce for more than she was willing to reveal.

Bea supposed she did owe Grace more than a simple apology. "I don't know if you ever realized, or ever witnessed, the lengths my father would go to have his way."

Grace nodded her head. "I witnessed what I am sure is a mild taste of what he was capable."

Beatryce could tell that Grace empathized with her predicament. Grace truly was a compassionate woman; it made Beatryce's actions toward her that much more difficult to bear.

"You have no true idea, and I wouldn't dream of describing to you, a relative innocent, the depths of his depravity. Suffice it to say, he was a very bad man.

"I also don't say all of this in an attempt to earn your pity or your compassion. I just...I just wanted you to know that my actions were born out of desperation. I realize that it doesn't excuse my behavior, but I just thought you should understand why...to a point. And to know that it was nothing personal and that I am sorry for my part in trying to keep you and Stonebridge apart for my own gain. It is clear that you two suit."

Grace smiled then, and leaned forward to grab Beatryce's hands, which she had been twisting together in the folds of her skirt. "Oh Beatryce, think no further of it."

Then, Grace did something most unexpected, she pulled Beatryce into a welcoming hug. "I'm glad you are here...cousin."

Beatryce hesitated, but only for a moment. Then, she returned Grace's hug without reservation. And fought to hold back more of those infernal tears.

CHAPTER 33

"The course of true love never did run smooth; But
either it was different in blood—"
                    —Shakespeare, A Midsummer Night's Dream

The Bloomfield Stables...
Near Midnight...

"Trousers, Lady Beatryce?"

"Trousers, Lord Dansbury."

Dansbury smiled with approval, while inside he was a raving lunatic. A candidate for Bedlam without question. The trousers she'd found must have been made for a ten year old boy; they hugged her curves like a glove. It left nothing to the imagination. And she looked nothing at all like a boy. He wanted to take her against the wall. He wanted to hide her from the eyes of every other male around. It was barbaric, the unwanted feelings that churned inside. And it worked to keep his mind from dwelling on all of the revelations he'd learned over the past two days.

He swallowed his animalistic impulses and reined in his runaway thoughts. "So where did you find your, um, trousers, Bea?"

She sat taller in her saddle. "I commandeered them from a young footman."

"How..."

"I didn't have sex with him, if that's what you're thinking."

He hadn't been thinking it…well, perhaps a wee bit. Jealousy was a dangerous thing; it wreaked havoc on a man's common sense. But she also didn't have any coin…

"I admit I might have employed a heavy amount of flirtation in order to obtain them. I don't have any coin to my name. But these…" She ran her hand along her thighs and he squirmed in his saddle, suddenly overheated "…they were necessary." She looked at him and lifted her chin, daring him to question her methods.

He wasn't that much of a fool.

"Just for my curiosity's sake: Why trousers, Lady Beatryce?"

"La, that's easy. They're for just in case we need to make a fast getaway."

It was a practical plan; he'd give her that, but her acknowledgement of their danger made him want to demand she go back inside and lock the door. He wouldn't say it, of course. He was smarter than that. He knew women.

He knew *this* woman.

"Fine. Do you have a weapon?"

"More than one, in fact."

He looked at her a moment and debated asking her if she knew how to use them. But he relished keeping his privates in place should she take offense. And she would take offense. Instead he just smiled, and said, "Well, then. Let's see what our madman has to say, shall we?"

Dansbury and Beatryce left the Bloomfield Stables on horseback at eleven-thirty for their rendezvous with a madman. For safety, it would take half an hour to pick their way in the dark for they had to travel over open fields, riddled with rabbit holes and uneven terrain, to reach the abandoned mill. The night air was crisp and cool, but bright from a full moon. Perfect weather to face a lunatic. For surely that is what they faced. Deadly, sure. But a bedlamite nonetheless.

They travelled in silence, too caught up in their own minds to speak. This was it. He hoped to God this was where it all ended. He was ready for…well, he didn't know for what, but he was finished with running from this man. The seriousness of their impending confrontation helped him to focus his thoughts on how this would all play out, rather than on things that could not be controlled…such as the past.

The mill came into view right at the stroke of midnight.

They rode up to a split-rail fence jutting out from one side of the mill. Dansbury dismounted and turned to help Bea, but she had already jumped down on her own. Of course.

As they tied up their mounts to the fence, he smiled at her over the nose of his horse.

She glanced up briefly, smiled, and continued on with her task.

Damn, she was magnificent.

"It's nice to see you are prompt at least. Step into the moonlight so I might get a better look at the pair of you," came a disembodied voice from within the open entryway to the mill.

Dansbury grabbed Bea's hand as they walked over and stepped into a pool of light.

"Awww…isn't that sweet. Holding hands. Is it true love, then?"

Dansbury gritted his teeth in anger. Beatryce inexplicably stiffened next to him. He could sense an immediate change in her. He dared to look. He could see her eyes open wide, paralyzed with fear. The sight worried him. This was not her, his strong, courageous Bea.

"Bea?"

"Well, well. Do I detect a hint of recognition coming from the lovely Lady Beatryce?"

The man stepped out of the shadowy doorway to stand in front of them, his ever-present hood and cloak in place.

"You know who I am, don't you, Lady Beatryce? You recognize the sound of my voice, don't you?"

"Show your face, then, you bastard," Dansbury interrupted, dragging the man's attention to him.

Dansbury could barely contain his fury. This man dared to cower behind a hood and taunt her. At least she stood there, open and exposed. Three times braver than this coward.

The man pulled off the hood. Beatryce let out a loud gasp.

Had Dansbury not been forewarned by Stonebridge, he might have fallen to his knees in shock. It was all still somewhat unbelievable.

"Edward?"

"Ah, good. I see you recognize your own brother then. How fun."

Fun? He'd hardly call this fun.

"And I can see you remember me, too, Lady Beatryce. My but you have grown since you were a child of fourteen. Still cool and aloof…and unresponsive, I see. Pity. I guess my brother has not been unsuccessful in training you in the sensual arts. Perhaps I should have another go at it?"

Without warning, Dansbury charged. His brother's implications all but erasing sound reasoning.

But his brother was not without some skill, despite his apparent madness. Before Dansbury could tackle him to the ground, his brother sidestepped and drew a sword from a scabbard on his back.

Dansbury caught himself and twisted around. He crouched low now and faced his enemy. His own brother.

"Tsk. Tsk. Brother. Allowing your emotions to control your actions? I judged you better than that. Besides, I doubt she is worth it."

This time, Dansbury held his temper in check. Ironically, his brother was right about one thing. Dansbury knew better than to attack in anger.

"I'm not sure it's sporting of me to combat you when I am armed, while you are not," said Edward. He shook his head. "Pity, I'm not a sporting man."

Edward lunged, but Dansbury was quick, and evaded his slashing blade with ease. They faced off again and circled around each other. Edward slashed his blade through the air in a threatening manner. Showing off. Wasting energy unnecessarily.

Dansbury knew if he could get Edward maneuvered into just the right position, he could disarm the man with ease. It was a matter of timing.

"I bet you are wondering how it is I am here. Aren't you curious, brother?" Dansbury refused to respond to Edward's taunts.

The man continued anyway. "Father was prepared to turn the members of the Society over to the Crown, you see. Like the coward he was. And we couldn't have that, now could we?"

Dansbury did not like where this was headed.

His brother grinned, pleased with himself. "I'm sure you can see where this is going. I, your ingenious brother, planned it all out, you see. Mother and Father's demise. Made their deaths look like an accident. Faked my own, too, of course. It was perfect, but then I had to go into hiding, you see. And you, my oh-so-charming younger brother, got everything that was rightfully mine. Mine! Don't you see? It is not yours to have. I didn't die."

Years of training allowed Dansbury to keep his emotions in check—this time, despite how painful his brother's admissions were. Despite the earlier momentary loss of his head when Edward had taunted Bea. Apparently, she gave him strength and weakened him, both at the same time.

His brother was not so well controlled, despite his admitted knowledge of the need to remain level headed. Years of resentment had clearly taken their toll on his brother's mind. Even in the dark, Dansbury could see Edward's eyes were wild with madness. His entire body fairly shook with crazed anger. It would be his downfall.

The only question in Dansbury's mind now was...could he do it? Could he take his own brother's life if he had to? Despite everything.

His brother carried on with his ramblings. "I never mourned their loss, you know. Mother coddled you from the start, sparing no affection for me. As if you were the golden child. I was livid when she refused to take you with us, for I had hoped to put you, too, in a watery grave. And father was weak, a coward. You weakened his taste for vengeance. After you, he couldn't stomach what needed to be done to fulfill the Society's goals so he decided to sell us out. Had he not done that, I would have been able to live my life as I was meant to. And you wouldn't have a bloody thing!

"But," the man chuckled wildly, "I'm here to rectify the situation. To set things to rights, so to speak. To take back what is mine—what should have always been mine—by taking your life."

"But it is yours. Since you are still alive. Technically you are Dansbury."

That gave his brother pause, but he was too far gone down the path to insanity to understand this.

"Just shut up! You're trying to trick me." Spittle flew from his mouth as he spat out his angry words. "I have to do this; you are to blame for the fact that I have had to live my life in the shadows. For Father being weak. For Mother not loving me. Don't you see? It is all your fault, and I mean to make you suffer for it. Too bad you're unarmed and unable to defend yourself."

"He's not!" yelled Beatryce from out of nowhere as she tossed him his own sword. Clever woman. He'd kiss her later for that.

Dansbury caught his sword with ease and stood tall, the advantage all his. His brother lunged in anger. In madness. Whatever. It was his first mistake. Dansbury parried the thrust with ease.

Then, the fight began in earnest. Swords clanged loudly in the night air—ringing through the trees and into the valley below. His brother was a surprisingly good swordsman for all his insanity. But he was sloppy. Dansbury fought his brother off with ease as he tried to determine the best way to incapacitate him in order to take him back to Stonebridge without fatally wounding him.

Thrust. Parry. Slash. Advance. Retreat. Their swords clashed, the sound of steel echoing in the night.

Ten minutes later, Edward was visibly weakening; his energy almost spent. Dansbury was still strong for he wasted no move, thus conserving his energy. It was only a matter of moments and he would have the madman.

But all of the sudden Edward looked beyond Dansbury's shoulder and yelled, "Shoot her!"

Bang.

At the sound of a gun being discharged, Dansbury spun with a shouted, "No!" But there was nobody there besides Beatryce. And she was fine.

He turned back around to face his brother, but Edward was gone. The bloody bastard had duped him. Damn him, the coward.

"Come back, you bastard, and face me like a man!" Dansbury yelled to the trees. He didn't bother to chase the man; he would not leave Beatryce unprotected in case someone else was around. Despite her capabilities.

God. His brother had turned out to be a weak man. He supposed psychosis would do that to a man.

Dansbury turned back around and sought out Beatryce. There she stood, a beacon in the night; moonlight highlighting her pale hair and features. Damn, she was beautiful to behold.

But she stood there, arms crossed, shivering in the cold; this brave, strong woman. He went to her and pulled her into his arms. "Let's go."

She just nodded in agreement. Despite her strength, he still set her on his own horse after tying hers to his. Then he mounted behind her. He needed to have her near. She was shaken. Badly. Perhaps they both were.

Just as he began to turn the horse toward home, he spotted a man a fair distance into the woods. It broke his heart to see this man, their traitor, who had finally deigned to show his face.

The turncoat nodded at Dansbury once as if to say…what? "All's good? I approve?"

To hell with that. Dansbury pointed back at the traitor and said, "You. Are a dead man." His sign language was unmistakable.

Because in truth, Kelly's life was now forfeit.

CHAPTER 34

"Each night, when I go to sleep, I die. And the next
morning, when I wake up, I am reborn."

— *Mahatma Gandhi*

"You were right. My brother, Edward, is alive." Dansbury walked into the library, where Ambrose awaited news. He crossed directly to a sideboard and poured himself a glass of whisky.

Ambrose stood. "Cliff. I'm sorry."

Cliff took a sip of the fiery brew and turned to face his longtime friend. "Don't. There's no need. As children, he was unbelievably cruel. We were not close because of it. As an adult, he's simply unworthy, even of my pity. Certainly not my empathy." Dansbury shook his head as he walked over to take a seat in one of the club chairs by the fire, opposite where Ambrose had been sitting. Ambrose retook his seat.

"You know. I had always felt somewhat ashamed for never truly mourning Edward's death as I was expected to. I mean, we are meant to love our siblings unconditionally aren't we? And a very small part of me does carry some measure of guilt for not caring one way or the other about my own brother's life or demise or whatever we are to call it now." He took another sip of his drink and stared off into the burning flames. "...But I haven't mourned him; I do not mourn him, and I find I quite simply detest him."

Ambrose leaned forward in his seat and steepled his hands. "We don't get to choose our family. Just because someone carries your blood doesn't make them a good person or similar to you in temperament at all. These things happen. You are not less of a man because of it."

"Yea, I know it."

"I take it, since he's not here and you haven't said otherwise, he is still alive?"

Cliff looked at his friend. "Yea. He is. The coward distracted me and fled when it was clear he was going to lose our fight." Dansbury opened and closed his left fist, it was a touch sore. He must have bruised it during their scuffle.

"Distracted? You?" Ambrose's infernal brow shot up.

Cliff looked away. "It is unimportant. Anyway, he appears to be our assassin and the man who murdered the Earl of Swindon. He was prepared to murder both myself and Lady Beatryce tonight. And..." he looked back at Ambrose "...he appears to be mad."

"Mad as in..."

"As in a prime candidate for Bedlam."

"I see."

"I believe he is tortured by the fact that he had to give up his birthright in order to remain in hiding all this time. At least, his eyes seemed to go wild with madness when he spoke about it."

"It is possible...and probable."

Dansbury didn't mention that Edward knew Lady Beatryce. That fact would remain private if at all possible. Besides, the point was completely irrelevant to their investigation, at least at this time. "It does make him somewhat dangerous because he is unpredictable."

"Of course."

"And he is reasonably skilled with weapons. He gave me a good run with his sword."

"That is saying something considering you are the best."

Dansbury shrugged, a habit he'd picked up from his many trips abroad working for the Crown.

"What of Lady Beatryce? Where is she?"

"In her room."

"And?"

"And she was magnificent."

"Cliff..."

He shot his friend a pointed look. "Don't. I told you earlier, she is not up for discussion."

"I remember. But do you remember…"

"I remember, all right? I just…I know what I'm doing, so leave off."

"Well, you spent a good six months warning me off the very same woman, I only thought to return the favor."

"There's no need. I know her. Besides, it's irrelevant. I'm not about to marry her."

"Sure." It didn't take a genius to hear the sarcasm and, more importantly, doubt in Ambrose's voice.

"Can we get back on topic?" Before he took out his frustration on his best friend by tackling him to the floor and using his face for target practice for his fists.

Ambrose nodded his head for him to continue.

"We have another problem. Kelly is working with the Society. He's our traitor."

"You're sure?"

He just looked as his friend as if to ask, *Are you really questioning my judgment after all these years?*

Ambrose chuckled. "Right. Forget I asked. Just tell me what happened."

"Kelly was on lookout in the woods. He was the distraction Edward used to get away. Kelly shot his gun into the air on cue, to make me think he'd shot at Lady Beatryce. As I turned to look, my brother ran away. I didn't want to leave Lady Beatryce behind without knowing who else might have been hiding in the woods, thus I did not pursue."

"I'm surprised by that. There was a time in the past when you would have done anything to get your man."

"Yes, well." The two men cleared their throats. Cliff took another sip of his drink. "There's still time yet."

"Why do you think Kelly let you see him? You and I both know you only saw Kelly because he wanted you to."

"Good question. It was deuced strange. He nodded to me as if to say, 'well done.'"

"And your response?"

Cliff grinned into his glass before taking another sip. "My answer might have been a tad…strong."

Ambrose just looked at him with that infernal brow raised. Again.

"I might have told him he was a dead man and made an unmistakable rude gesture in his general direction."

The duke shook his head and chuckled lightly, but he spoke in all seriousness. "It is odd, and something we'll have to consider. So, what is your recommendation?"

"I plan to scout the area. I don't think my brother is very far away. Then, we lure him out and take him. After that, we go after Kelly."

"Good. We'll start in the morning."

"I'll be ready." Cliff tossed back the remainder of his drink.

Now to hear from Lady Beatryce exactly how she knew his brother, Edward. After he fortified himself with another drink. Or two.

* * * *

She was unresponsive. Immobile. Lifeless. Even the loud grunting above did not appear to break through her indifference. Her bed shook in spasmodic waves. She ignored it all.

Her headboard hit the wall with one overzealous thrust, and the landscape hanging there rattled its protest. Yet she did not wince. Not even a flinch. And the sweat that dripped down from above, hitting her face and sliding down into her ear, did nothing to turn her gaze from the miniature of her mother on her bedside table.

Oh, Mama. Make it stop. Please, make it stop.

Lady Beatryce willed her mother to intervene, but it was no use. Besides, the damage was done. She was no longer a maid.

Oh, Mama…Would you have warned me about this? Would you have cried? Helped me? Stopped him? Stopped them all?

Oh, but her questions were pointless; Mother had died giving birth to her little more than thirteen years before.

Beatryce cleared her mind and concentrated on the small, gilt-framed portrait next to her bed. Her mother's likeness conveyed strength and a certain protective amount of aloofness. She wanted to harness that power. Breathe it. Live it. Own it.

She cried, despite her efforts not to. Her tears were silent trails of moisture on her youthful cheeks. Mother's portrait stood solemnly erect on the table, but she could no longer make out the details through her watery veil. She stared at it anyway.

Lady Beatryce had fallen.

Suddenly, her room caught on fire. As if by magic, everything—the bed, the paintings, the wall, her mother's portrait, even the man raping her—was immediately engulfed in flames. She could feel the heat and smell and see the smoke heavy in the air, swirling around and above columns of fire. Yet she breathed with ease as if the air were clear.

Even her very skin was on fire, though she didn't feel any pain. She simply knew she burned with the certainty only found in dreams, where even odd things made perfect sense.

Then, everything went black. Not black, like standing outside in the dark where you can still make out the vague outline of things around you, but black as in nothing existed. The air was no longer hot nor cold; it was nothing. No breeze stirred, no sound could be heard. She couldn't even hear herself breathe or hear the beating of her heart. And the smell of smoke was curiously absent.

There was absolutely nothing around her but a dark abyss. She couldn't even discern whether or not her eyes were open or whether or not she even had a body. She tried to move, but she could not even tell if she had or could or did. She was nothing but a thought.

After a few moments, or an eternity, she could scarcely tell which, a small pinpoint of light appeared. It began to expand, and it grew in size until she could see everything around her once more.

She was hovering a few feet off the ground, floating as if on a cloud. She looked down. There was a small, peculiar pile of ashes on the ground beneath her, different from normal for the ashes were creamy blonde in color, like the color of her hair. The clump was perfectly formed and about the size of a small anthill.

She looked around. She was outside now, that much she could tell, and she was in a forest, or what was left of one. Everything within sight had been burned. The trunks of trees still smoldered and the smell and sight of smoke clung to the air. For some reason, the smell didn't bother her, quite the contrary; the smell made her feel alive, renewed. Birds chirped in the distance and the air felt warm, like spring.

Her surroundings were unfamiliar to her. Was she at Bloomfield Park? She certainly wasn't near her old home where the dream had begun.

Movement caught her eye, and she looked down again. Beneath her, the pile of ashes stirred as if something moved underneath. Beatryce stared, mesmerized, as the mound of ashes grew in size and shape. Before long the small pile was the size of a large animal.

Eventually, an orange beak poked out from the center of the growing pile, then a feathered head. A bird?

The thing springing forth from the ashes grew. And grew. Until it was larger than life and beautiful in its light, feathered glory.

It was a pale, blonde phoenix. Rising from the ashes. Resurrected from fire. The phoenix fluffed its great feathers, then looked up at Beatryce and caught her eye. The creature's eyes were blue, more specifically, the color of the Adonis blue. Her own eyes.

She was reborn.

Beatryce bolted upright in her bed, drenched in sweat. The dream. She hadn't had it since she was sixteen. Seeing Edward must have triggered her memories. But the ending.

The fire and the phoenix? That was new; she'd never dreamt that part before.

"How do you know my brother?"

Lady Beatryce let out a small squeak, in reflex, but calmed almost immediately. She knew his voice by now.

There, by the fire, sat Dansbury, sipping some sort of drink. Probably whisky.

This man knew more about her than anyone else in this entire world. Why not tell him?

"I met your brother, Edward, when I was fourteen. I did not know who he was at the time; he was never introduced to me by name. But I recognized his voice tonight, the moment he spoke. His voice is one I'll never forget, unfortunately. Nor his face."

Beatryce sighed, then sat a little straighter and clasped her hands in her lap. She had nothing to be ashamed of.

"When I was fourteen, your brother paid my father for my virginity. And took it by force."

Dansbury's reaction was immediate. He threw his glass into the fireplace. The flames within leapt with the added fuel; the glass shattered across the hearth.

He leaned forward and rested his head in his hands, his elbows on his knees. "Damn! Damn! Damn! Damn! Damn!"

He pulled at his hair as he yelled his curses.

Then he jerked to a stand and stumbled over to her bed, broken glass crunching beneath his booted feet with every step.

"S-scoot over," was all he said.

She did. He sat down and began the process of removing his boots. No easy task. Was he planning to stay?

"Do you need help?"

"No, I'll manage. Done it a thousand times on my own."

Once he had them off, he crawled into bed and pulled her into his arms. He didn't say anything else, and Beatryce was glad. Had he shown pity or tried to coddle her, she might have broken down. As it was, his actions showed his confidence in her strength. And besides, he was the worse for drink. She didn't blame him his walk with the bottle; his world had been upended. The man could certainly afford to escape, if only for a little while.

She also didn't press him to talk about everything that had happened, how he felt about it. He would speak if he wanted to unburden himself.

"Bea?"

"Hmmm?"

They both kept their eyes closed as they spoke, still held tightly in each other's embrace.

"Do you know the first time I saw you?"

Beatryce wasn't sure she wanted to hear this. "Tell me." She encouraged him to speak anyway.

"It was the night of the Rutherford Ball in May of '13. Do you recall it?"

"Somewhat." She answered noncommittally, though she tensed with worry.

"I was outside, on assignment and hiding in the shadows, when you stepped out onto the back terrace. Your laugh preceded you and I felt it all over." She remembered. That was him in the shadows?

"Could you see me in the shadows?"

"I-I knew you were there, but I did not know it was you. I could only see a vague outline of your form." She decided to be truthful; he probably wouldn't remember this in the morning anyway.

"I nearly broke my cover and introduced myself, then and there. I had wanted you at first sight."

"Did you?" What else could she say to that? Now more than ever she was sure she didn't want to hear this.

"Then Middlebury joined you on that terrace. Do you remember that?"

"Y-Yes." She would not be dishonest; she would own her actions.

"He touched you. I wanted to break his fingers. The desire to do so was unreasonable, but real…and strong."

Her heart fluttered at his admission, despite the base nature of his revelation.

"Then I became angry at you. I heard what you said, what you two discussed. You'd both ruined a girl on purpose."

"Yes, we did."

"I hated you then." She hated to know it. "Yet for a moment I thought

I saw regret and desperation flash in your eyes. Was I imagining things, Bea?"

"No. You weren't." She spoke honestly, confident he'd remember nothing in the morning for his speech kept getting lower and slower as he fell his way toward sleep. "I felt this inexplicable trust in you, hiding there in the shadows. As if you were my guardian angel, sent down from heaven to watch over me. For once in my life, I wanted to be vulnerable and allow someone else to protect me, to keep me safe. For some reason, I knew you were up to the task and I pled with you the only way I could. I willed you to step in and intervene. To take me away from my life."

"Guardian angel?" He laughed, inappropriate though it was to her admission of vulnerability, but then, he was the worse for drink. "And here I was battling far more base urges."

She couldn't help but laugh, too. It was in the past and so long ago; she'd long since overcome her fanciful imaginings that night, and her disappointment that she'd been wrong.

And his response was so typically…masculine. Base urges, indeed.

"Bea?"

"Yes…"

"I'm no guardian angel, but had I known…I would have tried my best."

His admission pierced her soul. She tried to laugh it off in order to hide its impact. "Dansbury, you truly are a charming man."

His answer was a snore; the man had fallen asleep. Thank God. She wasn't sure she wanted him to hear her last remark. She squeezed him tighter, wishing him a peaceful slumber. Her eyes burned with tears.

But then he hummed and spoke again, his voice tired and low. "Mmm…Bea?"

She lifted her head and looked at him. His eyes were still closed. "Yes?"

Nothing. Silence.

"Yes, Dansbury?" She prompted.

He smiled, but his eyes remained closed as he asked, "What?"

She laughed. "You called my name…"

He smiled again, and said, "Oh…"

She waited for him to say something else, but he said nothing. Then, he snored. She laughed again. "Good night, D." And laid her head back on his chest.

"Hmm…Bea?"

"Yes, D?" She said with a chuckle.

"It seems…" His voice trailed off a moment. "It seems fate has plans for us after all…"

Snore.

Oh, Dansbury.

Oh, this man, this man.

He could charm the socks off a snake. She envied the woman who would claim his heart.

But it would not be her. Not that she didn't consider herself worthy; she had far more confidence than that. Now. But she was finished with society. His world now was her past. She was looking forward to being gone from society for good. Her experience at the Pump Room had reminded her of that.

It was then that she recalled and realized the point of her earlier dream. Her life had been a living hell, but that part of it was over. She was free. Reborn from the ashes of her previous life. And despite everything that had happened this night, despite being faced with a nightmare of a person from her past, she was now free of that past. And she was all that much stronger for her trials.

Beatryce fell asleep rejoicing in her newfound knowledge. In her freedom. Life, for her, began now.

CHAPTER 35

"The curve of your lips rewrite history."

—*Oscar Wilde*

"Unexpressed emotions will never die. They are buried
alive and will come forth later in uglier ways."

—*Sigmund Freud*

The Next Morning...

Dansbury opened his eyes to a face full of blonde hair. Beatryce. She was still in his arms.

They'd fallen asleep that way, just as they were after her confession the night before, though much of it was fuzzy in his mind. Carefully, he leaned up on one elbow, the rest of his arm trapped beneath her, and looked down at her, so peaceful in her slumber. She wore a small smile on her face, and he was pleased that she slept well despite everything. He reached over with his free hand and gently brushed her hair out of her face. She scrunched her nose as the ends of a few strands tickled her there.

He wanted to remain where he was for a little while longer. All day, in truth. He was comfortable. Warm. It would be cold out from under these covers.

He felt surprisingly clear headed despite being concerned in liquor the night before. He'd drunk a lot of water before turning to his whisky. Perhaps that had been the key to his lack of a hangover, despite his best attempts at procuring one.

Sigh. But there was no use in delaying the inevitable. He had a madman to find. And a traitor. This, all of it, had to end.

Then, he had a sister to find.

He looked back down at Lady Beatryce and shook her gently on the arm. She didn't move. He laughed, she was decidedly not a morning person.

He shook her again. "Beatryce, love. Wake up." He leaned forward and kissed her nose. "Wake up, darling. Time to rise and shine," he said in a singsong voice.

Beatryce stretched and moaned with contentment. His thoughts threatened to turn decidedly south. He suppressed the impulse, for now was most definitely not the time.

"Come on, my dove. We have some bad guys to catch."

Beatryce blinked open her eyes, saw him, and smiled before she closed them again.

He suddenly felt adrift at sea, a man unmoored.

He fell back and stared up at the canopy above the bed. He was stunned; he felt as if he'd been punched in the gut.

What the hell was he going to do?

Nothing. Nothing! It was just a thing born of being in danger. Together. That was all. It had to be all. He was not ready. Not her!

He ignored his feelings as best he could and sat up, pulling his arm from beneath her and pretending to be his carefree self. He was good at that; he'd had to do the like many times before in his line of work. Inside he was in turmoil, but only he would know it.

Beatryce immediately rolled the other way, turning her back to him. He slapped her on the arse as he turned to get out of bed. "Come on, lazy bones. We need to get moving." She only snorted and grunted in response. Nice and ladylike.

He placed his feet on the floor. Shite. It was bloody cold.

"Hmmm. All right. I'm coming." Beatryce murmured, then promptly let out a soft snore. He laughed. Then, crawled back on the bed.

"Oh, no you don't." He sat up on his knees a minute as he thought about how to proceed.

God, he was in trouble.

He ignored that, too.

Then, he rubbed his hands together as he wondered if she was ticklish. No time like the present to find out.

Real trouble.

He placed his hands on her sides and began his torture.

Ah. That woke her.

She shrieked; then, started laughing as she yelled, "No. No. Dansbury stop! I can't…I can't take it. Oh my, no. No. No. Nooooooo…" between great guffaws. She pushed at his hands, but he was stronger. And relentless.

Well, he had an answer to his question. She was most definitely ticklish.

Eventually, he released her. Though he was loath to do so; he was having far too much fun. And making her laugh made it easy to ignore his inner turmoil.

She rolled out of bed on the opposite side now. Bent over and heaving as she recovered her breath. She looked up at him and narrowed her eyes. "Ooooh. You do know I give as good as I get, don't you?"

"Is that a promise, Lady Beatryce?" he taunted in return.

"Why yes it is, Lord Dansbury." She responded with a smile.

"Well, I'd like to see you try." He goaded as he darted off the bed and dashed for the door. He opened it and rushed out to make good his escape, but not before a big, fluffy pillow hit him in the arse.

He ran from more than just her retribution.

*

His behavior was more than a little bizarre. He'd just been faced with his psychotic brother who, it turns out, is alive after all these years—and clearly responsible for their parents' deaths, and yet he teased her and laughed as if he hadn't a care in the world.

Was he that kind of man? One who suppresses unpleasantness rather than face it head on? Who brushes off serious concerns with a joke and a laugh or two? One who would wait until the pressure built and built until he had no choice but to explode?

Or was he truly so carefree, brushing everything off with the ease of kicking the dirt from one's boots?

She was betting the former and it concerned her.

Self-preservation kicked in. With a madman on the loose, her very life was still in his hands. What would happen if he flew off into a rage at the wrong time? Would she be in more danger? Not from him, per se, but less protected while he wrestled with his demons?

That did it. She knew she was falling back on old habits. Again. But she wasn't truly safe until the madman was captured. So, she would dress. Then, she would find Dansbury and prod him in order to set him off before his burden grew and he detonated on his own, at the wrong time and place.

Her opportunity came a few hours later.

CHAPTER 36

*"My tongue will tell the anger of my heart, or else my
heart, concealing it, will break."*
                    —*Shakespeare, The Taming of the Shrew*

"So you haven't had it easy after all. You've just successfully buried your emotions and hid them from the world. Have you ever dealt with them? Or properly grieved? Did you even mourn your parents' deaths?" Beatryce attacked the minute she walked into the library. She hit low, regrettably, but her aim was true.

He'd greeted her arrival with a smile. She hated to see it fade from his face so rapidly. But it did; the change was immediate. Of course it was. She'd struck with the precision of a viper, guaranteeing a reaction from him.

He closed the distance between them in a few steps, all but marching in righteous fury. A violent storm in human form. She stood her ground.

"Fuck you!" He all but yelled when he was close enough for her to feel his warmth.

She suppressed the urge to hug him, but grinned anyway, pretending as if she enjoyed her attack. "We've already done that."

He just looked at her somewhat stupefied as if surprised she would say such a thing, anger and puzzlement warring in his eyes.

But she was relentless, her life might depend upon it.

"You've never had to work for a damn thing in your life, have you?" He sliced his hands in the air. "You know *nothing* about me."

Keep telling yourself that, D.

She didn't bother to argue that point. "Or are you just now realizing you are not perfect in every way?"

He stood there, shaking in fury, but otherwise, he kept his hands to himself. He was in her face now, though. Close and searching her eyes. She felt his breath, hot upon her skin. It made her uncomfortable as it sawed in and out. She nearly squirmed beneath the intensity of his gaze. She almost lowered her eyes. Almost.

Then he smiled.

Ah, hell. He's going to do it again.

"Those were cold and heartless things to say, Bea," he said with a soft, almost gentle tone as he brushed his hand against her cheek.

She tried to retain the upper hand. She lifted her chin. "But that doesn't make them any less true." She said it in defiance of his kindness. Besides, everything she'd said was true, though it was cruel of her to point them out in such a way.

"Sure. But I know what you're doing. That self-preservation instinct has kicked in again, hasn't it? Misguided to be sure, but rearing its ugly head."

"La, I don't know what you're talking about."

"Yes. You do. We had this conversation yesterday, remember? What do you hope to gain by provoking me this way?"

She realized she wasn't going to fool him, so she admitted the truth. "Self-preservation, what else?"

"How so? Explain your thinking."

She sighed. "I wonder if you have even dealt with things the way one should. That you are suppressing these emotions. A man like you needs to confront his demons head on, or shatter from the emotion within. But I can't let that happen. Don't you see? My life depends upon you." It sounded stupid now that she'd said those things out loud; her argument sounded weak, even to her own ears.

"And do you feel better now, having said all those things?"

Her shoulders slumped as she admitted the truth. "No. I feel bloody awful."

He took her in his arms. She leaned her head against his chest and could hear the vibrations from his voice through his chest as he said, "Ah, Bea. You're learning. A few weeks ago and you wouldn't have cared."

"I'm worried about you, all right?" Why did her mouth persist on admitting the truth? She should just stop now, but she seemed to be the one ready to explode, if only with the truth of her feelings. "I just don't understand how you can so easily set aside your emotions. I feel like mine are constantly bubbling just beneath the surface, threatening to overflow at any minute. I've always felt that way. So I exercise, at night, to give myself an outlet."

"You've always given me the impression that you are the same, that you've always been quite divorced from your emotions, though in a more negative way, I must admit."

"It may have appeared that way, but the appearance was false. I just worked extra hard to make everyone believe that. Self-preservation again. If people believed they could hurt you, they would try."

"That is a pretty cynical view."

"We're talking about *the ton*. I'm not so far off the mark, am I?"

"Too true. Too true. But back to the emotions churning just beneath the surface...perhaps I am the same?"

"Perhaps, but I doubt it."

"Don't. I've seen much. Things that would make even you squirm with the telling. And I've had to make hard decisions...the kind that have gotten people hurt. Irreparably.

Even killed. Those costs are hard on one's soul if one doesn't know how to manage it. But I am relentless in my pursuit of the truth. I will put people in danger if I have to, innocent people even, in order to see justice served." His eyes told of true horrors his mouth hesitated to speak.

He touched his forehead to hers, and in a soft, low voice said, "One of my closest friends had, or has, I should say, a brother. We were on an assignment in France. It was dark, but we had a plan. My plan. It should have gone all right, despite the high risk." He paused to inhale a deep breath.

"But it didn't?" She prompted, softly, slowly.

He rubbed his hands up and down her arms. "But it didn't," he answered back, "and it wasn't the first time, but this time the man was my friend's brother; his twin."

Oh, that must have been horrible, for all of them. She hesitated to ask, nevertheless, "Did he die?"

"No. But he was injured gravely and is forever disabled. Mentally. Unable to care for himself. Unable to say more than a few words...a three year old cloaked in a man's body." Dansbury's body seemed to shudder from deep emotion. "His family would have left him in Bedlam, but my friend broke with his family to care for him. For the rest of their lives." His voice cracked on the word Bedlam, demonstrating how deeply he felt.

Oh, Dansbury. "You feel guilty, don't you?"

"I am guilty. Yet I know I would have made the same choices were I to have the chance to do it all over again. That knowledge is difficult to live with; it takes a toll on one's soul."

Oh, did she understand the sentiment all too well. And perhaps he had finally realized that they were all too similar on that front. She peered up at him and brushed her hand across his brow; would that she could remove the troubled look in his eyes as easily as all that.

"Bea. Never…" He leaned in to whisper low in her ear as he slid one hand up her arm. Slowly. Gently. "…never doubt that I feel…" He paused and took in a deep breath; she felt it to her toes, it raised the flesh on her skin. Everywhere. The other hand was on her side, his thumb touched her just beneath her breast. "I feel…Bea. I feel deeply." Then he kissed her.

She lost her mind in his kiss. Relinquished all of her control. She poured the depths of her humanity into it, letting go of years of suppressed emotion. His mouth was soft, so soft. His lips warm and smooth as they caressed hers.

Then she opened for him and he claimed her with his tongue and his hands. She was rapidly losing control for this was no mere kiss, but a merging of souls.

"Ahem." A third voice interrupted her joy, her ascent into heaven.

Dansbury pulled back, but he did not let her go. He touched his forehead to hers and sighed. "Ambrose. How about knocking next time?" He kept his eyes closed as he spoke.

"I did. You were too preoccupied to hear." The duke was angry, Bea could hear it in his voice. She didn't blame him. His closest friend was kissing her, of all people.

Dansbury pulled back and looked at her. His eyes said he was sorry.

Hers told him not to worry about it. She was made of stronger stuff.

They turned as one to face the duke.

The man stood there, his arms braced on his hips. He was scowling, make no mistake. Beatryce just smiled.

Dansbury squeezed her hand. "Bea, Ambrose and I are headed out this morning to see if we can discover the whereabouts of my brother, Edward. We're hoping to find some clues at the mill that will give us a chance to come up with a plan of attack. We don't expect to apprehend him, yet."

She squeezed his hand in return. "Then I'll stay and keep your aunt company while you search. Good luck."

She was not the type to break down into hysterics over fear for his safety. She would suppress such emotion. Ironic, that.

CHAPTER 37

"A very small degree of hope is sufficient to cause the birth of love."

— *Stendhal*

Stonebridge and Dansbury rode out to the abandoned mill to search for tracks and gain some knowledge of where Edward had raced off to the night before. It was a long shot, but it was all they had at the moment. Kelly knew to go back and cover his and Edward's tracks unless they wanted to be found. Dansbury was a damn good tracker. They all were, but Dansbury was the best. And Kelly knew this.

Neither Stonebridge nor Dansbury spoke as they rode their horses to the mill. Stonebridge hadn't breathed a word about the kiss he'd witnessed in the library. It was only a matter of time, though.

The duke waited no more than five seconds once they'd reached the mill and dismounted to raise the subject.

"She stopped by Grace's room yesterday."

Well, that wasn't what he expected. No need to identity the 'she' in this conversation. "And?"

"And she apologized for everything."

"She did?" He was surprised, in a way. A spark of something flared to life in his chest. Was it joy? Appreciation? Pride?

"She did. Grace believes she was sincere. I have my doubts, of course."

"As you say."

"My wife is far too trusting. Sees the best in everyone." Ambrose smiled with pride at this.

He was entitled; Grace was a good woman.

"Cliff, she's been a very bad woman in the past. She's done horrible things to people."

"I know."

"She lies."

"I know."

"You're a right jackass."

"I can be."

"You were supposed to say, 'I know.'"

"I know."

Both men laughed at that. "Well, I'm glad we got that straight."

"I believe we've had a similar conversation before," said Ambrose.

Dansbury remembered calling his friend an ass not too long ago. "At least once."

"But our roles are now reversed."

"And that is why I'm telling you to leave off." He gave his friend a pointed look, a warning.

"But I wouldn't be a very good friend if I didn't try."

Cliff folded his arms across his body. "Fine then. You've tried. Now let it go."

"All right. I will leave you to hang yourself. You are a grown man and should know what you are doing. I hope you know what you're doing."

"I do."

Ambrose's words seemed like a premonition. For the first time in his life, Dansbury wondered whether or not he did, in fact, know what he was doing.

And his words also made him realize he held a small measure of hope in his breast. Premonition or not, optimism and anticipation sparked a small and steady light in his chest, like a distant thunderstorm...visible but too far to be heard. And it all led down a rough but perceptible path toward Beatryce.

"Come on, my friend. We need to search around the other side of the mill if he ran off that way."

Cliff set aside thoughts that were both troubling and joyful and focused on their task.

It didn't take him long to find his brother's trail; the horse's hooves left fresh divots in the earth. "I wonder why Kelly didn't bother to cover their tracks? He's practically left us signs proclaiming 'This Way to Bad Guy.' What is his game?"

Ambrose smiled but didn't laugh, his tone thoughtful but serious. "It is odd. Isn't it? I have no doubt this was intentional. I know Kelly."

"Why then? Do you think he's setting us up for a trap?"

"No. I don't actually." Ambrose spoke with confidence.

"What then?"

"I think he may be working for them under duress."

Dansbury shook his head. "No. I don't buy that for one minute. He put my life in jeopardy. He put Lady Beatryce's life in danger by setting those men on our trail."

Ambrose raised his damn brow. "Was your life truly ever in danger, Cliff?"

"Yes." He said it like a petulant child. Even though it wasn't the truth; he'd never felt his life was truly in danger. But it made him furious that Kelly would put Beatryce's life in danger even if the risk of injury was quite low.

Was he really that much of a hypocrite? Was he the only one allowed to place her in danger? The thought was absurd.

Unruly emotions did that to a man.

"Suppose Kelly realized you would manage for the time being. Perhaps he was biding his time until the opportune moment arose to hand us Edward without making it look like he had a hand in it?"

"Well, you know him best, Ambrose. Why would he do this?"

"I can only think they have something on him. Something that is coercing him to act on their behalf, half-hearted though it is. I think if he'd truly intended to betray us, you would have had a more harrowing situation on your hands."

"Well, you know him best. I'll take your word for it, though I want it noted that I have my reservations."

"Duly noted."

"Well, then, let us see where this trail leads. Shall we?"

"Lead the way."

*

The tracks led to a seldom-used game keeper's hut less than two miles west of the mill. They were still on Bloomfield Park lands…Damn the man for being so close to Aunt Harriet, to Bea.

They dismounted about twenty-five yards away and cautiously approached the house on foot. All was quiet save for the usual forest sounds…birds, squirrels and the rustling of leaves on the breeze. Nature. Small animals. But no horses.

The hut's lone window was absent any glass and was dark. No fire burned in the hearth. No flames flickered from candles. In short, the hut breathed an air of abandonment.

The short stone wall surrounding the house and its small allotment was intact, but in obvious need of repair. The front garden was not a garden as one might imagine, for it consisted entirely of stones, dirt, leaves, and weeds being that the house stood in a dense forest. A rough path led to the door, which was closed. Bloomfield Park hadn't had an active gamekeeper in five years, and the outside looked it.

Bits of paper and string from shot casings littered the ground outside the wall. Along with that mess, the shattered remnants of what appeared to be dolls fashioned of sticks and straw were also strewn about. Strange. Obviously, Edward had been target shooting in the front garden. With crude dolls for targets. They'd already concluded he was mad. Everything they saw served to support their theory.

An army of toy shoulders, bent and twisted, were scattered about the grounds as well—both in the garden proper and outside its wall.

By contrast, the cottage's interior was fastidious, almost gleaming. Certainly not the condition in which it had been found. Personal effects were lined up with exacting precision on a table, including the tools for making up additional shot casings, the means for sharpening a sword, and a man's pocket watch. The watch was polished to a brilliant shine and lay perfectly square to one corner of the table, its chain lined up horizontally with the table's edge. Precise. Bizarre.

A traveling valise lay on the small bed in the far corner. Squarely in the middle. And on top of bedclothes pulled taut and tucked tight with not a wrinkle to be found. Very bizarre.

And there wasn't a single inch of dust to be found. Someone had certainly spent significant time cleaning the one-room shack.

So Edward wasn't here, though it appeared as if he would be returning. Someone that precise would not leave behind his personal effects.

Dansbury tapped the table and turned to face his friend. "What do you think, Ambrose?"

"I think I'm surprised we found him so easily. And I think he'll return…what are you doing?"

"Messing up the bed." Dansbury had sat on the bed. Just sat. It was enough to add a crease or two.

"How old are you?"

Dansbury just grinned at his friend. Clearly, the question was rhetorical.

"Anyway," continued Stonebridge, "I'll not wait here all afternoon wondering when. Let us head back and prepare appropriate accommodations for our reluctant guest. Then, we'll return at dusk and extend our invitation."

As they left, Dansbury brushed his hand over the pocket watch's chain. He just couldn't resist.

CHAPTER 38

"There's nothing like eavesdropping to show you that the world outside your head is different from the world inside your head."

—Thornton Wilder

The Back Terrace...
Bloomfield Park...

The women were outside on the back terrace taking coffee. And talking. He just couldn't help himself; he paused near the open door leading outside and listened in on their conversation. Eavesdropping had helped him out of many scrapes in the past; it was a hard habit to break even when not on assignment.

He no longer thought of Bea as an assignment.

Fortunately, the doors had panes of glass covered by translucent curtains, he was reasonably shielded from their sight, yet he could make out both their profiles well enough.

Yet he only had eyes for one.

"What about your half-sisters, Beatryce? Why do you leave them? I can see you care. You care for them a great deal," asked Aunt Harriet. He had wondered the same. He held his breath as he awaited her response.

He could tell Lady Bea squirmed in her seat. She reached up to push a stray lock of hair behind her ear. "I do. I care, though they wouldn't know it. I've had to keep them at arm's length, don't you see? Especially Adelaide. Have you met her?"

"Yes, I have. She's the female equivalent to our Dansbury. Charming. Precocious. And cute as a button." The women laughed at the comparison; their mirth danced to his ears on the breeze, free and unfettered.

He wanted to chuckle aloud with them. He did rather like little Adelaide. No wonder.

"She is at that. You could see it right from the beginning. And my father, the bastard that he was, always kept me in line by threatening her well-being. It was his way…and met with far more success than any direct assault could. He said that if I didn't…obey…he would use her instead."

Aunt Harriett gasped. Cliff gripped the doorframe with no insignificant amount of force. In the blink of an eye, a shadowed veil enshrouded them. That bastard!

"And so you obeyed…" Aunt Harriett's voice was shaken.

"And so I obeyed. Everything he would have me do, I did." Bea's voice remained strong, but with a hardened edge.

Dansbury wished the man alive so that he could be the one to kill him this time.

"But he's gone now; he can threaten you no more." A faint trace of hope colored Aunt Harriett's voice.

Yes, he is gone. Thank God.

"He cannot, tis true. But despite his evil, he did offer my sisters some level of protection from the more unsavory men of his acquaintance…so long as I was there to do their bidding, of course."

It's in the past, ignore it. Ignore it.

Dansbury gripped the doorframe even harder. The wood gave a telling creak.

Bea continued, "But he's not here now, and that actually makes the girls more vulnerable than ever, especially should I remain. It is too late for me, don't you see?

Those…men—I hesitate to call them that—they know me; they have certain…expectations…based on our past associations…and will and would continue to venture into and out of my life should I remain in society, which means running the risk of them turning their attentions elsewhere when they grow tired of me or simply want more variety…"

Dansbury shuddered with revulsion. What sick, sick animals. They certainly weren't men by any definition of the word. A rat had more honor.

"But I would keep them from turning their attentions toward any of my sisters…by staying far, far away from them. I could not live with myself should one of them try to take advantage of Adelaide…or even Hetty or Sylvia…because of their connection to me."

Bea's voice held a slight tremble now. He could not even begin to imagine how she had endured it for so long. Suddenly, he had an all-too-real, all-too-horrific vision of what sort of hell Beatryce had lived in and with her entire young life. And despite it all, she was willing to give up a life of comparative ease to ensure her sisters' safety…the very definition of noble and utterly unselfish.

"Oh, Bea, you poor dear."

Dansbury echoed the sentiment. It was so odd, hearing such dark tales amidst such bright and sunny weather. For the weather was certainly fine. Yet Bea's past, her story, tainted the very air in shadow.

"Aunt Harriett, it is all right. Their threats are in the past, and I have come to terms with my future. I am quite looking forward to this new life I have planned."

Cliff admired her strength. Despite her shadowed past, she actually held onto some small amount of optimism and acceptance of her reality. At least on the surface. She'd kept that part of her character hidden from the world quite well. Quite well.

"But by yourself, Beatryce? No man, to aid you?"

Bea laughed. "A man, Aunt Harriett? I need no man. And I am surprised to hear that sentiment coming from you, of all people. I see no man gracing your drawing room, save for your charming nephew." Bea lifted her cup and acted as if she suspected she might find a gentleman hiding beneath it. The real Lady Beatryce was actually a witty, funny woman. Imagine that.

Dansbury had to stifle his own laugh, weighted thought it was with her revelations. Lady Beatryce certainly had his aunt figured out.

"You are correct, my dear. But there was one. Once. A long time ago." Aunt

Harriett's voice trailed off as if she'd left to live a little in the past.

He recalled a vague memory of a kind man, always smiling.

"And where is he now?" Bea prompted.

Aunt Harriett sighed and searched her hands. "I don't know…One day, he just left, and I never saw him again."

He remembered now, his aunt burdened by sadness for many months when he was young. It had upset him, seeing her that way. So out of character from her normally vibrant personality.

"You still love this man? I can see in your eyes that you do."

Cliff felt mildly ashamed, how could he not have suspected this?

"Strange, I know. But I do. I still do. No one could ever measure up after that."

Still, he was surprised by her admission. She continued to love that man, still, after all this time…True love was a powerful, enduring thing, wasn't it? "And you still don't know what ever happened to him?"

"I don't."

"Oh, Aunt H…"

"No, No. Don't you worry yourself over me. I've long since resigned myself to my fate. I've managed all these years; I'm not about to lose myself now. But you, Bea, you are young yet. Would you not choose to have a man with you, if only to keep you warm on a cold winter night?"

Oooh, what a devious little troublemaker, his aunt.

"Like Dansbury, Auntie H?"

Dansbury's thoughts froze at Bea's unexpected suggestion. Him?

Aunt Harriett fiddled with her cup, turning it in her hands this way and that. "Perhaps…"

What? More astonishing still was Aunt Harriett's confirmation of Bea's suggestion.

He wanted to hear more of what Beatryce would say to that, but at the same time, he feared it. He wasn't ready. He needed time to think. To know…

It was clear that this was his cue to interrupt. He slapped on his most charismatic grin. "I see you two are taking advantage of our unusually beautiful weather by relaxing outdoors…" he said as he strolled out onto the terrace. He hoped to God his cheeks weren't aflame.

The cool air blowing across the covered terrace felt unusually cold to his skin, so he doubted it. Unfortunately.

Perhaps the ladies wouldn't notice.

CHAPTER 39

"Why then tonight let us assay our plot."
—Shakespeare, All's Well That Ends Well

"Dansbury! You're back." Beatryce jumped up and rushed toward him, her eyes combing his body for any sign of injury. Worry was getting the better part of her common sense and composure. She wasn't used to fretting over someone other than herself.

"Did you find him? Did you find that madman?" She didn't waste another breath, desperate as she was to know what happened. Still, she continued to check him for holes that shouldn't be there whilst she spoke.

"We did," answered Dansbury. He just stood there, arms outstretched like a scarecrow and let her have her way.

She shoved him gently and looked at him. "And?" Sometimes men could be maddeningly cryptic, offering very few words when they had to know one wanted every single detail, no matter how insignificant.

Bea resumed her inspection of his body while she waited for him to answer.

"He's staying in an old game keeper's hut."

"Close by?" She prompted and only just stopped herself from stomping her foot in vexation over his reluctance to elaborate. There were no unexpected holes on his left arm.

"About two miles west of the mill."

She wanted to pinch him, she really wanted to pinch him.

"God. That close?" And none on the right arm either. Good.

"Yea."

"So...I take it he wasn't there?" She prompted.

"He wasn't."

Aargghh. Sometimes men were less talkative than the stones beneath their feet...and just as hard headed.

God, for once give me a garrulous man.

"What are you going to do now? And do not say 'Go back later.'" She would drag it out of him even if she had to pull the words from his mouth one syllable at a time.

She patted his chest once, finished with her inspection and satisfied he was whole, awaited his answer.

Dansbury smiled, the flirtatious teasing one that made every woman weak in the knees. "You know men so well."

"Arg. Just tell me." She was ready to shake his words loose.

"Arg? Tsk. Tsk. Such a ladylike noise, Lady Beatryce." She crossed her arms and glared at him.

"We are going to go back later..."

He paused just to needle her; she just knew it. "At dusk. We'll meet in the library an hour before and finalize our plans. You will be there, won't you?"

"Of course." As if he needed to ask.

She turned from him then, an uncomfortable feeling beginning to form in the pit of her stomach now that she wasn't focused on inspecting him for injury. She caught Aunt Harriett's eye as she returned to her chair. She looked away, then jerked her gaze back up to catch Aunt Harriett's meaningful look.

Bea did not want to see it, and she most definitely did not want to acknowledge it.

Bea sat and entertained a most ridiculous plan to avoid further eye contact or conversation with either one of them for the rest of the afternoon, while her thoughts began to swirl chaotically like the wind ahead of an approaching storm.

Aunt Harriett cleared her throat. "Yes, well. That was most...informative."

Everyone remained uncomfortably quiet for a moment; to Beatryce the very outdoors began to shrink in on her. The atmosphere seemed to take on a darker, more saturated hue with shadows hovering around the periphery of her vision; the plants became more focused and defined, darker. Heavier.

All three of them knew Aunt Harriett was not referring to Dansbury's loquacious recount of his morning reconnaissance.

"Well, as these old bones are no longer suited for such dangerous assignments, I'll leave the planning and such for you young folk," she admitted.

Aunt Harriett rose to leave.

Dansbury stood out of respect, and Bea followed suit, though her eyes remained fixed on her own twisting, knotted hands. She couldn't look just now, not with her mind in such a whirl.

Aunt Harriett walked across the slates, her cane tapping the surface with every step. Like a clock ticking the seconds, marking the passage of time. One. Step. Two. Step. Three.

Bea couldn't help but look up and watch her now that Aunt Harriett couldn't see her.

The woman paused beside her nephew, and lay a hand upon his arm. "But Clifford, darling, remember, life is grim when you lose what makes it joyful…" She looked back at Beatryce, then turned to face Cliff again. "Be cautious, son." And she looked back once more at Beatryce before she took her leave.

Bea started and sought Cliff only to find he was already regarding her with troubled eyes.

She could not bear the weight of such a gaze. "I must see to…I must take my leave…as well."

And she followed in Aunt Harriett's wake.

But as she passed Cliff, she heard his unmistakable voice. "Coward…"

His words sounded more a plea than an accusation.

She did not let them halt her departure.

CHAPTER 40

*"All men should strive to learn before they die, what
they are running from, and to, and why."*

—*James Thurber*

Beatryce returned to her room with a fast step, yet heavy feet. La, she had jumped up and fawned over Cliff the same as she had in her role as Mrs. Churchmouse.

And everyone knew it.

Except this time, she wasn't play-acting. This was real.

They knew that, too.

And it scared her to death.

Ha! As if she couldn't see this coming. She'd feared this for days now, though she'd desperately tried to ignore her feelings and focus on plans for the future.

Yes, she saw it coming all right. Like a coach and four barreling toward her at great speed. She couldn't not see it.

She was in love with Cliff. In. Love.

Her...

How could she not be? He was good. He was kind...even to the likes of her. Now, at any rate. She snorted at that.

He was strong. Trustworthy. Dependable. Witty. Fun. He was...everything. Any fool would love this man.

Oh, D.

And she was the biggest fool of them all.

She'd practically run toward love with open arms…but also toward certain heartbreak, she'd known that as well, try as she might to ignore it.

Why couldn't she have held out a little longer and fallen in love with a simple man? From a small village or a farm in the middle of nowhere. Hell, a blacksmith or a costermonger. A butcher or even a cobbler. Or maybe, just maybe, a poor, lonely gentleman, searching for comfort and companionship.

Not a Marquess! He was of a world she must relegate to her past. She had to…She swallowed.

She could not go back. She refused to go back. She didn't want to go back.

Even for him.

For so long, she had doubted anyone else, besides herself, would ever see her worth. So why did he, of all people, have to be the one who just might be capable of doing so?

Oh, God. This was going to hurt. This was going to hurt in a way that defined the very word despair. Already her soul began to mourn his loss.

And they hadn't yet said the words…good bye.

A sob caught in her throat and her eyes began to burn at just a hint of what it was going to be like to say good bye to this man. Forever. She nearly doubled over from the pain just by brushing the edges of that thought.

Oh, God!

She wanted to throw herself on the bed and weep. Rather, she paced the floor; her strength of will the only thing keeping her from doing just that…burying her face in the pillow and sobbing until she was shriveled and dried from a lack of water. As it was, silent tears were now streaming in copious amounts down her cheeks—memories over their time together rolling out in liquid form. She couldn't stop them; the same as she couldn't stop her lungs from taking her next breath.

Gasp.

She shuddered as a sob tried to break the last of her composure. Her jaw felt like it would crack from the strain.

La, there was only one thing she could do at that moment—to manage the emotions threatening to burst forth uncontrollably…The one thing she always did when her emotions endangered her good sense…

She began to strip off her clothes, the act almost symbolic. She dropped off each article of clothing to the floor as she made her way to the clothespress where she found and put on her borrowed, manly trappings—just the trousers and a shirt.

She spun and dropped to her knees to hunt for her boots; they were somewhere under her massive bed.

Once she found them, she sat right where she was and pulled them on, while her all-too-informative eyes continued to reveal her every emotion whilst blurring everything in sight, like rain on a chalk painting.

She stopped by her vanity, swiped at her eyes, and pulled back her hair, tying it into one long tail with a strip of knotted linen. Then, she left her room and… She ran.

She ran until her sides ached. Until her knees hurt. Until she could barely breathe from her exertions.

She ran to the mill. She ran to the lake. She ran around the lake three times. Then once more for good measure.

Her hair was loose and billowing behind her now, her tie having fallen out before she'd run her first mile. The sleeves of her shirt flapped in the wind. The muscles in her thighs twinged and twitched from their efforts as she pumped her arms and wrung every bit of strength from her body.

She coughed a little; her lungs expelling built-up crud from the air, and gained a stitch in her side in the process. She slowed and bent at her waist toward the bothersome ache and breathed through her nose until it went away. Then, she bolted forward at full speed once more.

She felt great; she felt alive. Because for brief moments, she could almost forget.

She must have traveled more than four miles in less than an hour. And she wanted to keep going. Perhaps if she ran far enough or fast enough, she could outrun the misery that chased her. She could feel it nipping at her heels already. Every moment she lost her concentration on her run, her reason for it barreled its way to the forefront of her mind.

She finally stopped at a spot she'd scouted by the lake. It was well hidden…a place she could go to be by herself, to perform the rituals she'd always employed to purge unwanted emotions from her mind.

She stopped and bent at the waist, her hands on her knees as she caught her breath. Every part of her body throbbed with life.

Before the death of her father, she'd do this in the wee hours of the morning. In secret.

La, she had secret places deep in the gardens of every one of her father's homes, where she would exercise her body until she nearly collapsed from exhaustion…until she could no longer think. Or feel anything but the burn from her exertions.

It was why she was so slender, she was sure. But it worked, it always worked, to suppress her overwhelming thoughts and anxiety.

It would this time. It had to.

She dropped to the ground and laid on her back in the grass, her knees bent, hands behind her head. She crunched her body into a ball, then stretched out straight again. She repeated the action over and over until the muscles in her stomach burned and cramped.

Then, she rolled over to exercise her arms.

"What are you doing hiding out here in the shrubbery, Bea?" She froze an inch from the ground.

La, Dansbury had come…

CHAPTER 41

*"But now I am return'd, and that war-thoughts have
left their places vacant, in their rooms come thronging
soft and delicate desires."*
                              —*Shakespeare, Much Ado About Nothing*

She collapsed the remaining way to the ground in surprise. Fortunately, she hadn't been standing. She had been horizontal to the ground, stomach down, working her arms by lifting and lowering her body. She partially rolled to her side and looked over her shoulder to the man that drove her to be here in the first place.

Dansbury...Cliff. He was leaning against a nearby tree. Casual and calm, his arms crossed.

And staring at her ass.

"Stop looking at my ass, D."

He grinned. The heart-stopping, tongue-wagging, charismatic grin that was a deadly weapon in his sensual arsenal.

"Stop flaunting it in tight trousers, Bea." He said it and chuckled while he removed his boots.

"Fuck you!" Yes, she was coarse. Unladylike. Her revelations made her edgy, vulnerable, scared, and angry—despite her attempt to exercise her feelings into submission.

"We've already done that. Now, I want to make love to you." He threw one boot aside.

"You…What? You what?" She was stunned by his admission and the implication behind it. It disarmed her.

"Come here." He crooked his finger at her as he tossed aside his other boot. He remained otherwise fully clothed.

God, he was barefoot and dressed. Why did that sight of his feet planted in the grass seem more erotic than him standing there totally nude?

She rolled fully onto her back and leaned back on her elbows. She shook her head; she wasn't daft. "No. You, come here." She gave him her best smile.

Am I really going to do this?

Instead of stepping forward per her command…he began removing his clothes.

Piece by piece.

Her heart picked up its pace.

Am I really going to do this?

He untied his cravat and slid it from around his neck, his actions frustratingly slow.

She resisted the urge to fan herself. Just.

"Faster…" The word simply exploded from her mouth.

He moved to his waistcoat, undoing the buttons one…by…one.

He laughed as he did. "What was that, Lady Beatryce? I didn't quite catch that." If anything, he slowed his pace.

Liar. The neighbors six miles away likely heard her. But she didn't answer, just scowled at him while he continued his agonizingly slow show.

I'm really going to do this, aren't I?

He never once broke eye contact while he worked.

Her eyes darted back and forth between his eyes and his hands. She wanted to watch the desire in his eyes…yet she wanted to watch his body as it was revealed. Bit by bit.

"My patience…" She had to catch her breath "…wears thin, D."

It seemed like ten years had passed before he twisted out of his waistcoat and began on the buttons of his shirt.

He just smiled as he carried on. Unrushed, but steady.

There were too many buttons!

Slowly and steadily, his gleaming, smooth chest was exposed.

She squeezed her thighs together. "Goodness, Cliff, faster."

I am going to do this.

"Tsk. Tsk. Patience is a virtue, Lady Beatryce. I assure you, I am worth the wait."

La, how vain of him to be so sure of his appeal…not that it wasn't obvious based on the many whimpers of impatience she could scarce control.

The breeze changed and with it she caught a whiff of…herself.

Oops.

She broke eye contact and surreptitiously sniffed near her left arm to be sure.

Ugh.

Of course, she would smell. She'd been exercising for over an hour…

She peeked up at Dansbury, and her jaw nearly fell to the ground. He'd released all the buttons of his shirt down to his breeches, where a trail of hair, the only hairs on his massive chest, disappeared beneath the fabric of his breeches like an arrow pointing the way to treasure. His treasure.

No. Her treasure.

He began to pull out the tails of his shirt.

She nearly stopped breathing, momentarily forgetting all about her malodorous problem.

His shirt fluttered to the ground. Poor thing.

But more importantly, he reached for the buttons of his breeches. And Beatryce's mouth went dry in response.

He freed the first button of his fall front.

She felt the movement in her gut; she licked her arid lips.

He freed the corresponding button on the other side.

She could feel him watching her. She was sure of it. But she didn't truly know; she was watching…his hands.

She whimpered again and gave up all pretense of looking him in the eye. His hands and what they were doing were far, far too fascinating.

When all four buttons of his fall were released, he paused. Dammit. He paused. He seemed to hold the flap in place for an eternity. Her heart ratcheted up with each second he made her wait. And wait. She wanted to look him in the eye and demand he get on with it, but she didn't dare look away from the front of those breeches…

Then…

He let the flap fall…

Mmm…

She groaned out loud. She could not control it. He wore no smalls. No. Smalls.

She looked her fill. She wanted to beg him to step out into the light so she could see him more clearly. His cock was hard and upright and trapped by the top of his breeches. His manly, bushy hair peeking out from the opening covered by the fall front and hiding the real prize inside.

He reached for the button at the top of his breeches and released it…The fabric pulled apart revealing the tip of his long, hard shaft as it peeked out, its first taste of the air. It beckoned her…called her name…signaled Dansbury's intense desire, which echoed hers.

It seemed an eternity passed while he released the remaining buttons…slowly revealing his glorious manhood. Lord, she was close to orgasm just from watching him undress.

He dropped his breeches.

His cock, freed now, bowed to her in greeting.

Her feminine core twitched in answer.

He stepped out of his breeches and took one step in her direction.

She scrambled to her feet and held up her hand, her thoughts finally forming some sort of cohesive thought and with it the memory of her little smelly problem.

"Stay."

"Now, you want me to stay?" He was incredulous. He shaft bobbed as if to underscore his impatience.

"Yes." She swallowed. "For the moment."

It was her turn to undress now.

She began with her shirt. She rejoiced as his eyes smoldered with heat. Yes. Two could play this game.

"You play with fire, Lady Beatryce."

"I love fire, Lord Dansbury."

She watched his cock while she attended to her buttons. He was so hard, his staff stood out as if pointing to what it wanted: Her. It was beautiful. And it jumped with every button she released.

She smiled at him then, and they shared a laugh at his cock's antics.

She reached for the buttons of her trousers. She heard him growl as she released the first one.

She paused, for just a moment. La, he was right. Enough was enough.

She made quick work of the rest of her clothing, but instead of stepping toward him, she stood still and threw him a cheeky grin.

Then, before he could move a single muscle, she spun around and dashed for the lake.

She was not going to do this smelling like foul sweat.

She dove headfirst into the cool water. Ah, it was so refreshing. The juxtaposition of her overheated body and the nippy water rolling down her back brought goosebumps to her arms. Her nipples beaded even harder; it'd feel wonderful when he finally joined her and suckled them.

She came to the surface a dozen yards from the shore and immediately turned to seek out Dansbury.

He stood in the full sun on the shore of the lake with his hands on his hips; his cock distended and ready…thick and hard. She knew it would be hot and pulsing with his desire. He wore a smile that made her tingle from her head to her toes. His eyes blazed with a promise of the ecstasy to come.

"Are you ready for me, Bea?" His voice was low and carried an intensity that seemed to vibrate the air itself. She felt it as much as heard it.

Yes, I am going do this.

He didn't give her a chance to respond.

He dove in after her.

He swam underwater. To her. And her heart sped up with each second he remained below, swimming closer and closer. To her. Oh God, to her!

Her heart seemed to stop altogether when he broke the surface right before her. Water sluiced down his chest, over sculpted muscle. She wanted to drink from his skin. Her tongue darted out in reflex.

The lake was reasonably shallow; he stood on his knees and the water fell to his waist. She was also on her knees, but sat back on her heels, so she was covered to her shoulders. Modest—ha! He ran both his hands up his face and pushed back his hair, ridding himself of excess water. Then, with clear eyes, he reached for her.

He pulled her up and close, pressing her body to his, and kissed her. She didn't hesitate; she opened her mouth to the touch of his tongue and lost all pretense of restraint.

Her nipples were pointed darts, sliding around his slick, wet skin. His cock prodded her legs beneath the surface. His hands ran up and down her back and over her ass…it was a full on assault and she loved every minute of it.

"Bea…I need you."

She simply groaned in response; words escaped her. Thought only just made its presence known in her mind. His every touch was heightened by her awareness that she loved this man. This man. Being in his arms, being loved by him, made her feel hopeful, inspired, provocative…and playful. A plan formed in her mind.

She ran her hands down his sides and back up…then made an attempt…to tickle him. It was an unexpected revenge. He broke the kiss and laughed. She aimed higher. He fell sideways, bringing her with him.

"Oh no…" he chuckled "…you don't."

It was difficult to take him seriously when he was laughing like that. She laughed too, until her cheeks hurt, as she attempted to regain her balance in the water and to tickle him again and again. He finally reached for her, threw her over his shoulder, and waded to the shore. She was laughing too hard to protest…not to mention she daren't complain about the glorious view she had of his unclothed backside.

His ass was firm and flexed with every step. She reached down and squeezed his buns.

He squeezed his cheeks together in response, and they both laughed again.

He walked right out of the water, but didn't put her down. Not until he found a sunny patch of grass nearby.

He laid her down with care; his eyes turned serious, but no less intense.

"I'm going to make love to you now, Bea. You know that, don't you?" He spoke tenderly as he brushed his hand across her forehead and down the side of her face; his touch burned a trail of fire across her skin.

But it was the look in his eyes that robbed her of breath; all she could do was nod her head in agreement. She suspected he loved her. But did he know it? And did it even matter? They had no future.

She brushed aside such dark thoughts. They would ruin the mood. Instead, she looked him dead on and spoke her answer with her eyes. The words to accurately express how badly she wanted this didn't seem to exist.

"Good. I've wanted this for so long. So long." He ran one hand down her side. Down her hip. Across her thigh. Then, back up until he reached the source of her femininity. Her very core, which was slick and throbbing with need.

He closed his eyes. "God, you are so wet and hot here…it's taking all my energy to go slowly…"

"Then don't."

He looked at her then. "But I want to savor this moment, this perfect beautiful moment. Here beneath the sun with nothing else but us, the birds, and God's green earth."

She didn't think she could possibly love him any more, but his words echoed in her soul, making the sensation of love flood her heart...her mind...her body. It rendered her speechless in the face of such overwhelming emotion.

She reached up and brought his lips to hers.

She widened her legs and cradled him there. She felt the length of his manhood twitch upon on her leg.

His fingers toyed with her feminine bud, ratcheting the sensations humming throughout her body. It was light out, but she closed her eyes and stars seemed to float and shine in the darkness of her mind's eye. She was so close.

"Cliff, I'm close. I need you inside me when I come."

His answer was to remove his hand and place it on the ground beside her. They both moaned as he flexed his hips and slid into her. Slow. Steady. Hard...Heaven.

Her orgasm exploded around her right away, before he'd made it fully inside. The stars swimming before her eyes blazed brighter before bursting in a riot of colors. The feeling of his hard shaft buried in her core as she contracted in waves of ecstasy worked to ratchet the sensation higher than before. More intense. Hotter. Wilder.

Or perhaps it felt like so much more because this time, she was in love with this man above her. With her. In her. Cliff. *Oh, Cliff.*

He was completely sheathed now. And as such, he paused and pressed his forehead to hers. They both needed to catch their breath. She squeezed her eyes. Tight. Hoping to hold on to this moment. This memory would have to last a lifetime.

It took a few minutes. Then he pulled back, ever so slowly. And thrust forward once more. An upward lift that rubbed the head of his cock in just the right spot.

Again.

And again.

Her core was extra sensitive from already having one orgasm. And each rub of his shaft in just that spot was extra responsive. Extra sharp. Oh, the agony of such delirious ecstasy. She was riding the wave of another orgasm already. He thrust again. And again. Slow, but strong. Deliberate. Though she could feel he was on the edge of losing control.

She felt the orgasm barreling down. There was no stopping it now. She began to stiffen. To clench. She squeezed his ass.

And he lost it. He thrust hard. Rapid. Frenzied.

And she soared to the heavens. With him. He screamed, "Bea!" as he poured his essence into her. It was glorious. Brilliant. Life-changing.

CHAPTER 42

*"What is that you express in your eyes? It seems to me
more than all the words I have read in my life."*

— Walt Whitman

*"The face is the mirror of the mind, and eyes without
speaking confess the secrets of the heart."*

— St. Jerome

Bloomfield Park...
The Library...
A Few Hours Later...

"Out with it. What is the plan?" Ambrose marched into the library with a determined step. No greeting. No discussion of the weather. Straight to the point. So like the man Cliff had known for a lifetime.

Ambrose was dressed to perfection and held about him a serious air. Of course he did. It made perfect sense; they faced a madman bent on killing them, after all.

Nevertheless, Cliff, on the other hand, had dressed after he returned to the house...but hadn't bothered with a waistcoat or a cravat. He was one hundred percent comfortable. Relaxed.

And thoroughly well-loved. And debauched...and ruined...and...

Cliff turned from his view of the back garden with a smile on his face, one he suspected would remain planted there for some time. Optimism all but throbbed through his veins affecting his outlook on everything, despite the gravity of the matter at hand.

He joined his friend in the club chairs by the fire. He knew Ambrose despised his 'let's wing it and see what happens' approach to spying. Ambrose was a planner. Cliff was one only when he deemed it necessary.

This wasn't one of those times.

"Why don't we wait for Lady Beatryce? She'll be here momentarily," Cliff suggested as they took their seats. Though it wasn't really a suggestion so much as a command couched as one even though Ambrose was really the one in charge.

"Why don't we not wait for her," stated Ambrose. "Last time I checked, she wasn't a member of my team."

Cliff relaxed deeper into his chair. Still at ease, yet he refused to budge on this point. "She has a right to be involved."

"By what right?" countered Ambrose; his fingers tapped the arm of his chair, a telling sign the man was slightly agitated.

"It is private." And it was. He would never reveal Bea's secrets. Even to his best friend.

"Have you forgotten to tell me something?" As one might have anticipated, the duke's rather active brow rose to the occasion.

"Like what?" Cliff covered his mouth with one hand and tucked his chin; he nearly chuckled over his friend's predictable facial expressions. "If I knew that, I would not have asked."

"No." He laid his hand back down, though his lips threatened to twitch as he wrestled with inappropriate humor. Regardless, his answer was to the point, leaving no opening for debate.

Ambrose halted his haphazard assault on the armchair and stared at him, that brilliant mind working furiously. "I thought you were beginning to care for Lady Beatryce."

Cliff remained silent, humor all but flying out the window. He hadn't sorted his feelings in his own mind; he certainly wouldn't voice them aloud prematurely.

When he didn't respond, Ambrose spoke, "Cliff. This is one thing we will never agree on, isn't it? I just cannot see how you can willingly and consciously put someone you care about in danger like this. I would never put Grace…"

Dansbury sliced the air with his hand. "He is a madman that must be stopped. At all costs. I cannot let my personal feelings get in the way of that."

He rubbed a hand through his hair, the only outward sign of the distress hovering in the back of his mind, yet he refused to acknowledge it. He might have agreed with Ambrose if he didn't know Bea so well. She was capable. And part of this. Edward was a madman who had to be stopped. His personal feelings mattered naught, so considering them further was pointless.

And threatened to ruin his rather enjoyable after-loving glow. "But can you live without her, if the worse should happen?" Damn the man for trying to darken his mood with a dose of reality.

"It won't." He refused to entertain the idea for a minute.

Ambrose stared at him with that infernal brow. "Sure about that, are you?"

"Good afternoon, gentleman."

He and Ambrose stood as Lady Beatryce entered the room, saving him from answering a question he did not want to consider much less own up to.

She was like a breath of fresh air, radiant and…well-loved. His mind was desperate to return to the lake. Hell, he wanted to return to the lake.

The three of them met in the center of the room, for there were only two chairs by the fire.

"Cliff and I are having a moral debate. Aren't we Cliff?"

Cliff just nodded his head in agreement, his eyes never leaving hers.

"It amounts to the idea of whether or not the end result justifies the means to get there. I suppose I don't have to ask you which side you support?"

Beatryce didn't hesitate to respond. "La, I'm sure you can accurately judge that for yourself. You know me well enough. We were nearly married, after all."

She never broke eye contact with Cliff as she spoke, a telling sign. Yet for some inexplicable reason, Cliff's heart dropped at the thought of her almost marrying Ambrose.

Even though it hadn't happened.

And wouldn't.

"Indeed," was all Ambrose said to that.

Ha! Ambrose didn't know her at all, actually. Cliff was glad. No one in this world knew her like he did. No one.

He felt lighter of a sudden.

"Unlike me, Cliff here thinks it's worth putting the people we care about in harm's way in order to get our man. I find I disagree with him on that front." Ambrose pushed.

Beatryce didn't answer right away. She just continued to stare at him, her heart shining in her eyes.

Hell and damnation, she loved him. He could see it as clearly as he could see the sun shining in the sky, though that celestial orb wasn't nearly as bright as her smile…nor as vivid as the light gleaming from her eyes.

Yes. Right then he knew. She loved him. Him.

His heart began to race. His world shifted. Again. His entire After Bea world.

He scarcely heard the remainder of their conversation, though he knew she was agreeing with him. How could she not with her history?

His mind was scattered. He couldn't concentrate on any one thing, only glimpse the tail ends of ideas where they hovered just out of reach of his mind's eye. He nodded his head when it seemed appropriate, trusting Ambrose to plan their course of action.

But in reality, he was useless at the moment. The only refrain playing out in his mind, over and over again, was…*she loves me. She loves me. She loves me.*

He knew her so well; she didn't even need to say it for him to know it.

"So we're in agreement then…"

"Sure." He didn't know what he'd just agreed to…he was just going along with it. For the first time ever, he was unable to control his thoughts. To stop the relentless chant in his mind.

She loves me.

She loves me.

She loves me.

"Cliff?"

She loves me.

CHAPTER 43

*"Tell Wind and Fire where to stop," returned
Madame; "but don't tell me."*

    —Charles Dickens, A Tale of Two Cities

*"Before you embark on a journey of revenge, dig two
graves."*

                                              —Confucius

Dusk...

N o one spoke as their horses tore across the fields behind Bloomfield
Park. The wind whispered loudly in their ears. The sun dipped and colored
everything a hazy orange.

Trees and greenery were all but a blur as they raced toward danger.

For Dansbury, the cool air served to refresh his mind.

And made him doubt his choices for the first time in his life.

He looked to his right. Lady Beatryce rode next to him. Keeping pace.
Of course. She was a sight to behold, so strong riding bent forward astride
her borrowed stallion. Confident even. Completely unafraid.

The problem lay with him. For the first time ever, he questioned the
wisdom in putting someone he...possibly...lo...well, someone
inexperienced...someone he mildly cared about...in the line of fire. What if
something happened to her?

He pulled up on his reins suddenly and rubbed his chest where an ache appeared out of nowhere.

Bea and Ambrose followed suit.

"Something amiss?" called out Ambrose.

"Er…No."

Both Bea and Ambrose looked at him strangely. Yes, he was behaving oddly. He knew it and couldn't help it.

He looked at Bea, and was lost there for a few minutes.

He looked back to Ambrose who rested his hands on the pommel of his saddle and threw him an "I told you so" smirk.

Damn him.

Damn them both.

"Bea…" He hesitated, knowing this wouldn't go over well with her. "Er…Bea? Perhaps, it'd be best…" She started to scowl. Yea, not well at all. "…if you went back to the house. To…"

He never finished. She nudged her horse with her knees and took off.

Damn.

Ambrose laughed.

"Oh, stuff it." He'd never been so at a loss for words. So concerned for another.

Despite his past.

Ambrose just threw his head back and laughed some more.

"It's not funny."

"Oh, it's very funny. You should see the bewildered look on your face. I wish I could sketch it. I've never seen the like. On you, at least. I've seen it on others though, usually when a man realizes he might be in l…"

"Don't say it."

"We'd better move. She's fast; we might never catch up."

That did it. Dansbury kneed his horse and they took off at top speed. He sensed his very future lay before him. He chased it down.

*

Her thirst for vengeance sprang forth out of nowhere. But when it arrived, it seized ahold of her and refused to let go. Bea embraced it wholeheartedly.

That man, Edward, had raped her. Raped her. She had only been a child…a veritable babe lost to a hard dose of reality far too soon. She didn't even realize she still harbored such durable resentment.

233

So she was relieved when Cliff had slowed to a stop. It gave her the opportunity to get ahead of him. To get to the madman first.

She wanted revenge against the man who took her.

She wanted to protect Cliff from making a mistake that might haunt him forever. The man was his brother, for crying out loud. Let him be angry at her. Not his kin.

So while D was lost in hesitation, she took off at break neck speed. She didn't give either man a clue as to her purpose.

And they wouldn't catch her. She rode Bloomfield Park's fastest horse. She'd made sure of that ahead of time. In addition, she was lighter than either man.

They didn't stand a chance. And they had no understanding of her intentions, so they didn't try to run her down as they would if they knew her plans.

She arrived a few hundred yards from the cottage and dismounted right away. She did not look back, but she knew from the quiet that she was far ahead of Cliff and Stonebridge. She had enough time. Just. Provided she hurried.

She walked up the dirt path to the hut and walked inside without preamble. Without a single moment of hesitation.

"Welcome, Lady Beatryce. So nice to see you again."

Edward sat in a chair behind the room's lone table; his hands folded on the surface in front of him. Various items lay about him, all set out with exacting precision. Candles were set out everywhere, all lit. It brightened the room considerably for it was near dark outside. It was as if he'd known they were coming.

She suppressed a shiver that threatened to make her question her resolve. She placed her hands on her hips and looked him in the eye. "I cannot return the sentiment."

Ugh. This man. The man who had haunted her dreams for years simply nodded his head in acknowledgement.

"Then what brings you to my humble accommodations?" He waved his hand about the room. "I cannot imagine you are here to renew our previous acquaintance, are you not?"

She tapped her finger to her chin as if thinking about that. "Huh. Well, you do have some sense, I'll give you that." She let the sarcasm ooze from her lips. The man disgusted her. She didn't even try to hide her feelings on the matter.

Edward's smile said 'I'm humoring you.' Oh, she couldn't wait to see it fall from his face.

"I see. Well, please, my lady. Enlighten me so that I might understand; I'm only a simple man, you know." He was toying with her. That was fine. She was toying with him, too. She had a few minutes to spare.

She turned and walked the perimeter of the room. Making him wait. She ran her hands along the lone windowsill. No dust. She noted the bed, perfectly made. She allowed her hand to catch the top edge of the quilt and pulled it slightly out of place. She thought she could hear Edward grinding his teeth, and had to force herself to suppress a giggle. She perused the small alcove making up a rustic kitchen. Clean as a freshly minted silver penny.

Finally, she turned to face him once more.

And pointed her pocket pistol directly at his heart.

"It's quite simple really. I'm here to kill you."

His answer was a smile. Perhaps a hint of admiration, but she could still see the madness hovering around the edges of his visage. He thought he was confident.

She was more so.

He clapped. Slow and steady. Yet she didn't allow him to threaten her resolve.

"You surprise me, Lady Beatryce. I hadn't realized you were so...tenacious?

Willing? Strong? You've grown up, little girl."

"You'd be surprised by how much."

"But can you live with yourself if you take my life?"

"Without question."

Her quick response must have shaken his confidence. A hint of fear began to drift about him.

"I see."

She smiled. "Any final words you'd like to impart? Words of wisdom? Tales of who's behind all this?"

He laughed. "Ah, you think I'll tell you about Himself? The man is nothing. He is next on my list to die."

"Well, that is a shame. Since you aren't leaving this place alive."

A moment of shock crossed his features. He tried to hide it, tried to act like he wasn't even the tiniest bit concerned. She could see his mind working...looking for a way to distract her or stall her.

"My brother won't be happy with you, should you kill me. They'll want to question me. Discover what I know."

"You are right. And for that reason, I've considered just detaining you here until they arrive."

He looked marginally relieved by this. "Of course, they're on their way, aren't they?"

"Imminently. In fact, I am running out of time to decide whether or not I should leave you to them or go ahead and take my revenge." He jerked his head just before he reached for his gun.

He was fast.

But not quite fast enough.

Bang. Bang.

Two shots fired, almost simultaneously. Hers hit the mark. She saw the very life leave his eyes. Just as Dansbury bolted through the door.

She turned to look at him. His face was frozen in terror. And it felt like he was moving further away rather than racing towards her. How was that possible?

He yelled her name. She could see it was so as he reached for her. She saw his lips form the words. But his voice sounded muffled and distant.

It was the last thing she remembered before she fell to the floor.

CHAPTER 44

"Only in the agony of parting do we look into the depths of love."

—*George Eliot*

Bloomfield Park...
Day Two of a Different Sort of Torture...

He was altered, forever changed. He had known nothing before that moment...nothing of true pain; true horror...until Bea had fallen to the floor, her life's blood blooming across the breadth of her shirt...every expanded inch of the ever-widening circle of red another dagger to his heart.

And since that unforgettable moment, he was living a nightmare. One that felt as if it might never end.

It had to end.

Cliff leaned back in his chair beside the bed and dragged his hand through his hair and down his face as he took in a deep breath; as he'd done a thousand times in as many minutes. His action momentarily dried the tears that seemed destined to fall from his eyes for an eternity, a slow and steady stream of remorse and fear...and love...in liquid form.

Bea'd been shot in the shoulder. She'd live. Of course she would.

She must, dammit!

His head knew that; his heart feared it all a wicked lie...fate laughing over his shoulder, punishing him for every misdeed or spiteful thought aimed in Bea's direction.

Why, oh why had he even considered putting her at risk like that? How could he not have realized the danger? Hadn't he been through this sort of thing before?

Sure. Of course. But not like this.

Yes, he'd spent many hours atoning for his sins…for the lives of the people he'd placed in harm's way. Many hard hours that would never come close to making up for the heartache and pain caused by his actions in service to the Crown.

Yes, it was a risk they all knew in advance. And accepted. However, that knowledge never made it easier to face the aftermath when things went awry. And things eventually did go wrong. When it did, it threatened his very sanity every single time and was the reason he normally had such control over his emotions. The alternative was chaos.

Bedlam.

Usually.

But this was different.

He hadn't loved the others like he loved her.

Yes. The realization made his heart sing. He loved her! Lady Beatryce— who would have ever thought it? Oh, God, did he ever lover her! She kept him grounded, strong. She wasn't afraid to tell him when he was acting the fool or just plain wrong. She was practical and fearless and reasonably selfless despite all outward appearances to the contrary. She was willing to give up money, servants, prestige—everything—all for the safety of her sisters, who would never know the truth. The very definition of honorable— doing for others without any desire or hope for acknowledgement or returned favor. Many would do better to be half so decent.

She stood up to him. She wasn't afraid to disagree…Hell, she completed him. In every single way.

Every breath he took was for her. Without her…

He swallowed, though it was difficult to do so given the boulder-sized lump in his throat. No. He couldn't travel that path.

She would live, dammit!

He pulled at his hair, again, in frustration and misery. Then reached for her hand and leaned forward in his chair beside her bed. Placing his head on the back of her hand where he lay it on the bed near him, he prayed. And he never let go. He hated to break their connection, even for a moment.

Her hand was burning hot.

He looked up, though, when he heard a soft moan...His eyes automatically sought out her face. She was too wan. Too thin.

She started to twist and turn in her sick bed...again; the fever had yet to abate. He jumped into action though panic all but threatened to immobilize him. He forced his limbs to move across the room to the table that held a basin of water and squares of soft linen.

"I need more water," he yelled as he dipped the downy cloths into what little he had remaining.

He took the bowl with him and climbed on the bed next to her to bathe her, trying desperately to cool her overheated body.

He crooned soft words and sung sweet endearments while he wrestled to keep her alive. He fought with a desperation he'd never known.

"Bea, sweet, you must come back to me. I cannot..." He swallowed hard. "Love...I see you now. I see you; the real you you've kept hidden from the world. The real you who would sacrifice her life for her sisters even knowing they'd never realize it. The real you who would leave behind a life of ease to keep them safe even knowing they'd think you'd abandoned them. The real you who would do whatever it took to survive, even distasteful things that would cower a lesser man."

Desperation threatened to seize control; his voice became threadbare and worn.

"Bea...I need you to...well, dammit, who else am I going to tickle at night? Who else am I going to admire in snug breeches? Who else am I going to tease? What other woman could ever be as strong? Could ever compare? You were made for me...just me. You are wonderful..."

He froze. Had she made a sound? He looked up and saw her eyes were open. She was still fevered, her eyes too bright. But she smiled when their eyes met and it was the most beautiful sight in the world.

His heart felt as if it expanded in his chest to double its size.

He leaned in close. "What is it, dove? What are you trying to say?"

Her voice was barely a whisper. "I won't die, you blockhead."

Despite his fears, he smiled—a wide grin pulled from the very depths of his soul.

Yes. That was her, his Bea. Confident despite the seriousness of her condition.

His tears renewed their outward flow.

She spoke again. "It's about time you saw me, you fool."

He laughed. Yea, she'd live. Like him, she was too stubborn to leave this world too soon.

CHAPTER 45

"I loved you madly; in the distasteful work of the day, in the
wakeful misery of the night, girded by sordid realities, or
wandering through Paradises and Hells of visions into which
I rushed, carrying your image in my arms, I loved you
madly."

—Charles Dickens, *The Mystery of Edwin Drood*

Bloomfield Park...
Beatryce's Room...
One Week Later...

"Now that I know you will live, I could kill you for what you did."

Beatryce merely laughed. She was pretty much out of harm's way; her strength nearly returned. She was strong, his love. A fighter.

But her laugh didn't hold a trace of humor. She was testy. Probably due to an entire week of inactivity.

Well, that was fine. Cliff was mad, too.

She crossed her arms and glared at him.

He glared back. He was taller. And bigger. And thirty going on two.

"I did what I had to do. I won't apologize for it, either. If you're expecting one, then you don't know me half as well as you think you do." She countered.

"No, I know you're not going to be reasonable and say you're sorry for endangering yourself and driving me half mad with worry. But I wish you would consider for one single moment what kind of hell you just put me through. You could have died!"

"What of it? At least that madman wouldn't have been around to hurt anyone else.

Do you think I was the only woman he'd hurt? I doubt it."

That stopped him. Hell, he hadn't even considered that. He felt a moment's pity for the other women who'd had to endure his brother's depravity. The horror they must've endured. He resolved to find them any way he could and make amends.

But for now…

Beatryce turned and faced away, a moment of sadness seemed to envelop her.

"Bea?" He reached for her and pulled her in his arms. "What is it? What is the matter?"

She snuggled closer and squeezed him. "I'm just feeling a slight…" She looked at him and smiled "…slight, mind you, pang of…worry about my future. It'll be vastly different now, though I know I'll manage…It's just become real to me now." Her voice trailed away as if she was momentarily lost in her thoughts of the future. He had an answer for that, too.

But he let her continue; clearly she had more to say. "For a moment there, I simply didn't know how I was going to carry on. It's so hard."

"You could marry me?"

"What?"

"I said…"

"I heard you. I just cannot believe those words even came out of your mouth in reference to me. You do realize I'm not some broken, stray dog for you to fix?"

"Aren't you?"

She almost laughed. Almost. She shook her head, no, instead.

"How can you love me when I'm so bad?" She said instead.

"Damned if I know…" She looked at him, surprised. She started to sputter out a response… "Bu…But…I…"

He laughed.

"I admit you have been…bad. But, I think, if I'm not mistaken, that you have some sense of remorse…" She looked at him with some doubt. "…a small hint of remorse…" She yet held on to that reservation. "…a wee, tiny, barely noticeable minute morsel of doubt…" She laughed; he with her. "Does it excuse your behavior? Not always; not entirely. But then who in this world is perfect? Certainly not me. Perhaps you have been worse than others, but no one else has ever had to walk in your shoes…to endure what you've endured and survive…to protect your family at the expense of their love for you…to do what you must, no matter how distasteful, in order to make your escape…I get it now. I do."

She smiled then. A full smile that lit up her face and made her eyes all but glow.

"Bea, the truth is…I want to laugh with you until our sides hurt. I want to dry your tears, and you mine. I want adventures with you by my side; I want boredom until we both want to cry. I want to break fast with you each morn and sup with you each night. I want you in my arms when I go to sleep, and there again when I wake in the morn. I want to experience joy with you, and sorrow. I want all of it…the good, the bad, and the mundane. I want life. With you." He touched her face. Then, he said…

"I love you."

Bea looked down and touched her forehead to his chest…not quite the reaction he was hoping for.

She shook her head, but her hands wandered his back, a contradiction to her implied no.

"Cliff…" His heart picked up speed. She called him by his given name. It gave him hope.

She pulled back and looked at him; held his hands in hers. "I am flattered…"

He heard the 'but' before she said it…He saw her lips form to make the sound of a B and started shaking his head no preemptively.

She ignored that and said that hated word anyway. "But I don't see how we can possibly have a future…" She held her hand up. "Don't interrupt. You see me, now please, hear me." She swallowed and took a moment's pause. Then, on a sigh, she began, somewhat less steadily. "I-I was raped by your brother as a child. I know that isn't your fault, you had nothing to do with it. Yet I still feel it is a problem that stands to come between us if we're not careful. If that is not bad enough, I killed your brother. I know you never held a high regard for him. He was cruel, and you were young when you thought he'd died. But he was still your brother. Your flesh and blood. And the thought of me killing him would weigh heavily on your mind at

243

times…do not deny it, for I wouldn't believe you. It would threaten to come forth whenever we had a fight. And we would fight, from time to time.

"And if only that were all…" She shook her head. And continued.

"I have no remaining respect in society. I don't care nor do I wish to return to that life. I cannot risk my sisters' safety to be a part of your world. But it is your world; you have no choice. You have an obligation to the marquisate you cannot ignore." Her voice trailed off. He could see the pain in her eyes despite her words of rejection. She wanted to say yes; he could see it as plain as day.

"Are you finished?" He couldn't give her a chance to continue. She'd find something else and something else…excuse after excuse.

She nodded her head.

"None of that matters to me. You're smart. I'm smart. We'll manage. I love you.

And do you know one final reason…the best reason…why we should marry?"

"No…but I suspect you're going to enlighten me." She looked skeptical.

He smiled then, wide and full. He tried to exude confidence with his grin, but beneath the surface he was scared to death.

He tilted her chin and spoke carefully. "You love me."

She smiled at that, though a little surprise was evident.

He continued, "I've seen it in your eyes when you let down your guard. I know you do."

She didn't try to deny it.

"You have to trust me, Bea."

But she didn't. Nor did she change her mind.

He could add stubborn to her list of characteristics.

CHAPTER 46

*"Three grand essentials to happiness in this life are
something to do, something to love, and something to
hope for."*

—*Joseph Addison*

Bloomfield Park...
One Week Later...

She was gone. Off to her little cottage. Living on her own.

And he was lost within this great big house with only the servants, Aunt Harriett, and Grace and Ambrose for company.

They were all present under this massive roof Aunt Harriett called home. But he wasn't. Present that was. Oh, sure, he was here physically. But his heart wasn't. It was ten miles down the road in a little cottage beside a field of green. It belonged to a woman who was stronger and braver than anybody he'd ever known.

And he was slightly the worse for drink because of it. As he had been all week.

He rolled over in bed on a groan and rubbed his face in his pillow. Back and forth. Back and forth. Until he thought he might have rubbed away his eyebrows. He would suggest this to Ambrose. The sensation was somewhat numbing to his face.

What was she doing right now? It was mid-morning. Was she in bed?

Lighting a fire? Exercising?

God, why did he torment himself this way? Wondering about her. He should be trying to forget her. She'd made her choice. He esteemed her enough to respect her decision.

What he really wanted to do was grunt like a beast, beat his chest, and claim her as "Mine." His emotions ran the gamut of feelings. From irritation to misery to numbness to…nothing.

He made a wide berth of grief. He feared if he looked too closely at despair, he might never recover.

He wanted to growl. He wanted to hold on to her and force her to stay. Give her absolutely no choice whatsoever.

Of a sudden, the door to his room opened. He sat up in bed, cursing the additional light and the interruption to his misery. He was hung over and irritable and on the brink of utter grief. He knew it was true—he could feel it creeping up on him slowly but surely.

He was certainly in no mood to deal with people who would interfere with his wallowing.

But it was Aunt Harriett. He couldn't very well kick her out.

And she was scowling. Which provided him with something new to be concerned about.

Worse, she had a hold of her umbrella.

The Umbrella.

She walked across his room with It clutched firmly in her grasp. She was headed straight for his side of his bed.

She didn't speak.

She didn't look away.

And she most definitely wasn't happy.

When she reached his side, she didn't pause. She raised that infernal Umbrella and whacked him right over the head with it. Without even a moment's hesitation or a single sign of remorse.

And then, she simply turned on her heel with a huff and left; or at least, that was her intention. She was certainly headed toward the door.

He rubbed his aching head. "Ow…what was that for?" He was convinced she'd just hit him so hard, she'd bent It, her favorite umbrella. It would be ruined. He should point that out. He wouldn't buy her a new one either, dammit.

Had she really made such a habit of this? Bashing people with The

Umbrella such that he'd known what she was about the minute she walked through his door?

Normally, Aunt Harriett wouldn't answer. He knew that, too.

And he really hadn't expected her to this time. Surprisingly, she did.

"You let her get away, you fool." She yelled back to him as she marched across his room. She didn't miss a step and never once looked back.

"But I tried," he called out. He sounded like he was two again. He only just stopped himself from throwing out his lip, crossing his arms, and attempting to kick the footboard.

Was this what he'd become? A whining, simpering fool because he couldn't have what he wanted. Was it his way of avoiding just how unpleasant the thought of losing her was?

Or perhaps, he didn't yet truly believe she was gone for good.

Whatever, his near-whine gave Aunt Harriett pause, but she still didn't turn around to look at him. Instead, she simply said, "You didn't try hard enough," as she faced the doorway and the hallway beyond.

Ha! As if he'd let Bea go with ease. "She wouldn't have me. You should speak to her if this displeases you." He all but pouted again and crossed his arms. Yea, he sounded three at best. This time he did stomp his foot.

It made little impact in bed.

"Yea, well, I did. Saw her yesterday, in fact. And I beat her over the head, too."

He laughed and cocked his head. "You did?" He couldn't help the smile. He could imagine the sight quite vividly in his mind.

This time Aunt Harriett half turned to face him, one brow raised in question. Maybe Ambrose adopted his habit from her?

"Do you doubt me?"

"No." Was there any other answer he could give?

"Then stop asking questions. You are ruining my dramatic departure. Don't you know I'm supposed to hit you without saying anything? Haven't we played out this scene once or twice before?"

And then she did leave. Without another word.

Ambrose entered only a scant few minutes after her departure.

Damn if Cliff's head didn't still smart somewhat painfully…

"Was that Aunt Harriett I saw…" Stonebridge pointed a thumb over his shoulder.

"…with The Umbrella."

"Yes."

"The One she bashed me on the head with when I let Grace flee to Oxford?"

"The very One."

Stonebridge cringed in solemn empathy. "Ouch."

"Yea."

"I take it this means she approves of Lady Beatryce."

"Quite so."

"So what are you going to do about it?"

"I'm working on it." He rubbed his hand down his face as if that would help.

"Yea, you sure look like it. Well, while you're stuck here making your plans, do you have a quick moment for a little Crown related business? You know spies, murderers, traitors, and all that?"

"Sure. Might as well. I'm certainly up now."

"It was a shame we lost your brother before we had a chance to question him." Ambrose held up a hand to forestall Cliff's intended interruption. "I don't blame you...Or Lady Beatryce, for that matter. Besides, all is not lost."

"What do you mean?"

"We have Kelly."

"In custody?"

"No...but it is only a matter of time. I've sent MacLeod after him."

Ambrose would know precisely what thought went through Cliff's mind with that admission. "I know. I know. It's something you feel entitled to do..." Cliff nodded his head in agreement.

"...but you have something more important to do right now..."

"Such as?"

Ambrose made his way toward the door, shaking his head as if he, Cliff, was an utter dunce. "You have to find a way to get your woman back." Cliff smiled. He sure did.

He got out of bed and began to dress.

Lady Beatryce had better be ready.

He was coming for her. And she was not going to walk away from him again.

CHAPTER 47

"Journeys end in lovers meeting, every wise man's son doth know."

—Shakespeare, Twelfth Night

"The pain of parting is nothing to the joy of meeting again."

—Charles Dickens

A Few Miles Down the Road from Bloomfield Park...

Lady Beatryce walked out her front door, paused on her front stoop, and shaded her eyes from the brilliant sun. It was still difficult to believe that everything before her: this house, this garden, the walkway—all of it, was hers. It was perfect, even idyllic—with its small garden, thatched roof and solid stone walls. It was clean; the previous owners had maintained it well, and the garden was in superb condition as it had been tended daily by a gardener from the nearby small town of Chester so that it would still be manageable when a new owner took residence. Her.

An overabundance of flowers were in full bloom and freshened the air with a fragrance so pleasant she wished she could bottle the smell so she could enjoy the scent the year round. She would have to see about drying the blooms and creating a potpourri.

The house itself boasted no more than one room off the main room— a bedroom— within which was a bed just large enough for two, a clothespress, a wash stand, a ladies vanity, and a small, black, single-drawer table beside the bed. One leg might've been a tad shorter than the others, but it was functional and it was all hers so she didn't quite care. It even boasted a fireplace, unheard of for a cottage of this size, and a screen behind which was a copper bathing tub. She didn't think that was original to the house, yet she couldn't imagine how it came to be there.

Well, it was hers now. And she was thrilled to have it.

In the main living area, she had a dining table that seated two, two club chairs by the hearth and a kitchen with all the basic necessities she needed to prepare her meals. A giant rug warmed the floor.

Outside, she had a small lean-to behind the house for a horse, should she ever decide to acquire one, and enough split firewood to last her two years, at least.

In all, it was the perfect home for a simple lady living a quiet, unassuming life.

So perhaps there was a touch of loneliness in the air...but it would pass. She was sure of it. It had to.

Most importantly, she was free. Free from society. Free from her past. Free from everything she had ever feared in her life.

She was tired, sure; she hadn't slept solidly in a week. But without servants, there was no rest for the weary. And if she didn't tend to her chores, they wouldn't get done. That's all there was to it.

Bea stepped off her stoop, her skirts brushing the tops of her bare feet. She'd taken to going about unshod since she'd discovered how much fun it was to do so. She walked along her garden path, her destination the little kitchen allotment on the side of the house. Today, she needed to begin preparations for her fall vegetables.

She'd read everything she could find about kitchen gardens back when she'd lived at Beckett House in London. Her father had owned a surprising amount of books on the subject, and she had devoured every one at the time, never realizing that the knowledge would become so useful to her one day.

Yes, that understanding was proving worth its weight in gold now that she was living on her own without assistance.

She rounded the side of the house and lightly rubbed her stomach. She was feeling somewhat nauseated and it gave her a moment's pause. She wasn't with child, she knew that much for certain. But the feeling had been there, humming in the background like an annoying fly, for the past week.

Today, though, the sensation was intensifying. She couldn't quite explain exactly how she felt, only that she felt off. Wrong. Different. Empty?

She tried to shake it off. She didn't have the luxury to ignore her responsibilities. She looked around with more purpose in a desperate attempt to ignore the feeling of abject…wrongness…that seemed to be barreling down upon her and threatening to weigh her down until she could no longer stand.

She looked down and saw, there before her, a single dandelion. A simple, lone dandelion. And that was all it took to bring back the memory of Cliff—his love for the weedy, yellow and green plant.

And like a balloon that burst, that was all it took for her pent up emotions to completely overwhelm her…to flood her mind and drown her soul. She fell to her knees right there in the garden and began to weep.

She'd tried to push away thoughts of him, but his memory was damned persistent. She didn't want to feel. She didn't want to think about their separation because she was afraid that once she gave it a moment's consideration, she'd become overwhelmed in a grief from which she would never recover.

Ah, but it was too late now. The gates were open and she could no longer deny that her heart had been ripped in two with their separation.

She loved that man. Completely. Thoroughly.

She tried to take in a breath, but breathing had become as difficult as if she were attempting it under water. Or buried beneath the ground.

And she knew she'd been right. She would not recover from this. She loved him too much. Dansbury.

Ah, God, she couldn't do it. She couldn't spend her life without him. Even if it meant returning to society. Even if it meant giving up everything. Even risking her sisters. And that was a painful thought to admit. It made her feel selfish.

But he was hers…and she would do anything to remain by his side forever. Here. There. It didn't matter. Nothing mattered but being with him…being his partner. Hadn't they shown how well they worked together? How they complemented each other as if they were two sides of the same whole?

Without another thought, she wiped her tears on her sleeve. And pulled herself to her feet.

And then she ran.

Just up and left it all and ran with the wind. Not across fields of grass and wildflowers, but down the main, well-traveled road. Not in the dark, when the odd carriage or horseman would be practically nonexistent, but in the bright of day, where any person traveling through the countryside might see her.

And not in the normal male garb she usually wore for her exercises, but a proper, practical day dress for puttering about in her garden. It whipped about her legs and twirled about in her wake, but it didn't matter. Nothing mattered but getting to Bloomfield Park and him.

And yes, she still wasn't wearing shoes, nor did she take a moment to grab a pair before sprinting off down the road.

She didn't care. She ran as fast as she'd ever run in her life.

No, faster.

But this time, she wasn't running from her emotions or trying to suppress them. Rather, to them. To her future.

Ten minutes passed. Then thirty. Before long, it was noon and she'd already covered five miles. She had five more to go and she was still running. Five more would see her returned to the arms of the man she loved. And would have her running farther than she'd ever run before in one go.

She didn't have a carriage. Or a lot of money to rent one. Or even an acquaintance she could call on to borrow a horse. Or dash off a note. All she had were her feet and her knowledge that the love of her life was only ten miles east of her little cottage in the country.

So she ran on. And on. Dodging ruts in the road and kicking up dirt that no amount of washing would ever remove from the bottoms of her skirts.

She didn't care. She just ran.

The ground evened out to a smooth, better-maintained patch of road, with no immediate ruts visible to her eye, so she looked ahead for as far as she could see. On the horizon, she could just make out the shape of a horse and rider headed her way.

Her heart beat that much faster if such a thing were possible. It might be a mirage. But it might be…

It night be him.

She ran even harder. Even faster. Her smile widened with each pounding step until her cheeks hurt and she could barely see from squinting. And from crying. Crying tears of joy.

Her lungs sawed in and out. She got a stitch in her side that needled her angrily.

But she kept on running.

She was three hundred yards away from the rider.

Then two hundred.

A few yards more and he literally leapt off his horse.

She put on one final burst of speed and flew into his outstretched arms.

"Cliff…"

"Bea…"

They spoke at once. And they laughed at once. She worked hard to catch her breath while he squeezed the daylights out of her and refused to set her down.

He spun her until she thought she'd be dizzy.

She had to speak first. It was imperative. Yet she couldn't catch her breath to utter more than the single syllable of his name.

She tried to force her breath in through her nose and out through her mouth. To slow her breathing. God, it wasn't easy. She'd run five miles as fast as her legs could carry her.

In the midday heat. Without a hat.

She undoubtedly sported unfashionable freckles.

She didn't care.

A million years passed in a second while she caught her breath. And all the while he held her off the ground. Which was fine. She didn't want to be anywhere else in the world.

When she could finally speak, she said, "Cliff, let me down. I have something important to say."

"No. I'm not letting you go. You'll just have to talk like this."

She laughed. This man. This crazy lovely man. And then she kissed him instead. His lips melded with hers and she tasted heaven in a moment of pure bliss. This kiss was frantic with need. So many words were spoken without uttering a sound.

I love you.

I miss you.

I need you.

I want you.

Don't ever leave me again.

Eventually, their enthusiasm slowed as their hearts began to recognize that the other wasn't about to leave. This time. Or ever again.

She grabbed his shoulders; she could barely move within his embrace, but she managed to pull back enough to look in his eyes. It was all he'd allow her. She reached up, grabbed his face, and directed his attention to her. "Clifford Ross, 7th Marquess of Dansbury, you were right. You were so very right. I love you. More than anything in this world. And I need you like I need air to breathe. You are the love of my life and I cannot live another day, another hour, another moment without you. Will you…" She swallowed past the lump that suddenly filled her throat and started again. "Will you marry me?"

He didn't appear to think. Nor hesitate. He didn't prevaricate at all. He simply swung her around and shouted to the sky. "Yes! Yes! Yes!"

EPILOGUE

"It is the one of the great secrets of life that those things are most worth doing, we do for others."

—*Lewis Carroll*

Bloomfield Park...
One Month Later...

It was supposed to be a small affair. Stonebridge and Grace, MacLeod, Aunt Harriett and The Umbrella, the Priest, the servants, and of course, the bride and groom.

Beatryce waited, with only a smidge of anxiety, for the ceremony to begin. She'd been here before, after all. But this go round was far more important. And, hopefully, far less likely to be called off.

Still she'd feel better when it was over, and her man was all hers. For better or for worse. Forever.

Dansbury walked out of the drawing room and into the hall where she was waiting. He wasn't supposed to do that.

"What are you doing? I am meant to enter the drawing room and you are supposed to wait for me in there."

"I know, but Bea, I have a wedding gift for you that I need to give you before we make our vows."

Leave it to Dansbury to break all the rules.

"A gift?"

He nodded his head. "One I think you'll enjoy."

"All right…"

"Follow me…"

He led her to the library. She grew more and more curious. She'd expected something smaller; something he might carry in a pocket or already have in his hand.

He stopped at the door and turned to face her, placing the door behind him. "You are the world to me, Bea. My heart. My love. My soul. I'll care for you for the rest of my days. And…And I'll care for your family…our family now." Then, he turned and opened the door.

Bea stepped through and there before her stood her sisters. Adelaide at six, Sylvia at twelve, and Hetty at sixteen all lined up before her, dressed in their wedding finery. All of them were holding handkerchiefs. And all of them, like her, were crying.

She nearly fell to the floor and would have if Cliff hadn't been standing there beside her. Sharing his strength.

For a moment, she couldn't decide whether she wanted to grab up the girls and hug them for an hour or bury her face in Dansbury's shirt, her heart overflowing with love. Either way she'd be crying. She was crying.

Dansbury squeezed her hand, and she looked up at him, letting all of the joy and love in her heart shine through her eyes and speak for her. At the moment, she could not form words. She could barely see his smile in return through the copious amount of tears blurring her vision.

Then, she looked at her sisters, fell to her knees after all, and opened her arms wide.

They ran as one into them.

"Oh, Hetty, Sylvie, Addie…Oh, how I've missed you. How I've wanted to tell you so many times how much I love you all."

It was Addie, the youngest, who spoke for them. "We know it. We know everything. Lord Dansbury wrote to us and told us aaaaalllll about it." She looked down at her feet a moment, then back up at her. And in a quiet, almost shy voice, said, "You are very brave, Sissy."

Bea closed her eyes a moment and held on to the sound. To hear her sister refer to her with affection—she'd called her Sissy!

She was so overwhelmed with joy at that moment. She had never, ever experienced the like. She swallowed, put her hands on either side of Addie, and touched her sister's forehead with her own.

"So are you, my love. So are you."

Addie giggled. Then, pulled away and looked back at a woman standing apart and behind them. For a moment, Bea didn't recognize the woman.

Then, her eyes widened with surprise. "M-Mary?"

Her stepmother dipped her head in acknowledgement and smiled. "Yes, dear."

It was a smile Beatryce had not seen in over fifteen years, if ever. La, Mary had changed dramatically. And for the better. She looked happier. Healthier. Kind.

The world momentarily felt upended.

The sight gave her hope and brought her joy.

Dansbury cleared his throat and everyone turned to look at him.

"I'm happy to see you all reunited…but I am also quite anxious to marry my bride."

No further words were necessary. They turned as one and headed for the drawing room. Everyone bursting with excitement.

Dansbury on her arm.

*

It was a small, simple ceremony. With swaths of bold jewel-toned fabrics draping the room and bunches of wildflowers gracing every horizontal surface in the space. And the closest of friends and family.

As they left the drawing room, Beatryce turned on Cliff and in front of everyone, announced, "Now, I have a surprise…a wedding gift…for you, my love. One I know you will adore."

She grabbed both his hands and backed her way down the hall. Guiding him, again, toward the library.

This time, it was she who paused with her back to the door.

"You are the world to me, Cliff. My heart. My love. My soul. I will care for you for the rest of my days. And…And I'll care for your family…our family now." His eyes began to water; she saw disbelief war with pure joy at her intentional use of his exact words. "I have found…" She swallowed around the lump in her throat as tears, yet again, filled her eyes. For the thousandth time that day at least. "Darling D, I have found your sister…"

The succession of emotions that flew across his face in the span of a heartbeat was endearing to behold. She loved this man. She could not say it, could not think it, enough.

She quickly pushed open the door and made to get out of his way before he bowled her over to get inside.

But when she turned to look in the room, the place was empty. His sister was gone.

From behind Cliff, a Scottish burr spoke above the crowd, who'd begun exclaiming all at once in excited chatter.

"Och, I'll find her."

And without another word, as was his norm, Alaistair MacLeod turned on his heel and left.

THE END

Stay tuned for Lord Alaistair MacLeod's story…

PUBLISHER'S NOTE

Please help this author's career by posting an honest review wherever you purchased this book.

ABOUT THE AUTHOR

Amy Quinton is an author and full time mom living in <u>Summerville, SC</u>. She enjoys writing (and reading!) sexy, historical romances. She lives with her husband, two boys, and one cat. In her spare time, she likes to go camping, hiking, and canoeing/kayaking... And did she mention reading? When she's not reading, cleaning, or traveling, she likes to make jewelry, sew, knit, and crochet (Yay for <u>Ravelry</u>!).

<u>https://amyquinton.net/</u>